Religion in
New Zealand Society

Religion in New Zealand Society

Brian Colless
& Peter Donovan

T. & T. CLARK LTD.
36 GEORGE STREET, EDINBURGH

Printed in New Zealand by
The Dunmore Press Limited
P.O. Box 5115, Palmerston North.

for

T. & T. Clark Ltd., Edinburgh

ISBN 567 09303 4

First printed 1980

Foreword and Acknowledgements

This book can claim to be a unique conflux of distilled waters of knowledge on the place of religion in New Zealand. Ultimately, however, its source lies in the symposia on this subject held during the past decade at Victoria University of Wellington and the University of Auckland. The proceedings of these various working sessions were duly published, but in unwieldy fascicules that were too high to fit on a normal-sized library shelf. It has fallen to the lot of those who teach the study of religion at Massey University (in Palmerston North, on the highway between Wellington and Auckland) to direct these streams into a more manageable container. Accordingly, the editors wish to present their heartfelt thanks:

First to Keith M. Bennett, Director, Victoria University of Wellington Department of University Extension (and other members of that Department involved in producing the series of seminars on religious studies held from 1974 to 1976) for permission to use the papers by P. H. de Bres from *The Future of Religion in New Zealand - Seminar I* (June 1974), Ian Breward, E.H. Blasoni and Colin Brown from *The Future of Religion in New Zealand – Seminar II* (October 1974), and Michael Hill, Colin Brown and David Pitt from *Religious Pluralism in New Zealand – Study Papers* (1976).

Second to Rev. Dr. John Hinchcliff, editor of *Dialogue on Religion* (1977) for permission to use papers by L.H. Barber and Colin Brown (on the charismatic movement), and for his enterprise in organising the annual Colloquium on Religious Studies at Auckland University since 1974.

Also to Lucy Marsden, reference librarian of Massey University library, for compiling the select bibliography and standardizing footnotes. To John Dunmore and Patricia Chapman of the Dunmore Press for encouraging and enabling us in this publishing venture. And finally to Sharon Cox who did all the real work on her typewriter.

Contents

FOREWORD AND ACKNOWLEDGEMENTS   5

THE EDITORS' INTRODUCTION
The Religion of the New Zealanders, *Brian Colless and Peter Donovan*   9

THE HISTORICAL ASPECT
The Religious Dimension of New Zealand's History, *L. H. Barber*   15

THE MAORI CONTRIBUTION
Maori Religious Movements in Aotearoa, *Pieter H. de Bres*   31

THE CATHOLIC CONTRIBUTION
Can Catholicism Contribute to an Indigenous New Zealand Religion, *E. H. Blasoni*   57

THE PROTESTANT CONTRIBUTION
Have the Mainline Protestant Churches Moved out of their Colonial Status? *Ian Breward*   67

THE ECUMENICAL CONTRIBUTION
Ecumenism in New Zealand: Success or Failure? *Colin Brown*   81

THE CHARISMATIC CONTRIBUTION
How Significant is the Charismatic Movement? *Colin Brown*   99

THE SECTARIAN CONTRIBUTION
Do Sects Thrive While Churches Languish? *Michael Hill*   115

THE JUDAIC CONTRIBUTION
The Jewish Community in New Zealand, *David Pitt*   133

THE INDIAN CONTRIBUTION
Religious Movements of Indian Origin in New Zealand, *Kapil Tiwari*   149

THE PLURALIST TENDENCY
Pluralism and the Future of Religion in New Zealand, *Lloyd Geering*   171

THE ACADEMIC CONTRIBUTION
Religious Studies: New Zealand and Worldwide, *Albert C. Moore*   185

BIBLIOGRAPHY   195

INDEX   205

The Editors' Introduction

THE RELIGION OF THE NEW ZEALANDERS
Brian Colless and Peter Donovan

New Zealanders are notorious for reading books about themselves. But if Kiwis didn't read New Zealand books, a cynic might ask, then who in the world would? Alternatively, some observers might see in this an immature preference for imbibing only what is comfortingly familiar. An amateur psychiatrist might even go to extremes and diagnose it as pathological introspectiveness, the books being merely a respectable cover for clandestine contemplation of the navel, and perhaps other private parts too. Nevertheless, we who are the participants know that the study of Aotearoa's history, culture, and contemporary life offers more than just the comforting reassurance of familiar names and opinions.

In fact, though we would be reluctant to solemnize it as 'a search for identity', a serious interest by New Zealanders nowadays in the question 'Who are we, and why are we the way we are?' marks a growing awareness that interesting things are yet to be found out, hidden behind the more obvious landmarks of our society and its ways. New Zealand religion is one such little-explored area.

Tangible evidences of religion in New Zealand are unspectacular enough to be taken for granted most of the time. We have no holy cities, and few sacred shrines. Every traveller up and down the country sets foot, at some time or other, in a vaguely 'historic' church. But, for the most part, places and buildings with religious uses, whether they be churchyards or maraes, temples or Kingdom Halls, chapels or New Life Centres, get little attention from the daily passer-by. Like the buildings containing government departments, we only know which is which and what they stand for if we happen to have done some business with them ourselves. Otherwise religious buildings signify nothing much to us, empty and closed as they generally appear to be.

To ask acquaintances what local church they attend is not readily accepted as a part of polite Kiwi conversation. Nor is it felt important, except on a very small number of moral issues, to enquire about the religious inclinations of politicians and public figures. What a Mormon Minister of Labour (if we had one), a Jewish economist, or a Baptist mayor might happen to believe about the divine origins and destiny of the human race would be thought to be of little significance. As long as they looked and sounded much the same as other politicians, economists, and mayors, the assumption would be that their religions were their own private affair and could safely be ignored in assessing their views on matters of public importance.

For all that, we are basically a Christian nation, it would be widely agreed. But just what that means is another matter. The Christianness of New Zealand does mean, at least, that the history and traditions on which people draw, and the institutions and language by which our religious self-expression is shaped, are chiefly those of the Christian Churches and the Bible. These have set the patterns of belief (and disbelief) about religious matters, for the great majority. Our history has simply excluded other alternatives.

From that fact arises a common assumption that the religious life of New Zealand society comes down to the present day from a distant source, distant in time and place, rather like water drawn from an unseen and remote reservoir. This system of spiritual irrigation, it is felt, is increasingly in danger of drying up in our secular times, as the traditional Christian institutions and teachings through which it has flowed seem extended beyond workability.

A quite different view can be argued for, however, if the source of society's religiousness is located not so much within ecclesiastical traditions and institutions, as in the permanent possibilities and continuing experiences of personal and social life. On this view, the inherited institutions (in our case, the various doctrines, customs, and churches of Christianity) are not the suppliers of religion so much as its chief regulators. They make their contribution in stimulating the religious tendencies of society: they channel and amplify them, help to express them, and provide for their continuity. Yet the religious institutions are not the sole source of these tendencies. Nor can the life and health of the institutions be taken as fully representing the extent of the religious life of society at any particular time.

With this in mind, recent students of religion in society have looked for terms by which to draw attention to religious features of society existing outside the churches. Of the many terms offered, 'civil religion' and 'folk religion' are the most useful.[1]

In present scholarly opinion, 'civil religion' is regarded more as an exploratory idea than a proven reality. It refers to the way a state or nation, in its laws and practices and official functions, uses forms of words and rites and ceremonies evoking emotions and expressing commitments very similar to those associated with religious attitudes and behaviour.

A few examples from New Zealand society illustrate the idea. Oaths of allegiance required for naturalization and other purposes end with the phrase 'so help me God'. Words in the Sovereign's official style and title ('Elizabeth the Second by the Grace of God') imply a higher-than-earthly authority for our laws and government. Prayers to open Parliament 'humbly acknowledge the need for God's guidance in all things'. A cross of stars appears on our flag and coat of arms. Our war dead are given solemn commemoration on Anzac Day (a day which still arouses at least as much indigenous religious fervour as does Good Friday and Easter). Our National Hymn is a prayer to the 'God of Nations', asking that 'God defend New Zealand'.

Advocates of the civil religion theory would deny that these practices show merely the lingering influence of the established churches of the colonial homeland. For it is the United States of America, they argue, which has most firmly rejected the idea of a state church, that gives the best examples of civil religion, with its sacred history of Pilgrim Fathers, its ideal of 'One Nation under God', and its motto 'In God we trust'.

New Zealand lacks some of the features which make up American civil religion. It has no solemn office of President to make high-priestly pronouncements on significant occasions. Its myths of origin (the Pakeha ones at least) are more mundane than those of the American settlers. Waitangi Day does not, for most, approach the significance of the Fourth of July, and there is nothing at all in our customs to match the family ceremony of Thanksgiving.

Yet for all that there may be sufficient sanctity and piety in the forms and practices of our civic life to embody a faith of a religious quality: minimal, no doubt, but more uniformly New Zealand's own than the faiths of the particular churches. It would be, if you like, a religion of patriotism. But the true object of such a civil religion would seem to be not simply the nation's institutions, whether parliament, the governing party, or the apparatus of state at any given time. Its focus is something transcending those particular features of society: perhaps God (liberally defined, rather than doctrinally specific), an abstraction like Democracy or the Welfare State, or simply the ideal of 'a better way of life for New Zealanders'. It is to such a final, transcendent focus for hope and aspiration that political parties ritually appeal, in the solemn pledges of their manifestos (at least for the few weeks leading up to a general election).

Civil religion, as a concept, has its critics. Theologians and historians have been quick to point out how history is full of lamentable instances of governments and heads of state claiming supreme authority for themselves, and drawing on the powerful forces of religion to entrench their positions, rather than allowing the state to serve the higher objects of its people's faith, as a church serves God. Thus when President Nixon in his second inaugural address in 1973 called for a renewal of 'faith in America' there were those who saw this as a device to silence criticism of his policies, by making critics appear guilty of disloyalty, impiety, and something approaching blasphemy.[2]

More relevant for us, however, are the criticisms of civil religion made by those who fail to find sufficient sociological support for it as a reality touching the everyday lives of the majority of people. By contrast, the idea of folk religion, the religious ways of common people outside both religious and political institutions, does seem a more substantial field for investigation. Like civil religion, folk religion in New Zealand could be too readily dismissed as simply watered-down church religion. Church-goers sometimes scorn what they see as merely token or nominal Christianity reflected in such things as 'Xmas' cards and celebrations, grace at formal dinners, hymns at funerals, 'Good night and God bless' said by T.V. announcers, the semi-sacred formalities of lodges and service organizations, blessings at ship-launchings and foundation-stone layings, Scouts' and Guides' promises, the R.S.A.'s moment of silent remembrance, school songs and mottos, and popular references to 'God's own country'.[3] Yet it could be argued that things like these are the common currency of a genuine non-sectarian New Zealand piety.

However, like the instances of civil religion given earlier those examples fall mostly into the category of polite behaviour reserved for special occasions. Others have insisted that true folk religion is what comes alive in more spontaneous emotions and responses: the swearing we do when we feel things deeply, the ways we show grief and sympathy, our greetings and farewells, customs for marking important events in family and community life, and other such unselfconscious expressions of our way of life. The question of how such Pakeha ways and customs compare with Maori and Polynesian ones would be well worth sensitive investigation.

A thorough study of folk religion in New Zealand would have to include also the cultic aspects of certain sports and recreations, school traditions, nature-protection movements, popular opinions about the supernatural or occult, alternative ways of coping with illness or despair (chiropractic, yoga for health, horoscopes, weight-watchers, Alcoholics Anonymous, and so on), the kinds of wisdom expressed on talkback sessions or in advice columns, and the annual Telethon appeal (a remarkable display of joyful fervour and cheerful giving).

Is this religion at all? Yes and no. Once we have moved beyond official religious institutions and admitted wider categories such as civil and folk religion the borders are far less well-defined. Much useful work waits to be done, to see if religious parallels can throw light on broader social phenomena.

This book keeps chiefly to the forms of religion more or less defined by recognized religious institutions, these providing the most manageable and available material for an introductory work. But it should be remembered throughout that beyond the institutions, and keeping them going from year to year, are the lives and experiences of New Zealanders living within a distinctive social environment which to a large degree makes them the people they are.

This environment is being enriched by newcomers bringing their own culture: Polynesians, Asians, Americans, Australians, and Europeans embracing various forms of Judeo-Christian and Hindu-Buddhist religions. Many of them see New Zealand as 'Paradise' or 'Godzone Country'. At the same time, thousands of disillusioned people are migrating out of 'the Land of the Long White Cloud'. At their point of departure they are asked to fill out a brief questionnaire. Regrettably, from our point of view, emigrants are not required to state their religious affiliation. If we had such information we would know whether, for example, Jews were leaving in significant numbers, or Methodists, or Presbyterians, or Muslims, or Baha'is, or Mormons.

We who have remained may now take the opportunity of contemplating the various contributions that religion has made to New Zealand society. In the first place the historian Dr L. H. Barber highlights 'The Religious Dimension of New Zealand's History'. Next, Rev. Pieter de Bres outlines 'The Contribution of Maori Religious Movements to Religion in New Zealand'. The Catholic and Protestant contributions are presented by Father E. H. Blasoni and Professor Ian Breward, who respectively ask 'Can Catholicism contribute to an Indigenous New Zealand Religion?' and 'Have the Mainline Protestant Churches moved out of their Colonial Status'. Mr Colin Brown examines two streams which are aiming for unity in the Christian Churches, namely the ecumenical and the charismatic movements; 'Ecumenism in New Zealand: Success or Failure?' he asks, and 'How Significant is the Charismatic Movement?'. Professor Michael Hill examines the sectarian contribution, addressing himself to the question 'Do Sects Thrive while Churches Languish?'. The place of 'The Jewish Community in New Zealand' is discussed by Professor David Pitt, while Dr Kapil Tiwari looks at 'Religious Movements of Indian Origin in New Zealand'. The pluralist and secularist aspects of the picture are scrutinized by Professor Lloyd Geering in his prognosticating study on 'Pluralism and the Future of Religion in New Zealand'.

Finally, since this book is certainly going to be read by students taking Religious Studies courses in New Zealand universities, Professor Albert Moore of Otago University puts in a brief word for the academic contribution to our understanding of religion. On a visit to New Zealand in the 1930's, George Bernard Shaw was moved to declare that our university students (especially aspiring politicians) should have 'a competent general knowledge of the Moslem and Hindu religions, of Buddhism, Shinto, Communism, Fascism, capitalism — and of all the forces which are really alive in the world today'. Universities where these things are not taught and discussed, he said, 'are not universities at all. They are booby traps'. Shaw cannot take all the credit for the present situation, with Religious Studies available in four out of the six universities in New Zealand. But there is today a greater opportunity for systematic and sympathetic study of religion in the academic realm; and as Albert Moore reminds us, 'there is a whole world of religion and religions to explore and rediscover'.

Notes:

1   See:
    American civil religion. Richey, R. E. and Jones, D. G. eds. N. Y. Harper & Row, 1974.
    Also:
    GLASNER, P. The study of Australian folk religion. *In Australian Essays in world religions.* Adelaide, Australian Association for the Study of Religions, 1977.

2   BELLAH, R. N. American civil religion in the 1970s. *In American civil religion. op. cit.* p.255-272.

3   Our thanks to Yvette Reisima and Jenny Sutherland for providing some of these examples.

The Historical Aspect

THE RELIGIOUS DIMENSION OF NEW ZEALAND'S HISTORY
L. H. Barber

Any attempt to explore the religious dimension of New Zealand's history is a risky venture. The main risk is that one's readers might give vent to a collective yawn, a natural enough reflex action to a subject dulled by the superficial, episodic, name-studded recitals of the 'church insular' that pass for denominational histories in New Zealand. There are few enough histories of New Zealand's churches, and these few tend to restrict the religious dimension of the Dominion's history to a recital of 'intra-mural' ecclesiastical affairs.

The Anglican Church in New Zealand has two major volumes that trace its development from the missionary period. Unfortunately, both Canon H. T. Purchas' *History of the English Church in New Zealand*[1] and Professor W. P. Morrell's *The Anglican Church in New Zealand*[2] provide little more than recitals of ecclesiastical events. In these two works processions of bishops, priests, and deacons move almost endlessly to their eternal rewards. The extramural involvement of the church receives only a nod. The two great wars are treated as affairs of chaplains and vacant parishes, while the Depression of the 1930s is dismissed with a few references to the difficulties met in maintaining parish solvency. Both authors restrict the dimension of religious history to the ecclesiastical ghetto.

Professor J. R. Elder's *The History of the Presbyterian Church of New Zealand*[3] has almost as little social context. There are some references to the hardships of pioneer life, and the role played by home missionaries as civilising agents, but in the main its perspective is also narrowly ecclesiastical.

The one comprehensive volume on the history of New Zealand Methodism is William Morley's *History of Methodism in New Zealand.*[4] The Wesley Historical Society has attempted to cover some of the history of Methodism since the publication of this work. The Society has produced many useful publications, but it has shown little interest in the impact of religion on society, and the impact of social change upon the church.

As for the Roman Catholic Church, it has commissioned no recent history of Roman Catholicism in New Zealand. The most recent history of the church is J. J. Wilson's two volumed *The Church in New Zealand,*[5] published in serial form from 1910. This work can only be generously described as parochial and disconnected. Students wishing to study Roman Catholic history in New Zealand must rely upon several learned articles and theses. Peripheral works such as R. P. Davis, *Irish Issues in New Zealand Politics, 1868-1922,* and Pat Gallagher, *The Marist Brothers in New Zealand, Fiji and Samoa: 1876-1976,* are useful.[6]

The Church of Jesus Christ of the Latter Day Saints has been active in New Zealand since the 1880s and B. W. Hunt's *Zion in New Zealand* is a reliable, though subjective, account of that church's growth.[7]

The Salvation Army scores the highest marks; although a bare pass at that. John C. Waite's *Dear Mr Booth* is an episodic, slender, and undeveloped account of the first eighty years of the Army's march through New Zealand.[8] However, Waite does make some attempt to relate the Army's work to changing social patterns, economic and political change, and to the advance of materialistic secularism. In Waite's book the Salvation Army meets William Pember Reeves, Richard John Seddon, Sir Peter Buck, the 'Young Maori Party', the Trades and Labour Councils, the Depression, and the liquor interests. While the social context is inadequately explored, it is at least there.

New Zealand's Jewish community is not without its historian and L. M. Goldman, in *The History of the Jews in New Zealand,* has provided a rather superficial account of Jewish participation in early settlements, problems of inter-marriage, reaction to Russian Jewry, and the involvement of New Zealand Jews in the arts, culture, and industry.[9] More useful is his discussion of Jewish religious practices within the Dominion.

This mainly dismal catalogue must come to an end. By this time it should be clear that the religious dimension in New Zealand's history has in the past been restricted to narrow 'intra-mural' confines by the denominational historians. However, in the last decade the perspective has broadened. Students now have access to a growing number of theses, articles and books, by Judith Binney, J. M.

R. Owens, Hugh Laracy, P. S. O'Connor, I. Breward and others.[10] These scholars have indicated something of the mixture of prejudice and principle, reforming zeal and intolerant bigotry, and racial prejudice and cultural inter-involvement, that have been part and parcel of the religious dimension — from the pioneer missionaries to the present time. The development of church history as a subject for theological college diplomas and divinity degrees has aided this move to a more sophisticated historical appraisal. These experts have frowned upon the hagiographic and anecdotal approach to New Zealand religious history. The appointment of professional church historians to the staffs of the leading theological colleges and seminaries has signalled a new respect for church history. These historians have been quick to interest themselves in New Zealand's history.

Religious Studies Departments have assisted in the formation of a broader perspective of New Zealand's religious history. The foundation and expansion of religious studies has, in some centres, challenged undergraduates to look more deeply at the claims, prejudices, and impact of religious groups. The South Island universities have a much better record than the northern universities. At Otago, Professor Ian Breward has a paper in ecclesiastical history; and at the University of Canterbury, the Rev. Colin Brown presents papers in 'Western Religious Thought', 'History of Religious Thought', and an M.A. paper in 'A topic or period in the history of Christianity'. At Victoria University of Wellington, Dr James Veitch is in 1979 introducing a paper on 'Religion in New Zealand' at Honours level. This course will attend to the Maori context, coming of the European, colonial stage and to denominational triumphalism within the colony. Considerable attention will be given to New Zealand religious history in the years following the first world war and students will be required to undertake field work and to present research essays in the fields of the Ratana Church, charismatic movement, and Judaism in New Zealand.

In universities without theological faculties or religious studies departments, the religious dimension of the nation's history still receives attention. At the University of Auckland, Professor P. S. O'Connor and Dr Hugh Laracy have given considerable attention to the religious component of New Zealand's social history. Professor W. H. Oliver, at Massey University, has a particular interest in millennialism and in religious pressure groups that have attempted to shape, and regulate by law, the behaviour of New Zealanders in the past.[11] At the University of Waikato, a history course was introduced in 1976 entitled 'Aspects of New Zealand Religious History', and has grown annually, to a class component of over thirty in 1978.

The Waikato Experiment

The three classes that have so far enrolled for the Waikato paper have faced several frustrations and challenges in their attempts to get to grips with New Zealand's religious history. No single volume textbook exists, and many of the decades studied have been neglected by church historians. Denominational bias was a problem to be faced in some of the early histories. Church statistics were found to be somewhat unreliable. There were sufficient journal articles about the missionary period and the sectarian strife of the First World War to allow exact study of these two areas of interest. Unfortunately, there are few learned articles to guide the student's understanding of other decades. These problems are not insurmountable. Primary documents were collected, reproduced, and made available to the students. Those who have completed the course have studied a variety of church reports, biographical comment, ecclesiastical statistics, theses, Parliamentary Debates, ecclesiastical and religious journals and church newspapers. The lecture programme involved a discussion of the colonial ethos, the evangelical alliance, anti-Catholicism, heresy in the nineteenth century, social crusading, revivalism, theological education, attempts at church union, and the growth and decline of minor ecclesiastical groups. During its first year the course covered the period from 1880 to 1940. However, in 1977 the terminal date was moved to 1967 — in order to include the Geering heresy trial. In two years' time the course may become 'Australasian Religious History'. This expansion will allow students to make use of the considerable and well-written corpus of Australian religious studies.[12]

For three intakes of students the course is now a distant memory. For me, the process of stock-taking continues. As part of this stock-taking and self-criticism that follows examination marking, I have attempted to clarify what religious dimensions of New Zealand history should be of concern to lecturer and students in future years. I wish now to share with you some of the basic religious issues that have so far identified themselves.

Where To Begin

One of the elementary problems that faced us was where to begin. There were very good arguments for beginning in the missionary period. After all this is the only developed field of research into New Zealand's religious history, and it is the only field that presents a set of published scholarly work. It has a further advantage — the scholars do not always agree — particularly Judith Binney and John Owens.[13] Their disagreements may be used to pedagogical advantage in forcing students to assess the evidence for themselves. At the University of

Waikato the present course begins its survey in 1880. This date was settled upon partly because Dr John Miller has for some years taught at third year level a course on race relations in New Zealand. (The History Department at Waikato certainly does not wish students to get double value for their labours!) There is, however, another equally valid argument for beginning at 1880. This argument holds that by 1880 New Zealand had developed sufficient patterns of urban and rural life, and the churches had been given sufficient time to consolidate their organisation – to allow valid comparisons with British and Australian models. Besides, by 1880 some of the great nineteenth century intellectual and emotional tides are in full flow. Darwinism, the challenge of higher criticism, middle class fear of syndicalism and socialism, and virulent anti-Catholicism are in evidence in Britain and New Zealand. New Zealand's reaction to these makes a fascinating story. However, against this selection of a late starting point it could be retorted that the 1880s can only be properly understood in the light of settlement religious attitudes and practice, and that missionary-Maori culture contact before the Land Wars is a basic foundation to New Zealand's religious history.

If another university decided to pioneer another course in New Zealand religious history, and decided to begin with the missionary period, its lecturer might well note the surprising insularity of much of the study done so far. Despite the steady trickle of ink spent in assessing missionary diaries, reports, and correspondence, the net result is surprisingly insular. Far more attention could be paid to comparisons of the New Zealand missionary experience with the Hawaiian, the Pacific, and African missionary period. More attention could be paid to the ideological baggage and inherited prejudices brought by the missionaries to New Zealand. For example, it is significant that a branch of the Evangelical Alliance was formed in New Zealand in 1847 by the Reformed Church of Scotland Minister, James Duncan, within a few months of the Association's foundation in England in 1846.[14] Most missionaries reacted to the pressures of antipodean hardship by closing their ranks and becoming even more fixed in their denominational loyalties and their ethical rigorism. Therefore, greater attention could be paid to the state of their home churches. Considerable work remains to be done in tracing the impact of the Evangelical Alliance in stiffening the Protestant ranks against popery and Puseyism; and in creating a climate of fear towards French-Catholic ambitions in the Pacific basin.

The treatment afforded the New Zealand missionary years raised the question 'How can insularity of approach be avoided?' I found that students came to the course knowing little of the religious history of Europe and the United States.

This defect had to be quickly rectified. Through reading Alex. Vidler's *The Church In An Age Of Revolution,* and more specialised examinations of the state of British and European religion in the Victorian and Edwardian ages, students gained a context for their survey of the religious section of New Zealand's history.[15] Only when this contextual knowledge had been gained was the student in a position to recognise and understand the problems that his documents raised. Without this background he could make little of the adjustment of Anglicanism from its position as an established church in England to its colonial role as a free church in a free state. Unless the student knew something of Scottish church history, the saga of New Zealand Presbyterianism's development from an Otago enclave of Free Church of Scotland émigrés, to the second most numerical of New Zealand's religious professions, was meaningless. Similarly, the change of status for Baptists and Methodists, from 'dissent' to denominational equality only assumes a significance if one is aware of the history and place of 'chapel' in British society in the nineteenth century.

A Variety of Models

In the period 1882-1940 the religious dimension of New Zealand's history was sizeable and consequential. Our students used a variety of models in their appraisal of this period. One student tested the involvement of the churches in secular life by asking how effectively they performed the Old Testament roles of prophet, priest, and king. Their prophetic role was in evidence in Rutherford Waddell's dramatic denunciation of 'the Sin of Sweating' in 1888;[16] and in his role on the Royal Commission on Sweating set up by the government following his allegations. The expansions of networks of parishes, church schools, and lay missioners, into the 'backblocks', reveals the church's endeavour to provide priestly services, and a moral guardianship at the advancing rural and surburban frontiers. Attempts by religious pressure groups to cajole, bribe, and threaten parliamentarians into amending the Education Act of 1877 shows the church involved in government. Endeavours to close the public-houses of New Zealand, enforce the Scottish Sabbath, limit gambling, and impose a more rigorous censorship on the stage, showed that some of the traditional churches assumed that they were still God-ordained authorities in matters moral and legislative. They believed that New Zealand's parliament, the parliament of a Christian country, was bound to take notice of the judgments. They assumed that the state was bound to take notice of them, and some statesmen did. The doctrine of the 'two swords' was not dead in late nineteenth century and early twentieth century New Zealand.

A further testing of the impact of religion on society in New Zealand, and society on religion, was made by several students who analysed the involvement of the churches in the wars. The two world wars, and the Boer War that preceded them, allow for a study of the reactions to the demands of patriotic jingoists, imperialists, xenophobic anti-Germans, and the persecutors of pacifists. In all these cases, the major churches showed themselves conformists to the demands of government and popular hysterical pressure. They seemed to lack in prophetic zeal. There were several exceptions – Ormond Burton was one.[17] The involvement of the church in the suppression of his prophetic message, and the failure of the churches to denounce the persecution of émigré Germans and pacifist Jehovah Witnesses, makes a sad chapter in New Zealand's history. Both world wars acted as watersheds. After the First World War, the aims of the religious social crusaders ceased to be viable propositions. Prohibition and Bible-in-schools increasingly became minority opinions; the size of the minority dwindling yearly. The Second World War was followed by an expanding secularisation of society.

Students were quick to note the involvement of religious issues in civil rights conflicts in New Zealand. From the 1920s civil rights contests have been more frequently the concern of those New Zealanders daring enough not to be intimidated by Austin Mitchell's 'clobbering machine'. James Gibb intervened on behalf of F. F. Wolter, a refugee from Prussian militarism, and a naturalised British subject, who found himself during the First World War deprived of his citizenship, incarcerated on Somes Island, and subjected to vindictive xenophobia.[18] The late Archbishop Liston was arrested for sedition, following a speech made during the St. Patrick's Day celebrations in 1922.[19] The bishop had described the suppressive tactics of the British Army in Ireland as 'murderous'. On this occasion, a sensible judge, Mr Justice Stringer, refused to accept the view that New Zealanders opposed to British policy were *ipso facto* disloyal. Liston was acquitted. The Archbishop's prosecution is particularly interesting. Anti-Catholicism went to considerable lengths to pay off old scores in New Zealand in the 1920s.

The dismissal of two teachers, Ormond Burton and F. Page, from the teaching profession, for refusing to take the oath of loyalty, an oath they believed to compromise their conscience over New Zealand's militarist stunts, and Alun Richards' deprivation of civil rights are all issues that raise profound religious questions.[20] In this period many oft-repeated Augustinian questions were again raised: the priority of God's laws, the right of dissent, the responsibilities of Christians to the state, and government's responsibility both for defence and for the maintenance of civil rights.

New Zealand was not without its millennialist movements and in the 1920s and 1930s these captured a considerable following. Arrogant Pakehas had long predicted the further decline, and possible extinction of the Maori race. Josiah Strong's racial social Darwinism was not without its New Zealand disciples. The 'Young Maori Party' had awoken the race before its death-rattle had commenced; but the people needed both leadership and their *raison d'être*. Students were quick to note the importance of the indigenous Maori millennialist movements—especially Ratana's.[21] Tahupotiki Wiremu Ratana gave a prophetic leadership that brought Maori and Pakeha in their hundreds to Ratana village — seeking healing of both body and soul. Historians have interpreted him as an advance guard for Maori nationalism. My students suggested that he owed far more to Judeo-Christian religious concepts than had hitherto been ascribed to him. They noted that in the tradition of the Old Testament prophets, the Mangai saw a cloud come from the sea as a vision from God; and that he interpreted the washing up of two whales on the coast as a word from the Almighty. Ratana's call for the destruction of the power of the *tohunga* could be likened to the Old Testament prophetic denunciations of the prophets of Baal. They held that the Mangai, well-versed in the Bible, had assimilated many of the Old Testament concepts. He saw the Maori people as a remnant to be saved. The influenza epidemic of 1918 was a sign of God's wrath. His hostility to tribalism owed as much to the Yahwist as it did to Maori Nationalism. Ratana insisted that the Maori people were meant by God to recover their strength and become a power in the land, and his conviction that they were the elect of God strengthened the religious growth of his church.

The uncertain economic climate of the 1920s and the Depression of the 1930s also sent many non-Maori New Zealanders in search of millennialist solutions. In most of the major churches individual clergy, and committees of churchmen, impressed by the panaceas offered by Douglas Credit, involved themselves in discussions on the reform of the monetary system. They turned to Douglas Credit, or Labour, or the New Zealand Legion, or to revivalism, for assistance. Frightened by the continuing inroads of materialist secularism on church attendance and church income, frustrated by the failure of life to return to pre-war normalcy, and disturbed by their further displacement to the periphery of everyday life, some of the clergy looked for help to this-worldly revolutionary solutions.

A study of revivalism in New Zealand allowed students to investigate the parallels that they thought might exist between the electorates' withdrawal into political conservatism and the periodic withdrawal of the churches into religious reaction. They noted the failure of parliamentary liberalism to bring an era of political stability and just economy to the post-war world. They saw this being accompanied by an increasing suspicion of theological liberalism. Anthropocentric theology, with its assumption that man was basically good, and that human progress was the natural order, was now greeted with hollow laughter. Biblical conservatism, fundamentalism, and the 'theology of crisis' — inaugurated by Barth and Brunner in particular — summoned men and women to take refuge in the ark before the flood arrived.

In the years immediately following the first world war, revivalists arrived in New Zealand in increasing numbers. Herbert Booth, the renegade son of William Booth (founder of the Salvation Army), was in New Zealand in 1919 and 1920. He demanded from his converts that they pledged themselves to a covenant that affirmed the literal inerrancy of all scripture, and required them to disavow 'any and every creed or argument tending to deny his [Christ's] deity, or diminish his glory'.[22]

In 1922 a small army of revivalists wandered through the countryside. The Rev. J. J. North, the Baptist college principal, found it necessary to rebuke one — the Rev. W. Lamb. Dr North complained of Lamb:

> He is a very faithful minister of Christ but we believe he is thoroughly mistaken in many of his identifications . . . The discovery of Ireland in the book of Daniel is a piece of sheer, almost fantastical surmise.
> . . . The business of the church is not to rival augurs and soothsayers but to preach the everlasting gospel and to live in expectancy of Christ's glorious realm.'[23]

The revivalists were pessimistic and judgemental. So were the theologians of crisis — Barth and Brunner. These 'theologians of the Word', made a considerable impact on the Presbyterian and Congregational ministers, especially at the time of the Fascist and Nazi menace to civilisation. Their impact dwindled in the early 1950s.

Secular historians have been very much involved in analyses of the Labour movement in New Zealand. I was particularly interested in this course to trace the impact of the churches on the working-classes. I suggest that the churches' greatest period of impact amongst the workers of New Zealand was at a time when the colony's labourers were disorganised, aspiring, and needful of leadership and spokesmen. I further suggest that it is in the 1880s, and through to 1910, that the labouring groups gained most from the churches. Clerical leadership in the sweating agitation, church support for liberal humanitarian legislation, and involvement in improvement associations (the Workers' Educational Association, Literary Associations, the prohibition movement, anti-gambling societies, and the like) suggested that the church was the guardian of social justice, and a civilising agency. The churches became less certain in their attitude toward Labour as Syndicalist and Marxian leadership asserted itself within the workers' associations, and as the Trade Union movement developed. The arrival of Australian agitators, and the dissemination of Pat Hickey's American trade union tactics, brought to the fore a middle-class fear of violence and upset to law and order.

The 1890 strike had been a warning. The 1911-1912 strike at Waihi, and the 1913 Waterside Strike clinched matters. In the main, church leaders denounced disorder and dressed down the unionists for demanding too much. Private property, and the capitalist system, were equated with the divine order.

The First World War worsened the situation. Dislocation, overseas revolution, and a fierce materialistic drive, made the church's leaders more fearful. The joint participation of clerics and labour leaders in the disarmament movement, through the League of Nations' Union, was small and short-lived. The Depression of the 1930s made matters worse still. The labour force was made hungry by a Coalition Government determined to balance the budget at any cost. How did the churches fare in this situation? As far as economic solutions were concerned the churches had nothing to offer. The realists joined the Labour Party. Nash, Nordmeyer, Carr, and other leading churchmen, threw their weight into the party that in 1935 swept on to the Treasury benches. However, my students were quick to remark that although H. E. Holland, the Labour Leader until 1933, had been a Methodist lay preacher, M. J. Savage, the new leader and Peter Fraser, his deputy and successor, were both secularists. Fraser was an admitted agnostic, especially opposed to any attempt to overturn the secular basis of New Zealand's education.

We came to the conclusion that the churches accepted, rather than applauded, the birth of the welfare state. It seemed that whilst most New Zealanders concentrated their attention on new social welfare legislation, improvements in housing, and developments in education, the church leaders seemed to have been busy berating those who spent Sundays at the beach, rather than in their pews. A terrestrial heaven had arrived, but the church appeared as a complaining dowager who had lost her place during the advance of time.

Did the Second World War worsen the churches' liaison with the working-class New Zealander? Soldiers returned with materialist ambitions — seeking farms under rehabilitation loans, asking for government assistance to buy a garage, or to conclude a university degree. They had little time to give the churches. Their wives, many of whom had become workers during the war, had to a large extent lost touch with the church. Old and retired ministers, and lay preachers, had ministered to congregations made up mainly of women, whilst even the very young and very old men drilled on Sunday in the home guard. The church seems to have done very little to assist New Zealanders in their post-war readjustment.

What of the 1951 Waterside Strike? The churches spoke out against government interference with civil rights, and especially against the Police Offences Amendment Bill, but they had little to say about the right of the militant unions to a fair hearing, and the rights of all sections of the New Zealand community to a distribution of the new wealth gained from wool sales abroad. Law and order were again their vital concern.

In the 1960s and 1970s the churches seem to have become even less relevant to the labour movement. The churches' interest in New Zealand's involvement with the Third World does not concern the New Zealand worker, let alone ally him to the church. Occasionally, clerics and labour leaders join hands — in opposition to a rugby tour or to a visit by a nuclear warship. One of my students suggested that their juncture was like a rare meeting between an emissary of China and one from the Grand Duchy of Lichenstein.

Yet another set of questions was raised by the recurring problem of theological certitude faced by New Zealand's churchmen in our period. The conflict between dogmatism and variety of theological subscription began early in our colonial history. William Salmond, a Presbyterian minister employed as Professor of Moral Philosophy at the University of Otago, was in 1888 arraigned before a church court for daring to question the *Westminster Confession's* suggestion that unbaptised infants were damned.[24] James Gibb, later to unite the two Presbyterian churches of the colony, was himself found guilty in 1890 for asserting the same 'heresy'.[25] In the 1930s, John Dickey, a Presbyterian Professor of Theology, was attacked for his thoroughly orthodox book, *The Organism of Christian Truth.*[26] Maurice Gee's recently published novel, *Plumb,* tells another story of ecclesiastical intolerance.[27]

Heresy-hunting in New Zealand has been a predominantly Presbyterian sport. One of my students provocatively argued that this was because the Presbyterian clergy contained more intellectuals, and was always at pains to make a rationale for its faith. However, the Anglican Church in New Zealand did excommunicate Ratana for making too much of angels, and tried a few excessively High Anglo-Catholics; and the Methodists did depose Burton for the heresy of being out of step with current patriotism. A few Roman Catholic priests have, from time to time, been banished to ecclesiastical Siberia, but, even so, the real public heresy trials have all been Presbyterian.

These trials, especially the Geering trial of 1967, allow students to analyse the claim to credibility made by theologians and preachers during our history. They also revealed the growing challenges made to traditional dogma, from both within and without the churches.

The 1967 Geering trial raises a number of important problems. To what extent have the New Zealand churches always marched a step behind the British, American, and northern European churches, in their acceptance of theological and moral restatements? Has the development of charismatic groups within New Zealand religion expressed an escape from the tension of struggling to present a relevant and credible faith? Is it a compartmentalising of religion away from everyday life? What is, and has been, the attitude of New Zealanders to theological colleges and theologians? Are theological teachers regarded as dangerous radicals? Does this reflect a continuing pioneering suspicion of intellectuals, and of elitist groups? Another question raised by the trial was that of 'vestigial belief'. Were many of Geering's public accusers merely reacting to a challenge to long-held myths, associated with happier family or Sunday School days? To what extent were they really debating doctrinal issues? Did some regard the beliefs challenged in a way similar to their respect for grandfather's top-hat — to be venerated but never worn? The Geering trial, and the heresy trials previous to it, allow students every opportunity to analyse the changing challenges of secularism and science to New Zealand's religion.

Conclusion

The religious dimension of New Zealand's history is broad and encompassing. There are many areas open to investigation that we did not touch in our course. In the future, attention could be given to the role of religion in protecting the pioneer from the barbarism of the rural frontier; in promoting the myth that rural life is more virtuous and morally healthy than town life, and in asserting that remarriage is to be made as difficult as possible for New Zealanders. New Zealand's attitudes to Jews, Polynesians, Mormons, and the representatives of other world religions, also deserve attention.

However, over the last few years, extra-literary records have become available to the student of religious history to assist in the task of assessment. The archives section of Radio New Zealand, and the availability of reproductions of video-tape, have allowed a cross-section of ecclesiastical viewpoints and liturgical activities to be retained and analysed. In our library and language laboratory we are able to replay Bob Lowe's interviews, General Synod debates, and samples from 'Morning Comment' and 'Faith and Works'.

Religion is far more than the worship and charity of the devotee. A person's religion is the scale of values that motivates his daily acts. If this is so, the secularist inroads of the 1960s make the study of New Zealand's religious history increasingly difficult. Religion need not any longer be a matter of church affiliation, nor of conscious allegiance to a code received from any one of the churches. I suspect that W. H. Oliver was right when he stated in *Comment,* July 1962:

> The Christianity which characterises the bulk of the New Zealand people is a vestigial sort which is manifested fitfully, in moral attitudes rather than in explicit beliefs or overt behaviour. It is enshrined, not in any building, but in such phrases as "giving a man a fair go", "doing the decent thing", "playing the game", and "lending a hand" − colloquial debasements of the Golden Rule.[28]

If this is so, and our 'religious' behaviour and values have existed for some time beyond the fringe of church activities, then it is obvious that the significance of the religious dimension of New Zealand's history is far too potentially important to the student of New Zealand society to be left to the confining category of 'church history'.

References
1. PURCHAS, H. T. *A history of the English Church in New Zealand.* Christchurch, Simpson & Williams, 1914.
2. MORRELL, W. P. *The Anglican Church in New Zealand; a history.* Dunedin, Anglican Church of the Province of New Zealand, 1973.
3. ELDER, J. R. *The history of the Presbyterian Church of New Zealand, 1840-1940.* Christchurch, Presbyterian Bookroom, 1940.
4. MORLEY, W. *The history of Methodism in New Zealand.* Wellington, McKee, 1900.
5. WILSON J. J. *The Church in New Zealand.* Vols 1 and 2. Dunedin, N.Z. Tablet Printing and Publishing Co. 1910-1926.
6. DAVIS, R. P. *Irish issues in New Zealand politics, 1868-1922.* Dunedin, University of Otago Press, 1974.

GALLAGHER, P. *The Marist Brothers in New Zealand, Fiji and Samoa, 1876-1976.* Tuakau, New Zealand Marist Brothers Trust Board, 1976.
Amongst the best of the theses is:
LARACY, H. M. *The life and context of Bishop Patrick Moran.* Thesis, M.A., Victoria University of Wellington, 1964.
Attention is also drawn to:
SNOOK. I. A. Religion in schools, a Catholic controversy, 1930-1934. *N.Z. journal of history 6:* 169-177, 1972.

7. HUNT, B. W. *Zion in New Zealand; a history of the Church of Jesus Christ of Latterday Saints.* Hamilton, Church College of New Zealand, 1977.

8. WAITE. J. C. *Dear Mr Booth: some early chapters of the history of the Salvation Army in New Zealand.* Wellington, Salvation Army Territorial Headquarters, 1964.

9. GOLDMAN, L. M. *The history of the Jews in New Zealand.* Wellington, Reed, 1958.

10. BINNEY, J. *The legacy of guilt: a life of Thomas Kendall.* Auckland, University of Auckland/Oxford University Press, 1968.
O'CONNOR, P. S. Sectarian conflicts in New Zealand, 1911-1920. *Political science 19*(1): 3-16, 1967.
O'CONNOR, P. S. Mr Massey and the P.P.A. – a suspicion confirmed. *N.Z. journal of public administration 28*(2): 69-74, 1966.
O'CONNOR, P. S. Storm over the clergy – New Zealand 1917. *Journal of religious history 4:* 128-148, 1966.

11. OLIVER, W. H. *Prophets and millennialists: the uses of biblical prophecy in England from the 1790's to the 1840's.* Auckland, Auckland University Press/Oxford University Press, 1978.

12. The *Journal of religious history* (Sydney) provides a continued appraisal of the state of Australasian religious history.

13. See articles by:
BINNEY, J. *N.Z. journal of history 1:* 124-147, 1967. and by:
OWENS, J. *N.Z. journal of history 2:* 18-40, 1968; also review by OWENS of BINNEY'S book, *A legacy of guilt,* in *N.Z. journal of history 4:* 91-93, 1970.

14. For an extensive discussion of the inter-involvement of British religious moods and the New Zealand ecclesiastical situation see:
BARBER, L. H. *The social crusader; James Gibb at the Australasian pastoral frontier, 1882-1935.* Thesis, Ph.D., Massey university, 1975.

15. VIDLER, A. *The Church in an age of revolution, 1789 to the present day.* London, Hodder and Stoughton, 1962.

16. BARBER, L.H. *The social crusader op. cit.,* p. 74.

17. BURTON, O. E. 1893-1974. Burton's unpublished autobiography is deposited in the Alexander Turnbull Library.

18. BARBER, L. H. The Twenties; New Zealand's xenophobic years. *N.Z. law journal* 1976: 95-96.
19. The Liston trial deserves fuller treatment.
See *Otago Daily Times* 20-24 May 1922, and *Maoriland worker* 29 March 1922.
20. For a careful discussion of this incident see:
OPENSHAW, R. *Patriotism and the New Zealand primary school: the decisive years of the twenties.* Thesis, D. Phil., University of Waikato, 1978.
21. HENDERSON, J. M. *Ratana: the man, the Church, the political movement.* Wellington, Reed, 1972. (Polynesian Society memoir, vol. 36)
22. WORSFOLD, J. E. *A history of the charismatic movements in New Zealand.* Bradford, Julian Literature Trust, 1974. p.94-97.
23. *Ibid.,* p. 107.
24. BARBER, L. H. *The social crusader op.cit.,* p. 56-60.
25. BARBER, L. H. James Gibb's heresy trial, 1890. *N.Z. journal of history 12:* 146-157, 1978.
26. DICKIE, J. *The organism of Christian truth: a modern positive dogmatic.* London, Clarke, 1931.
27. GEE, M. *Plumb.* London, Faber, 1978.
28. OLIVER, W. H. The habit of establishment. *Comment 12:* 4-5, 1962.

The Maori Contribution

MAORI RELIGIOUS MOVEMENTS IN AOTEAROA
Pieter H. de Bres

Among the reactions against Western penetration of non-European countries and subsequent colonisation is the emergence of movements of a religious nature. A product of the introduction of the Christian faith by missionaries, they are organisationally independent and indigenous in that their own traditions are intermingled with newly introduced beliefs and in their own forms of leadership. In 'doctrine' they may sometimes deviate from the teachings of the Western churches to the extent of being not even recognisable as 'Christian'. The contents of the faith are largely drawn from the West, but recast in local patterns.

Among these movements we find the Maori churches and cults in this country. Although they have their specific New Zealand characteristics, they are related to the much wider group of so-called millennarian type movements and cargo cults outside New Zealand.

They are usually brought about when people are suppressed and frustrated. In contact situations the 'wealth' of the Western Countries fosters certain expectations the fulfilment of which leaves much to be desired.[1]

It applies equally to oppressed peasant groups in old European societies, to the 'city poor' in industrialised countries. Frequently contact has led to a degree of social isolation when kinship groups and cohesive local communities are broken up. Subsequently, disintegration of traditional social patterns, combined with forced acculturation, efforts to erase traditional culture and the presence of racial discrimination, have led to a quest for a cultural re-orientation, frequently expressed in religious terms. They are a new activating and unifying force, creating a new unity which transcends kinship and social loyalties. In many instances they are a pre-political phenomenon, a precursor of political awakening and a forerunner of a new political organisation. Though clothed in political apparel, they remain basically religious, having originated in societies dominated by religion. Their political message is couched in the language and images of traditional religions. In a situation of political helplessness at the time, they are outlets for extreme anxiety and depression.

Maori Religious Movements — Self-Christianisation

Maori religious movements are many and varied. Some date from the very early times of colonisation. An example is the prophet Te Atua Wera, whose activities are recorded as commencing in 1833. The Bay of Islands, centre of the earliest missionary activities, was the natural place of origin of such a movement. Te Atua Wera set a theme typical of many later emerging prophetic indigenous movements — the Maoris identifying themselves with the *Hūrai,* the Jews, claiming to be descendants of the 'lost tribes of Israel', and, like them, a chosen people, object of the special care and love of *Ihowa* (Jehovah). There were others, some whose names have been recorded, others who have been lost to history.

However, the major development of Maori prophetic movements did not take place until the 1860's, when the land wars stirred society and gave rise to new expressions of religion in Maori terms. Te Whiti, a Maori pacifist; Te Ua, the founder of the *Pai Marire* religion, a name which means 'good and peaceful' (ironically this group, Hauhaus, became a strong supportive force of the wars of the time); Te Mahaki; Te Kahupukaro; King Tawhiao, the second Maori king and founder of the *Tariao* or 'morningstar faith'. All these made their own contribution and influenced subsequent prophets, but none of them made an impact to the extent that they left behind lasting religious groups. They were very much time-bound and associated with political events of the day, particularly with the confiscation of Maori land.

There are only two prominent Maori religious leaders who left a permanent mark on religious life in New Zealand: the nineteenth century East Coast prophet Te Kooti, founder of the Ringatu Church and the twentieth century charismatic leader Tahupotiki Wiremu Ratana, who founded the Ratana Church. Lesser prophets supported these churches and played a role in their development. The prophet Rua was associated with the Ringatu movement, Maria Pungare saw her prophecies fulfilled in the emergence of Rua, and Mere

Rikiriki prophesied that the spirit of God would fall on Ratana. A prophet with a smaller following was Rapana, a Ratana dissident.

This phenomenon of the emergence of new religious groupings can be described as a form of self-Christianisation. On the one hand the teachings of the missionaries and the Bible form the sources of their faith, on the other they reject the interpretations of the missionaries. The leaders play an innovative role but always adjusted to the aspirations of their followers. Biblical figures like Moses and Jesus feature prominently, Christian symbols are used, but their role and place are made relevant to the actual situation of the times.

To the Hauhaus, Lyons suggests[2] the cross symbolised the crucifixion of the natives at the hand of the whites. Baptism was meant to consecrate the warriors before they went into battles which were fought with religious fervour as 'holy wars'.

Te Ua saw himself as a new Moses and thought that Jehovah would speak from the top of the Niu pole. Rua presented himself as the incarnation of the Holy Ghost, as a son of God and the younger brother of Christ.

Some of the movements were militant, like the Hauhaus. Others stood for non-violent resistance.

Te Whiti was particularly concerned with the problem of suffering and saw the suffering of the Maori people as part of God's plan. There was no tragedy in this, for through suffering they would attain grace. Their destiny was to be persecuted, the trials became a virtue, they rejoiced in them. He saw no point in fighting. God was a just God and would save his people himself. To quote Te Whiti's own words:[3] "The Master will not allow the doings of great and wicked men to be accomplished. Evil cannot be upheld. The wrath of God is upon the strange people, but He is supporting us, the small assembly gathered here this day." God was not a distant, remote God, but relevant to the Maori situation. He was not the Pakeha God but the Maori's own God. Te Whiti aimed at a higher and better quality of life. People who didn't fight would bring a little more love. Ultimately, he believed, a peaceful co-existence of Maori and Pakeha might emerge — that the races would be living side by side in peace — the white man to live among us, but the Maori no longer sub-servient to his immoderate greed.

Following the period of the activities of the early missionaries and of the movements which emerged during the land wars of the nineteenth century, a new development took place in the birth of the Ringatu and Ratana Churches, both of which are of contemporary significance as 'genuine Maori variants of Christianity'.[4]

These will be the main subject of the discussion. Occasional reference will be

made also to two subgroups of these churches, the millennarian movement of
the prophet Rua, which became extinct after the founder's death, and the still
existing, but very small, Rapana church.

The Sources

One of the major problems a researcher of Maori Religious movements has to
face is the dearth of documentary material, particularly if one tries to focus on
their 'religious quality', rather than on historical facts.

For many years the study in this area has concentrated on mythology and
religion in *traditional* Maori society. Shortland, Best, Johansen, Alpers, Orbell,
and Irvine are familiar names.

However, a number of monographs on various topics have been published.[5]
Gadd, Henderson, Sorrensen, Binney, and Clark have written from a historical
perspective. Bathurst made a psychological study of the Hauhaus. Winks wrote
on the doctrine of Hauhauism. Sociologists Arbuckle, de Bres, and Mol have
been concerned with religious affiliation of the Maori. Within the same category
one may place survey reports by Caton and Mirams. Greenwood published a
monograph on the Ringatu. Church leaders like Laughton, Laurenson, and
Rakena have written from a missionary perspective. Older missionary material,
found in the archives of the various churches, supplies the student with some
data, but often presented in a biassed form, emphasising those aspects of new
emerging religions which were out of line with traditional dogmas, and new
religious movements were often referred to as neo-pagan, deviationist and
heretical. Some worthwhile observations were made by Ngata and Sutherland in
their essay 'Religious influences'. Press articles by well qualified writers like
Dansey and Fowler are yet another source. Recent contributions to the study of
Maori religious movements were made by the anthropologists Lyons and Misur,
while Anne Gibson wrote a comparison of Pai Marire and Ringatu. Particular
reference should be made to the articles on Ratana and Ringatu in the symposia
edited by Michael King, written by Maoris, and which, in some respects,
represent a class of its own, an 'inside story'. Apart from the documentary
material of the Ratana Church, found in the archives of this religious group in
Ratana Pa, we note the complete absence of primary sources.

A new development is Maori Marsden's 'God, Man and Universe: A Maori
View'. It is, in someways, a further development of the approach taken in an
older paper, attributed to A. T. Ngata, 'The religious philosophy of the Maori'.
This approach has become of increasing interest to Maori Christians and

theologians, members of the main line churches, which are now showing a greater appreciation of 'Maori theology' than at any previous point in history, as Rakena has pointed out in an article on 'Maori Theology of Life'.[6]

Finally, some data used in this essay was gathered during the writer's fieldwork among Maori religious groups.

Ringatu and Ratana

The founder of the Ringatu Church is the Maori warrior Te Kooti Rikirangi (1814-1893), who spent some time in exile in the Chathams. It has been suggested that the Ringatu religion is a direct descendant of the Pai-Mārire religion. It is similar in so far as it is an adaptation of the Christian religion to the Maori situation, giving support in a most frustrating situation – with a particular reference to the destruction of Maori land rights and the repercussions on Maori society, but it was Te Kooti's intensive study of the Bible during his exile (particularly of the Psalms, Judges, and Joshua) that led to the establishment of the Church. Part of the attraction of the Ringatu church was that it retained many elements of Christianity but avoided identification with any of the denominational groups of the Pakeha. The religion, but not the church policy of the Pakeha, was to some extent retained. As a church, the Ringatu movement was officially recognised in 1938. At present it has approximately 6000 members.

An offshoot of the Ringatu movement was a strongly millennarian movement founded by the charismatic leader Rua Kenana Hepetipa, in the Ureweras, with Maungapohatu as the centre. Though there are still isolated believers in Rua, the movement as such has died down.

The Ratana Church was founded by Tahupotiki Wiremu Ratana, a Taranaki farmer, who had been strongly influenced by his aunt, the Maori prophetess Mere Rikiriki. As a Church, the Ratana movement was constituted in 1925. It is a distinctive Maori Church. Since 1918, the year when Ratana commenced his activities as a national faith-healer, the movement swept through the Maori communities and made a profound impression, changing the religious allegiance of a vast number of Maoris. "Here was something that broke abruptly through the traditional allegiances with the Pakeha missionary churches – a Maori religious movement with deep psychological appeal to the Maori mind, with a lure of nationalism and the promise of redress of the wrongs suffered by the Maori people."[7]

While the Ringatu found their followers in the Central and Eastern districts (Bay of Plenty and Ureweras), the Ratana movement spread from the

Wanganui-Taranaki area to the centre of the Island, and to Northland. The census membership is just over 35,000 but the actual membership may be higher.

Contrary to the Ringatu movement, which was firmly grounded in Maori culture, the Ratana church was a movement away from traditions, leading back to the belief in Jehovah, with emphasis on the abandonment of old beliefs and the social organisation of the tribe.

An offshoot of the Ratana movement, is the Rapana Church, founded in 1941 under the name Absolute Established Maori Church of Aotearoa, Te Waipounamu and Whare Kauri. This church is, in fact, a Maori protest against a Maori church. The founder, Te Aka Rapana, was concerned about the emphasis on political activities in the Ratana church: "You cannot preach the gospel and go into politics too."[8] The original centre was in Te Tii but most of the members now live in Tinopai. The total membership is below one hundred. Initially, they lived communally, sharing the profit of the produce of the land. They are encouraged to retain a close association with the family and community aspect of traditional Maori life, and are concerned that Maoris who are successful in the Pakeha world tend to let this lapse, because of their emphasis on the individual, which is the 'new civilisation's way'.

Apart from one article by Dansey no further information could be located on this movement.

Symbolism

It is proposed to discuss in the remainder of this essay the 'religious expressions' as represented by these Maori religious movements.

Prior to looking at the main aspects of religious expression it is opportune to refer to one particular characteristic of religion in Maori and Polynesian societies in general. In the area of religious studies the distinction has been made between endeictic and discursive modes of religious expression. The first category includes those which express religion 'in veiled form', that is, indirectly. The meaning is implicit. These forms are needed because of the inherent difficulty of expressing things adequately otherwise. The second category refers to more explicit ways. The discursive mode is direct and uses language in the sense of words. It is belief defined, it is more exact.

Western religions have developed discursive modes to the extent that to many this is almost the only acceptable form of expression, certainly when it comes to measuring the validity of purity of beliefs. In other societies, endeictic modes are more prominent, evident for instance in a much greater use of symbols. This we find in Polynesian societies, in traditional religion as well as in later religious developments.

The symbol is a manifestation of 'God'. It is something concrete, material, profane, in the sense of what does not belong to the sacred, yet is related to something spiritual. Symbols are never exact. They leave a great deal of latitude with respect to meaning. They may be interpreted in different ways. As an illustration, we refer to the symbols of water used for baptism, bread and wine of Holy Communion, or, for that matter, to the cross.

Symbols serve the function of helping the worshipper to apprehend spiritual reality.

An example from an earlier movement is the somewhat exotic symbolism of the Niu pole, associated with the Hauhau religion. The Niu pole, possibly a pre-European divination device, symbolised the link between earth and sky. Schwimmer[11] describes the Niu pole and its function as follows: "The Niu pole was to be over fifteen feet in height, straight, unbending and crossed by yard arms on the end of which sat the two gods Ruru and Riki. Riki was the war god, Ruru Te Ua's guardian spirit. Streamers would hang from the yard arms. Celebrants would march and dance and chant around the pole, thus drawing magic power which would drive the Pakeha from New Zealand and establish the millennium."

"It was believed that angels, carried by the 'Hau' (spirit), entered the bodies of the faithful by alighting on the Niu pole and descending by the streamers. Each time the dancer accidentally touched a streamer, a little of this spirit substance would be communicated to him. The dancing would become progressively more frantic and end in spirit possession, sometimes in collapse. It was believed that the *mana* thus obtained would make a warrior invulnerable to bullets."

Gibson[12] records a suggestion that the use of the Niu pole may derive from Christianity. "It is possible that the pole might have represented to the Pai Marire adherents the steeple of a church and the cross upon it. The steeple might have occurred to the Maoris to be a means of communication with God."

It has been suggested that the Ringatu church rejects all symbols and is more spiritual, yet the sign of the 'upraised hand' is a symbolic action and the Ringatu seal is a symbol. Rua built a temple as a symbol of the movement. The Ratana church has a number of symbols like the *patu* (club used in ceremonial dances) the rosette, the clover leaf, and, of course, the Ratana temple, where lines, stars, and crescents are used symbolically. Of some neither the origins, nor the exact meaning can be established. The temple contains also a symbol of God, namely the 'eye of God', a pattern of concentric circles. The most prominent symbol of the Ratana faith is the *Whetu Mārama,* the originally four and now five pointed star. The star and the crescent represent the shining light of Ratana's mission, proclaiming *Māramatanga,* the Kingdom of Light, waging a successful war against the King of Magic and the *tohungas* (witchdoctors).

The Ratana star has five colours: blue, representing the Father; white, the Son; red, the Holy Ghost; purple, the holy angels; gold the *Māngai,* colours found also in the colourful hues of the Ratana officials. The name T. W. Ratana is written on the crescent, and on either side one finds an A and an O, these representing Alpha and Omega – the beginning and end of Ratana's work.[13] This symbol, referred to as the 'Star and Moon badge' is the official crest of the Ratana church.

These symbols are meant to give the people a comprehensive form of the faith as the Ratana church interprets it.

Expression in thought, action, and fellowship

For the purpose of this essay and in our exploration of the wider field of religious expressions in Maori society, Wach's conceptional framework[14] has been adopted as a convenient vehicle for the ordering of the data. He offers a systematic and comparative study of various forms of religious experience and isolates three different areas.

Firstly, the expression in thought, the cognitive aspect of religious experience, the intellectual or theoretical expression, the articulation in thought of what has been experienced in the confrontation with the deity.

Secondly, the practical expression, the cultus, including forms of worship, the confrontation with the deity in ritual and values. The cognitive aspect and the cultus are naturally intertwined. As Wach[15] suggests: "No act of worship can exist without at least a *modicum* of religious expression."

Thirdly, the sociological aspect of religious experience, the expression in fellowship, characteristic of a body of people united in a particular group experience, members and leaders together, observing sacred times, having sacred places and sharing common economic obligations.

This method will now be applied to Maori religious movements.

Expressions in thought – doctrine

Doctrine formulates what the symbol implies, doctrine explains, it helps to preserve the purity of the faith in formulating what is considered to be the truth. Most religious communities have a variety of doctrines even though officially clearly formulated basic doctrines are accepted as standards of the faith. Different churches have different doctrines, the origins of which are many and varied. When, as part of Western penetration into non-Western societies, the Christian faith was introduced, new doctrines developed, due to cultural and sociological factors. It appears, however, that doctrinal developments initiated by missionaries and taking place in indigenous churches are seldom comparable to those in the mother churches. As regards Maori religious groups, they are doctrinally poor.

Laughton[16] suggests that the major weakness of the Ringatu church lay in its lack of a formulated system of doctrine which gave rise to numerous new claims, revolutions and impositions. As an example he cites the Ringatu dissident Rua Kenana, who made the most extravagant claims and yet remained a member of the Ringatu church.

The only formulated doctrine the Ringatu church possesses is embodied in eight covenants, given to Te Kooti during his time of exile.

In order to establish a 'Ringatu doctrine', one would perhaps have to follow Turner[17] who studied a large number of sermons preached by native pastors in West Africa. A study of this kind could well be fruitful in New Zealand if the churches concerned would be willing to co-operate and realise that it could make a contribution to the church itself as well as increase the knowledge of New Zealand religion.

However, one or two observations have been made. Firstly, the 'God concept' of the Ringatu is vastly different from the 'Western God' of the orthodox churches. It is basically the God of the Old Testament, conceived as the Maori's ancestral God and linked with the Io concept. They place also a particular emphasis on the locus of the Holy Spirit. Te Kooti himself was recognised as a prophet of the Holy Spirit and the original name of the Church was the 'Church of the Holy Spirit'.

It has been suggested that Te Kooti was reluctant to include anything specifically 'Christian' in his liturgy as he had suffered so much from the hands of the Christians, but certain passages of the New Testament, particularly those concerned with eschatology, are part and parcel of contemporary preaching in the Ringatu church. To them, wars and rumours of wars[18] point to the literally interpreted second coming of Christ.

To the Ringatu, the Bible is the supreme authority of the faith, though its use by members has been limited. It is only in recent times that the reading of the Bible has been encouraged. In their selection of Bible passages there seems to be a clear preference for those parts which are closest to their own thought patterns and experiences. In their recitals great care is taken not to depart from the written text. For this reason and because of their great emphasis on the Bible as the principal source of religious truth, the Ringatus may well be called the 'fundamentalists', or 'literalists' among the Maori religious groups.

It is interesting to note that this group, which in many ways has remained so close to traditional life, and believes in the existence of evil spirits, rejects (officially anyway) the belief in *mākutu*[19] and the traditional way of combatting it. Evil spirits are controlled by prayer, and traditional magical methods of exorcism are not practised.

The Ratana church has a concise Creed[20] comprising ten clauses. This meets the basic need for doctrine within a church which presents the claims of Christianity in a simple, practical, compelling form and resents the intellectual approach of the Pakeha as being too abstract. Basically, the Ratana Creed endorses the belief in the Trinity, creation, redemption, in a Christ-centred church, in the brotherhood of all men, in love and in justice as found in traditional Christian churches. It accepts the Bible as a record of Jehovah's greatest revelations.

There are, however, two clauses which show a considerable deviation.

Clause five refers to the Ratana belief in the Faithful Angels, Jehovah's workers and messengers, helpers of men. The Ratana believers experience great support from the Angels. They bring them closer to God, they protect and inspire, are guardians and intermediaries. Belief in angels is, of course, Biblical in origin and part of Judaism. In the Bible as well as in the Talmud, one finds many references to the angels as celestial beings and divine messengers. Michael, the chief guardian angel of Israel, Raphael the angel of healing, Uriel the light of God. Ministering angels accompanied men to the synagogue and on returning home. It was the doctrine of the angels which was the primary cause of conflict with the orthodox churches. It was not so much that they believed in angels, but because the Faithful Angels were associated with the Trinity and an extended formula was used in the rite of baptism.[21]

Yet, the angels were never placed on the same footing as the Holy Trinity: like Ratana himself they were only one further link between God and man. Ratana's conception of the channels of communication was that all prayers and supplications passed through him as a mouthpiece, (*Māngai*), thence to the angels, thence to God.[22] Raureti gives as a possible explanation of this aspect of the Ratana beliefs that it is rooted in the traditional Maori worship of Io, the supreme God. Io was so sacred that the ordinary mortal being did not have access to him. That right was preserved only for the tohunga and the highest ranking chiefs. "By the institution of the ministry of angels, Ratana catered for the old Maori concept of sacredness and indirect contact with God, at the same time conceding the European concept of the approachability of God. The intermediaries in the form of the *Māngai* and the *Anahera Pono* (angels), were compromises between the two modes of thought and worship."[23]

The place of the *Māngai* in Ratana beliefs is contained in clause ten of the Creed and gives Ratana a most prominent place in the religion. Later he was also referred to as Mediator, but it is questionable whether this was the same connotation as the concept of mediator in traditional orthodox beliefs. Ratanas believe that as Christ, a Jew, was sent to the Jews, so Ratana, a Maori, was sent to the Maoris.

The Rapana church has no known formulated creed. The preaching is Christ-centred. A formal creed would seem unimportant, since truth to the Rapana comes not so much through the study of sacred writings as through revelations which come to the spiritual leaders in dreams.

Expressions in action

1. In ritual

When we speak of expression in action we think in terms of acting out one's relationship to God. In the first place, acting out this relationship takes place in ritual, in the worship service. As indicated already, the Ringatu ritual is completely based on the Bible, mainly on passages from the Psalms and other parts of the Old Testament. These are recited and never read from the Bible. The leaders are Christian *tohungas* who memorise the prayers and teachings of Te Kooti like the oral traditions of old. Great emphasis is placed on perfection of performance. This has its origins in the traditional *tohunga* who was very conscious of the fact that a mistake made in reciting incantations *(karakia)* would be regarded as an ill omen. A mistake in a prayer could mean the rejection of a plea.

Traditionally it would mean that the power of the *karakia* would be lost and the god would punish the priest responsible. Hymns, comprising parts of the Bible also, are sung to traditional Maori Chant songs. Extempore prayers are permitted, but not common. During the recitation of prayers and the singing of hymns, the congregation stands.

A specific Ringatu ritual act is the raising of the right hand at the close of each prayer, following the words: "We glorify your holy name" – an act of reinforcement. This practice is another evidence of the literal use of the Bible, where the lifting up of one's hand is connected with prayer.[25]

The sign was first used by the Hauhaus, who believed that it would safeguard them from the bullets of the Pakeha; this is reminiscent of Moses' holding up his hand in the battle against the Amalekites.[26] The Ringatu church sees it simply as a sign to indicate homage to God. Included in the prayers is the Lord's prayer, but the phrase 'Give us this day our daily bread' is omitted. In the Maori Bible bread is translated by *taro,* a highly valued but scarce commodity in Te Kooti's days. Te Kooti considered that there was little use in praying to give taro every day when you would be lucky to get it once a year.[27]

With regard to the contents of prayers, in single sets of interrelated ideas, generally speaking they relate to the functions of the traditional Maori gods: safety in journey; preservation of life; success in harvest, in fishing, and in hunting; in wartime victory in battle. In other words, they are related to the events of everyday life.

During Ringatu gatherings, a number of services are held, each with their own emphasis. In these services recitations of passages from the Bible, psalms, and prayers go right round the meeting house, moving clockwise, and are led by different people.

The tunes of the chanting are all pre-European, indigenous Maori. Of special importance are the healing services including prayers for the sick. Communion services in the traditional sense are not a feature of the church. Te Kooti found this ritual repulsive, as the idea of taking Christ's body and blood reminded him of cannibalism. Their communion is of a spiritual nature.

The Ratana worship ritual is of a different kind and in many ways closer to that of the orthodox churches. The services are conducted according to the Ratana Service Book, which contains orders of services for various occasions: baptism, funeral, marriage, Ratana Festival days and the ordinary Sunday. It includes also seventy-one Maori hymns, mostly set to Sankey tunes.

The Bible is used, but sparsely. The sermon has a place within the framework of the service, is usually short and based on a proverb, a prophecy of the founder of the movement, or of some other prophet, or sometimes on a text from the Bible. It should be remembered that Ratana closed the Bible officially in 1927, out of fear of misinterpretations, particularly of the apocalyptical literature. The Ratana church journal, *Te Whetu Mārama,* assists the ministers with the preparation of their sermons. The weekly home or chapel service in places where there is a chapel follows much the same pattern as those at larger gatherings, but the latter are a much more colourful performance. Whoever visits the Ratana Pa on the 25th of January will see the church attenders marching to the Temple, headed by the brass, bands. The officebearers, at the front of the procession, wear their colourful robes and blazers — 'the garden of flowers', the Māngai used to call it. Other worshippers are expected to be well dressed, the men wearing jackets, the women cardigans or frocks with long sleeves — no shorts. Healing services and baptismal rites form part of Ratana worship. At the initial stages of the movement faith-healing was the main characteristic of Ratana's activities. His ability as a faith-healer had both traditional and Biblical precedents to draw on and had therefore a dual tradition.

Of particular interest is the hymn section of the Service Book. In these hymns, the name Ratana has been substituted for Jesus Christ. They sing: 'Soldiers of Ratana arise', instead of the traditional version 'Soldiers of Christ arise'.

One of the most popular Maori hymns[28] reads in the Ratana version:

> May the peace of God the Father
> Son and Holy Ghost
> With the Holy Angels
> Guard and watch over all of us
> May the Faithful Mangai
> Lead us in the right way
> In truth and righteousness
> To the throne of Jehovah.

2. In living

The second aspect of religious expression in action is the acting out of the relationship to God in everyday living, the upholding of the values of the religious community. The basic values of the Ringatu church are respect for people, reverence for life, and sensitive awareness of the Spirit of the Universe. They believe also that it is the Church's responsibility to conserve Maori values, adjusted to the contemporary world and the new social order. In their value system the *tapu* concept has remained of prime importance, the Bible and burial places being the most *tapu* objects. As the Bible is *tapu* it has to be treated, like every other *tapu* object, with great care and as a highly valued article, so sacred that it is sometimes hidden between the rafters of the home. Contact with the dead, or being at a burial place must be followed by some cleansing ritual. Everything connected with the preparation of food is *noa* (profane) and no cooked food should ever be taken into church buildings.

The Ratana church had originally a strict code for living which included that baptism and marriage had to be sincerely honoured, good care should be taken of children, cigarette smoking should be limited, and the Ratana Covenant included also a commitment to pray for 'power to eschew intoxicating liquor'. Playing football was frowned upon. Blasphemous use of the name of Christ was also strongly objected to.

The Rapana church instituted strict rules to distinguish their members from their environment. On joining the church, a prospective member had to pledge not to take alcoholic beverages, not to gamble, not to fight, not to play football, not to see films, not to read undesirable books. They were, however, allowed to smoke and dance.

Even though many of these rules have been relaxed, they apply to a certain degree still at official church gatherings.

Expressions in fellowship

Religion is to some extent an individual affair, the experience of a personal relationship to God, expressed in what is called private devotional life, including, for example, the reading of sacred books, prayers, and meditation. To measure the extent of this would be a difficult task. From observation of Maori society and discussions with individuals, one senses that individual prayer of the Maori does play an important role but perhaps in a less formalised form, as little devotional literature is available.

Frequently, extempore prayers are offered in times of crisis, when travelling or planting crops, in line with traditional rites. But religion is mainly a 'group affair'. In religious experiences, man behaves primarily as a 'social animal'. The old phrase 'one Christian is no Christian' contains a great deal of truth and may be applied to other religions as well. Before looking at religious communities, it should be said that to the Maori, as to many non-Western societies, the whole concept of a separate religious community was new. In traditional Maori society, the distinction between the secular and the sacred of life did not exist. There were no separate religious fellowships. Cults were tribal and religion was completely integrated with tribal functions. It remains still basically true that the Maori doesn't meet to worship but worships when he meets. However, due to Western influence, religious communities have emerged either built on tribal or kinship groups — as in the Ringatu and Rapana churches — or on a supertribal structure in the case of the Ratana church, where the spiritual brotherhood surpasses the physical ties between the brothers. How these communities function in worship and living has already been discussed in the previous section. This part looks at some other aspects, criteria of membership, leadership, sacred times, sacred places, and church economics.

1. Membership

To become a member of a religious group requires the acceptance of their beliefs and doctrines and conformity to the practices as held at the time. Like their traditional orthodox counterparts, the Maori churches practise infant baptism as a means to admit people into the membership of the church. Infant 'baptism' in the Ringatu church is either performed by placing the feet of the child in water or by a simple act of dedication. In the early days of the Ringatu and Ratana churches, a covenant had to be signed prior to admission to the church.

The members of the Ratana church will frequently wear rings, pendants, or other ornaments with the Ratana symbol, to identify themselves with their group. The Ringatu have no outward sign of membership. The Rapana church members have a customary dress during church functions only. The men wear dark suits, the women blue skirts with maroon blazers, while the young men, called wardens or doorkeepers, wear maroon blazers and peaked caps.

2. Contemporary Leaders

Each of the churches under review has its own body of leadership.

In the Ringatu church, the main governing body is a General Assembly, which meets bi-annually. The Assembly selects the leader or *Poutikanga* who administers the church with the assistance of a general secretary and an executive committee, comprising twelve men. The office bearers are divided into four different categories: the *ture,* persons versed in church law; the *takuta,* officials who conduct healing services; the *tohunga,* ordinary ministers; and the *pirihimana* ('policemen'), who are in charge of marae duties and discipline at Ringatu gatherings.

The organisation of the Ratana Church is different. The church is headed by a President, who may either be a man or a woman and preferably a close descendant of the founder. The largest governing body is the *Komiti Mātua,* the Central Committee, representing the four quarters of the Ratana church. The church is divided into a political and a religious wing. The religious wing is headed by a synod operating directly under the *Komiti Mātua.* The Synod in turn has a number of *Komiti* in which the ministers play an important role. Within the church hierarchy, the ministers have varied status. Highest are the registered apostles, distinguishable by their purple stoles; then come the spiritual apostles, wearing red stoles; while the lowest grade of ministers are represented by the *akonga,* who have gold stoles. The *āwhina,* or women assistants, wear purple robes; the Psalmists, golden robes; and the choir wear blue blazers.

The Rapana Church has an administrative head and a spiritual leader (*kai ārahi*). The ministers of the church wear blue ties.

Sacred Times

Even though religion is expressed in thought and action in many ways at all times, most religious groups have special sacred times or seasons which are of particular importance.

In neither of the churches has Sunday ever acquired the same importance as in their orthodox counterparts. The Ringatu church, due to its Old Testament orientation, does observe Saturday (the Sabbath) instead of Sunday as the day of worship, but weekly services are not common. Rather, the Ringatu people regularly meet for worship on the 12th of every month. The number twelve is chosen because of the significance of this number in the Bible. Of particular importance are the two annual festivals: the New Year Festival and the Harvest Festival in the seventh month.[29]

The Ratana church has two major days of remembrance, the 25th of January, when the opening of the Ratana Temple is commemorated, and the 8th of November, the day when Ratana received his first vision which led to the founding of the movement. Easter also has a special place in the Ratana church year. On each of these occasions large gatherings are held, lasting several days. The place of the Easter convention changes, but the other meetings are always held at the Ratana Pa with the Temple as the centre of the celebrations.

It is at these larger gatherings that the Ratana church really functions as a group, and these are far more important than the small weekly services.

The Rapana church observes Easter as the most sacred time. This is their Central Festival. At New Year the group celebrates that the past is left and the new is taken up. It is a time for the leader, who is seen as the channel between God and the people, to tell the group the course they should take.

Sacred Places

The Ringatu church has no church buildings which are distinguishable as such. Te Kooti and his followers built some carved meeting houses with the specific aim of using these for church gatherings. Kin groups have built meeting houses as centres of church activities. This may be expected in a church in which tribal and sub-tribal groups play an important part in each area. Winiata[30] refers also to certain *tapu* places where rituals and ceremonies were performed, known only to the leaders, who consequently were the only participants.

The prophet Rua built a temple in Maungapohatu, but this building has unfortunately been lost to posterity.

The Ratana church has as its main sacred place the Ratana temple, though the Ratana pa, the 'Mekka' of the Ratana church, has many other parts which have almost become sacred. The Ratana temple is the real spiritual centre of the movement and many Ratanas make pilgrimages to the temple during the festival seasons. Local Ratana chapels, in architectual design reproducing the main temple, are other sacred places, but not to the same degree. The only other sacred Ratana place is 'Te Rere o Kapuni', in Taranaki, an historic place where the founder of the movement used to deliver his famous sermons to the people. On special occasions, the Ratana people meet there to remember their leader.

Church Economics

The Maori churches have a comparatively low budget, as none of them maintain full-time or even part-time paid clergy. This may be related to the traditional belief that a priest should never be paid for his services as a teacher of ritual, as it might well destroy the psychic force of the spells and consequently the aims would not be achieved. Only the secretary of the Ratana church is a paid official.

In order to meet their expenses of the daily running of the church, which is virtually little more than administrative costs, the Ringatu church leaves it entirely up to the members as to what they want to donate. Collections are never part of church services. The only time offerings are asked is after the so-called 'Love Feast', an extravagant fellowship meal held during the Ringatu gatherings. It is stipulated that these offerings must be from money 'earned by the sweat of the brow'. A token contribution to the church is also expected when members cannot attend the gatherings, meaning that no offence is intended by this breach of discipline. The Ratana church acquires its finance through donations from members, through the sale of ornaments with the Ratana emblem, raffles, socials, etc. Their main need is the maintaining of the central buildings at Ratana Pa.

Contributions to religion: the wider context

Speaking in general terms, we may say that right throughout the period of religious contact the emergent religious movements, operating outside the established churches, have enriched and broadened the spectrum of religious life in New Zealand. More specifically they have produced churches expressing their faith in Maori idiom. "Here is emphatic evidence of the Christian impact upon

New Zealand life and of the 'New Zealand thing' in Christianity in New Zealand."[31]

Rakena has concluded that the churches have proved unable to relate the message to the Maori's spiritual outlook.[32] Mbiti argues, in relation to African independent churches, that the missionaries produced a written image of the faith and — in Africa — no positive attempt to incorporate ancestors, witches, song and dance in Christianity was made. Therefore, independent churches were formed which were closer to traditional aspirations.[33] Likewise, after an initial enthusiasm about the new religion, the Maoris developed their own religious synthesis, groups with which they could identify themselves and express themselves in a more satisfactory way than was possible within the Pakeha churches, adopting new forms, frequently with preference for endeictic rather than discursive modes. The European had assumed that the Maori would readily adopt European patterns of life and worship: in theology, in forms of worship, in the variety of the Church's ministries, in Christian education, in matters of finance and administration, of structure and law, adaptation to the European pattern was expected. These expectations were not fulfilled.

By way of a careful process of selective borrowing, aspects of religion were brought to the fore which had never received the same prominence in the traditional churches. An example is the revival of angelology. Angels play a very important part in the Ratana church, but not only there. Much earlier the prophet Te Ua spoke of the archangel Gabriel, who visited him in his dreams, suggesting innovations in religious observances. Even his action to exhume and dry the head of a certain Captain Lloyd, which thereafter became the means of Jehovah's communication with the Maori people, was based on instructions from the angel Gabriel.

One may refer to church policy, the building up of new structures of religious bodies, reminiscent of Pakeha patterns, but deviating from these in many ways. The Church's ministry on a non-stipendiary basis was developed in line with characteristics of traditional Maori society and independent of a similar phenomenon in some smaller Protestant sects. Startling are the new interpretations of the Bible found for instance in the use of the Old Testament by Te Kooti. He produced meaningful rearrangements of texts. Ratana interpreted the Biblical message in the Ratana hymns.

But still more important is the identification of Maori charismatic leaders with characters of the Old Testament, particularly with the prophets. Prophecy has been a characteristic of the Maori religious movements from the early days of contact.

Te Kooti identified himself with Joshua and the Judges. Rua saw his mission confirmed by the prophecy of Te Kooti, who had said that a star would herald the rising of a great leader who would set upright the canoe of the Maori. Te Kooti's prophecy of the two stars, one to arise in the East and one in the West, is seen as heralding the emergence of Sir Apirana Ngata (East) and Ratana (West). Ratana's mission was also prophesied by Mere Rikiriki, the leader of the Holy Ghost Mission and Ratana's Aunt, who said that a cloak of the *Wairua* (Holy Spirit) would fall upon the shoulders of her nephew, Wiremu. Ratana saw the vision of the two whales, representing the spiritual and political mission of the movement.

Sayings of famous Maori religious leaders, whatever group they represent, are distributed at Maori religious gatherings to keep their memory alive and make their message heard.

Another form of identification took place when religious leaders, allegedly, performed miracles which were related to similar events in the Bible. A striking example is 'the proof of Te Ua's divine selection to convey the promise of Jehovah',[34] which involved two stages both of which had Biblical parallels. He broke apart the ropes and chains with which he had been bound after an alleged assault of another man's wife: 'Thrice I was bound in chains and thrice I was freed by an angel,' a story reminiscent of Samson.[35] At some other time he was ordered to kill his son, but the wounds were healed by the angel Gabriel's intervention, a tradition similar to Abraham's attempted sacrifice of Isaac.[36]

Contributions by movements within the Churches and beyond

So far, the discussion has focussed on Maori religious movements outside the main line churches. However, simultaneously Maori members within these churches have made their own contribution. Very little of this has been recorded, but it is certain that a researcher who would record sermons and other forms of religious speech-making, would unearth valuable data about an emerging Maori theology. The few available papers give us only a glimpse of what is happening.

In an undated paper, 'The religious philosophy of the Maori', attributed to A. T. Ngata, the writer assesses the approach of the great faiths — he mentions Islam and Christianity — to other faiths they encounter. "The militant faith brooked no opposition nor paused to argue or compare, where native philosophies obtained. These were overrun or overlaid, driven to cover where they were not destroyed. The native proselytes were confronted violently with new and strange conceptions, clothed in forms undreamed of in the world they had known." Later: "It is no sacrilege to say that to very many Maoris even today, and more so in the two generations which preceded them, the Deity was seen as the God of the pakeha and happily or not as himself a pakeha. The paraphernalia of civilisation which accompanied him to this land were those of the pakeha and were imposed upon the native culture with little regard for its susceptibilities and pre-occupations."

Then he explains the Io concept, the God with many attributes, who brought the universe into existence from chaos. He was never born, had no wife nor had offspring, yet through him all things came into being. He was the beginning of all gods. Ngata's whole discussion is placed within the framework of the opening phrases of the Anglican communion service. He suggests that the Maori who participates in the sacrament virtually equates the Christian God with the supreme god of the Maoris, Io, arguing that Maori religion has evolved from a most primitive stage of beliefs to the belief in this Supreme God. He closes with the words: "Whether independently evolved or borrowed, there were minds among the Stone Age people of the Polynesian archipelago which could comprehend this elevated conception and dream a philosophy of things in heaven and earth to satisfy the cravings of mind and spirit. Of course there would be a place in it for 'archangels and all the host of Heaven and earth' "[37]

Here is a cry for a Maori theology as well as a tentative approach to develop one.

Another, very recent Maori theological treatise is Maori Marsden's 'God, Man and Universe'.[38] He compares Maori and Biblical concepts and asks how they relate. In his opinion *mana* includes the New Testament concept of *dynamis*, which empowers man to perform miracles. *Tapu* would be close to the Jewish idea of 'sacred' or 'holy'. Purification, required after the (inadvertent) violation of rules, is compared with baptism as a means of transmitting *mana* (charisma, spiritual power) to humans. *Te whakapā*, a consecratory rite, employed by a father before his death to impart the family *mana* to his chosen son, is similar to a related practice among the Israelites and corresponds to the Christian rite of confirmation. Marsden sees the office and function of the Christian priest in principle as being the same as that of the *tohunga* — for the welfare and benefit of the people. He compares Maori and Christian sacramental systems to show that certain spiritual principles are universal in application. In the remaining part of his essay he places these concepts within the context of the metaphysical, philosophical, and religious thinking out of which they originated and finally discusses at length the Io concept and the Maori world view. Here is a new and genuine Maori attempt to express the Christian faith in a new way, to interpret divine truth according to one's own conception of it and build up a new theology.

Gnanasunderam, a Sri Lankan who has been working in New Zealand for several years and has been in very close contact with Maori society, has written a paper 'The church and the Maori',[39] He discusses particularly the phenomenon of exorcism and points out the special significance of this concept to many Maoris and how they feel alienated by the church in this area. He suggests that this example of a Maori concept which appears to them as Christian and Biblical, should make the churches more wary of labelling some of the other concepts of the Maori as heathen and of no Christian spiritual value. He quotes a Maori academic who said: "In all, there still remains with us today many of the spiritual values of old. The beliefs and practices of the modern Maori are a cross between Christian beliefs and Maori beliefs. If Maori Gods die, they die very slowly. I believe that we have a duty not to allow our gods to die, because if they do die something dear to the Maori heart and mind dies. There is a place for these gods in the life of the Maori Christian. To deny them is to deny our own history, our literature and our ancestors." So the Maori feels that his Maori concepts can enrich his faith. To them the person of Jesus Christ is fulfilment of what was once but a shadowy apprehension of the true order of divinity.

The churches have become increasingly aware of the need of the Maori believer to develop his own theology and there is a growing conviction that the Maori has a special contribution to make to the enrichment of religion in New Zealand. The Maori within the churches feel their responsbility in this respect. This became evident at a meeting in Auckland in 1973, at which the majority of the clergy present were Maori and where the following resolution was adopted: "We now affirm and recommend that the Maori be encouraged as much as possible to develop his Christian life, worship and mission through his Maoritanga, so that he might be able to make his free and full contribution to the Great Church."[40]

The Maori section of the National Council of Churches in New Zealand has done much to foster these developments of Maori Christianity. The Reverend Rua Rakena [41] has pointed out that some advances have been made in the designing of worship services for special Maori occasions, some of which are in use already: a service for the opening of a meeting house, for an unveiling of a gravestone, for the blessing of a house from which a body has been removed. But, he suggests, it must go beyond this and include Maori religious expressions in architecture and other forms of art. As with service books, containing church ritual, what has been achieved so far is in many instances no more than Maori versions of what is, in essence, Pakeha.[42]

Besides the contribution through Maori religious movements outside and inside the churches, there is a third area where the Maori has made an impact on religion in New Zealand. In line with the traditional experience of religion which permeated the whole of Maori society, the Maori has contributed by making a religious presence in areas usually considered to be of a secular nature.. The involvement of the Ratana Church in politics springs to mind. For many years now (with only one brief interruption in 'Eastern Maori') the four Maori seats in Parliament have been occupied by Ratanas. Raureti suggests that members of the church tend to vote in block for the candidate as a church member rather than have any allegiance to a party.[43]

Political symbols are part and parcel of the church. The symbol of the rising sun on the Ratana flag commemorates an alleged treaty between the Japanese and Ratana, the latter being promised protection if the Japanese should ever land in this country. The symbol of the olive leaf commemorates the tour of Ratana to the United States in 1925.[44]

One may look also at the Maori view of. their culture as a sacred heritage. It is more than just a coincidence that the Ringatu church particularly has taken a strong stand as regards the perpetuation of Maori culture. Cultural activities are an essential ingredient of all large Maori church gatherings. People have fought and are still fighting 'religiously' for the preservation of the Maori language, to them more than just a means of communication. Maori church services have been maintained by almost all denominations. The Maori Bible, inadvertently perhaps, has not only been a contribution to religion in New Zealand in a restricted sense of the word, but has been a milestone in the battle for cultural identity.

Downey has made the comment: 'The Maori by his use of his own language in the church services and by the development of separate churches like the Ratana, has found a way of expressing symbolically his separate identity within a wide cultural framework, something the New Zealanders as a whole have yet to do.'[45]

Beliefs have developed a 'religious lifestyle' through the work of the Mormon Church, which has instilled values through the preaching of a very practical, down-to-earth form of Christianity, and has thus proved to be of great importance to many Maoris in their adjustment to urban life.

Maori religious movements have made their contribution to the *marae,* that sacred place where the Maori belongs, and which is more than just a community centre or a secular place; rather it is 'the spiritual focus of the group'.[46] The deep involvement of the churches in *marae* activities, foremost the funeral wake or *tangihanga,* has contributed much to the perpetuation of its function. Moreover, the approach to religious functions on the *marae,* where it is customary that all religious groups co-operate and share in one another's ritual, has made members of other religious groups, divided by seemingly insuperable barriers, look with envy at the almost natural way in which this has been accepted by their fellow believers of Maori descent. While Pakehas are involved in a never-ending discussion on union, the Maoris are offering a very practical solution. The different emphasis in religious expression, foremost a less doctrinal approach, has created an opportunity for innovation as well as tolerance for beliefs of others.[4 7]

Finally, one may refer to the land, which has such deep social and emotional significance for the Maori, based on a mystic, a spiritual connection between man and his natural environment, the domain of their gods. One could well hypothesise that this deep respect for the natural environment and his appreciation of the value of the retention of the resources of land, sea and forest, have contributed to a revaluation of these on the part of the Pakeha. The 'secular' Pakeha concept of conservation, has a deep religious connotation for the Maori.

Conclusion

The emergence and development of Maori religious movements outside and inside the older churches, plus the penetration of religion into many areas of life, together demonstrate the dynamics of religion, the variety of responses to the Divine, changing over time and adjusting to new situations. It is apparent that in a contact situation one religious system contributes to the enrichment of the other. In New Zealand the Pakeha has contributed much to Maori religious life, including fulfilling the role of a midwife in assisting with the birth of new and original religious groups, which in turn have contributed much to religion in the Pakeha world.

One may think of the Tuhoe proverb:

> Nāu tō rourou, nāku tō rourou, ka ora te manuhiri;
> Nāu te rakau, nāku te rakau, ka mate te hoariri.
> Your little baskets of food and mine will satisfy the guests;
> Your weapons and mine will destroy the enemy.

Notes:
1. ABERLE, D. A note on relative deprivation theory as applied to millennarian and other cult movements. *In Reader in comparative religions.*

W. A. Lessa and E. Z. Vogt, eds. New York, Harper & Row, 1962. p. 527-531.

2. LYONS, D. P. An analysis of three Maori prophet movements, p. 63. *In Conflict and compromise; essays on the Maori since colonisation.* I. H. Kawharu, ed. Wellington, Reed, 1975. p. 55-79.

3. GADD, B. The teachings of Te Whiti o Rongomai, p. 449. *Journal of the Polynesian Society 75:* 445-457, 1966.

4. SINCLAIR, K. *A history of New Zealand.* rev ed. Harmondsworth, Penguin Books, 1973.

5. The particulars of these sources are found in the general bibliography of works on religion in New Zealand, at the end of this volume.

6. RAKENA, R. Maori theology of life. *The new citizen.* 7 Sept. 1978: 5.

7. LAUGHTON, J. G. *From forest trail to city street; the story of the Presbyterian Church among the Maori people.* Christchurch, Presbyterian Bookroom, 1961. p. 20.

8. DANSEY, H. Simple, humble folk, all of us. *Auckland Star,* 1966.

9. In the essay the concept 'God' is used as a matter of convenience. It is not necessarily to be identified with the meaning attributed to it by traditional Christian Churches. Alternatively one could speak of the Deity, the Divine, the Holy, Ultimate Reality, the Numen, whatever one prefers.

10. GIBSON, A. *Religious organisation among the Maoris of New Zealand after 1860.* Thesis, Ph.D., University of California, Berkeley, 1964. p. 51.

11. SCHWIMMER, E. *The world of the Maori.* Wellington, Reed, 1966. p. 118.

12. GIBSON, *op. cit.,* p. 51.

13. RAURETI, M. The origins of the Ratana Movement. *In Tihe Mauri Ora: aspects of Maoritanga.* M. King, ed. Auckland, Methuen, 1978. p. 42-59.

14. WACH, J. *In The comparative study of religion.* J. M. Kitagawa, ed. New York, Columbia University Press, 1958.

15. WACH, *op cit.,* p. 15.

16. LAUGHTON, as quoted by GIBSON, *op. cit.* p. 95.

17. TURNER, H. W. *Profile through teaching.* Edinburgh, Edinburgh House Press, 1965.

18. Matthew 24:6

19. *Makutu* is a form of witchcraft.

20. HENDERSON, J. M. *Ratana: the man, the church, the political movement.* 2d ed. Wellington, Reed, 1972. p. 118-119.

21. Yearbook 1925, Diocese of Waiapu.

22. RAURETI, *op. cit.,* p. 51.

23. *Ibid.*

24. GIBSON, *op. cit.,* p. 20.

25. e.g. Psalm 28:2; 63:4; 134:2.

26. Exodus 14:21; 17:11. See COLLESS, B. The religion of Moses as the first cargo cult in history. *In The religious dimension.* J. Hinchcliff, ed. Auckland, Rep Prep, 1976. p. 72-75.
27. LAUGHTON, J. G. *Ringatuism – the Ratana Church.* Dunedin, Knox College, 1960.
28. Nā te Mārie.
29. Leviticus 23:24.
30. WINIATA, M. *The changing role of the leader in Maori society: a study in social change and race relations.* Auckland, Blackwood and Janet Paul 1967.
31. OLIVER, W. H. Christianity among the New Zealanders, p. 13. *Landfall 20:* 4-20, 1966.
32. RAKENA, R. *The Maori response to the Gospel: a study of Maori-pakeha relations in the Methodist Maori Mission from its beginnings to the present day.* Auckland, Wesley Historical Society, 1971.
33. MBITI, J.S. *African religions and philosophy.* London, Heinemann, 1969.
34. CLARK, P. *'Hauhau', the Pai Marire search for Maori identity.* Auckland, Auckland University Press, 1975. p. 10.
35. Judges, 16:10-12.
36. Genesis 22.
37. The section of the communion service, here referred to, reads: 'Therefore with angels and archangels and with all the company of heaven, we laud and magnify Thy glorious name; evermore praising Thee, and saying Holy, Holy, Holy, Lord God of Hosts, heaven and earth are full of Thy Glory: Glory be to Thee, O Lord most high.'
38. *In Te ao hurihuri.* M. King ed. Wellington, Hicks Smith, 1975.
39. GNANASUNDERAM, A. *Maori theology and black theology or a theology of liberation.* Auckland, Church and Society Commission, 1974.
40. *Ibid.*
41. RAKENA, See note 6.
42. This does not apply of course to Ratana and Ringatu service books. Particularly the latter is completely different and original in its composition.
43. RAURETI, *op. cit.* p. 50.
44. RAURETI, *op. cit.* p. 54.
45. DOWNEY, P. J. Being religious in New Zealand. *Landfall 20:* 31-37, 1966.
46. IRVINE, J. Maori mysticism in the north. *In Dialogue on religion: New Zealand viewpoints, 1977.* P. Davis, and J. Hinchcliff, eds. Auckland, Printed at the University of Auckland Bindery, 1977, p. 6-10.
47. GIBSON, *op. cit.* p. 95.

The Catholic Contribution

CAN CATHOLICISM CONTRIBUTE TO AN INDIGENOUS NEW ZEALAND RELIGION ?

E.H. Blasoni.

There are people who believe that the Catholic Church throughout the world is governed and directed in all matters by Roman authorities, and by the Pope especially. They believe that the Catholic faithful are handed down an official teaching on every conceivable question. These people could not be further from the truth. Even a cursory reading of the documents of the Second Vatican Council (hereafter Vatican II) will show how far from the truth they are.

Vatican II was the most recent general council in the Catholic church. And in the Catholic church a general council is the highest teaching authority. It is convoked and presided over by the Pope and comprises all the bishops who are in union with him.

Vatican II, which ended in December 1965, brought a renewed spirit of openness to the Catholic church. It made two things possible: greater decentralisation in administration and wider variation in the form of Catholic life. It is in fulfilment of the hope of that Council, especially, that the Catholic church in New Zealand can contribute to an indigenous New Zealand religious life.

However, there is a major constraint. The Catholic church believes that Christianity is a religion of a completely different order from all others. It is not an expression of a human search for God; it is the result of God's search for man. God enters the history of man. He does this definitively in Jesus Christ his Son.

Because God has entered human history in a definitive way through his Son's presence on earth, Catholics believe that the Church cannot invent another message of salvation and never will.[1] So while the Catholic church can contribute to an indigenous New Zealand religion, there are limits to what it can do.

Some things are possible. First, there can be development of doctrine. The church can achieve greater understanding about the meaning of God's intervention in our history and can express this understanding in clearer ways. Over the centuries clearer and more precise language can be found to express the same truths.

Secondly, the principles of Christ's teaching have to be applied to new moral and social questions. For example, we must work out the implications of using nuclear weapons and the implications of associating with other nations which use them.

And then there can be adaptations in Catholic ritual and discipline. However, none of these developments, applications, adaptations, can be allowed to lead the Catholic church to a teaching or way of life which is entirely new. They must all take place against the backdrop of the definitive teaching of Jesus Christ and they must be judged by the teaching authority (called 'The Magisterium') of the church.[2]

These limitations may suggest that the Catholic church has little to offer in the development of indigenous religious forms. But indigenization is not only possible, it is essential in Catholic life. An important characteristic of the Catholic church in New Zealand today is its growing awareness that while the nature of the Church is essentially unchangeable, it is also essentially a historical community.

The mission of the Catholic church is a tension between the demands of the Gospel on one hand and the continually changing situation of the church and human society on the other. Human society is the context in which the church lives and the object of its apostolic concern.

The renewal which is taking place in the Catholic church now is the result of theological and Biblical studies, philosophical movements, and developments in social sciences which were unknown or scarcely in their infancy in the last century or the early part of this century. So we can expect to see changes.

The Form of Catholic Life in New Zealand

The Catholic church in New Zealand, like all other Christian churches, has had a form of Christian teaching and life which is not noticeably different from that in European countries. Maori and Pacific Island people have been expected to accept a western form of Christianity.

Therefore, the Catholic church in New Zealand has not yet fulfilled its original mission. The mission was to bring the Maori people into the community of the Catholic church. When they began, the missionaries followed a policy of changing local customs only gradually. At that time they were not aware of the possibilities of incorporating Maori thought and customs into a Christian way of life.

After the first wave of missionaries there was a major reorganisation in the Catholic mission. In 1850 the first missionaries were transferred to the newly created diocese of Wellington under Bishop Viard, while Bishop Pompallier recruited a new group of priests for the diocese of Auckland. The withdrawal from Auckland had serious consequences as far as Catholic work among the Maoris was concerned. From that time the main thrust of the Catholic mission was a ministry to European immigrants and descendants. The wars of the 1860s aggravated the situation.[3] Catholic missionaries in the nineteenth century confirmed the policy of ministry to European immigrants:

From the point of view of the Roman authorities the provision of Irish clergy for Irish laity was part of the task of catching up with Roman Catholics who had travelled ahead of the church in the vast population movements of the last century. The migrants' religious needs had to be ministered to and the normal structure of the Church – its institution and discipline – built around them.[4]

Other external factors help explain the limited success of the Catholic church's original mission to the Maori people. Sectarian bitterness was a factor. But, more importantly, the Catholic missionaries arrived long after missionaries from other churches. They may also have erred in concentrating their first efforts in the area north of Auckland where other Christian churches were becoming well-established. There were administrative problems too. Even the poverty and unworldliness of the missionaries were handicaps.

But now the Catholic church acknowledges internal reasons for its lack of success in establishing a church with distinctive New Zealand character. The early missionaries could not have guessed that the concept of the superiority of European Christianity would be called into question in the middle of the twentieth century. Nor could they have known that the Catholic church would look increasingly towards indigenous and contextual factors as the vehicles for its mission. Catholics now appreciate that western forms of Christianity are not the only possible forms.

The Catholic Church: Present and Future

The changes which have been taking place within the Catholic church this century were consolidated in the teaching of Vatican II. More than any previous council, Vatican II affirms the value of pluralism in the church. The universal Catholic church is seen to exist in a fraternity of local churches. Once again catholicity has come to mean that Christ's Gospel enriches the cultures of the various peoples who profess faith in him.

The phenomenon of dechristianisation also brought a new appreciation of the meaning of local church. Every supposedly Christian country has thousands of people who no longer consider themselves believing Christians. The teachings of Christ are familiar to them but the church finds itself engaged in the transition from a uniformly instituted Christianity to a Christian life with local expression.

Vatican II shows very clearly that the Catholic church is involved in the same transition. It is part of the historical process. Catholics are reminded that they must divest the church of traits that pertain too narrowly to past civilisations. The Catholic church, seeking to renew itself, is prepared to take on new forms and structures as the needs of various times and cultures may require.

So now there is less tendency to identify Catholic faith with a particular verbal expression. People of non-western cultures are encouraged to formulate the Christian faith in thought patterns and vocabulary that owe more to their own religious heritage and less to western tradition. [5] Secondly, Vatican II reflects a serious commitment on the part of the Catholic church to the world and its development. The world is no longer viewed simply as a place of trial or as the hostile environment from which Catholics must protect themselves as best they can. Instead of standing apart from the human quest, Catholics are called upon to participate in the striving for peace, justice, and a richer human life for all.

Thirdly, even more strongly than the documents of earlier councils, Vatican II stressed that it is God's will to save every person. The Council recognised the spiritual, moral and cultural values of other religions, but in no way suggested that these offer alternatives to the Christian teaching which is, by divine, public, positive institution, a definitive intervention of God in the world. [6]

Finally, Vatican II in its *Declaration on Non-Christian Religions* set a precedent by its positive and optimistic approach to other religions. In seeking to build upon what is positive in other religions, the Catholic church is not departing from its missionary responsibility to call all people to faith in Jesus Christ. Nor is it denying orthodox Christian teaching.

Possibilities for Indigenous Growth

Together with other local churches in the universal Catholic community the Catholic church in New Zealand is becoming more aware that some aspects of its life may require local forms of expression. By searching for these the Catholic church will make its contribution towards a religion with distinctive New Zealand character.

A New Zealand Theology

Vatican II indicates clearly that the Christian message may, from time to time, require new formulations and expressions. These must take account of concepts, language, thought patterns, values, and even customs of different times and cultures. So, in New Zealand, we have to take account of Maori and Pacific Island cultures as well as European culture.

After cautioning that "it is sometimes difficult to harmonize culture with Christian teaching" the Pope and bishops in the *Pastoral Constitution on the Church in the Modern World* state that:

"Furthermore, while adhering to the methods and requirements proper to theology, theologians are invited to seek continually for more suitable ways of communicating doctrine to the men of their time. For the deposit of faith or revealed truths are one thing; the manner in which they are formulated without violence to their meaning and significance is another." [7]

The same thought is repeated in the *Decree on the Missionary Activity of the Church* with reference to the young churches.[8]

It is not to be expected, from a Catholic's point of view, that entirely new dogmatic formulae or liturgies will replace Christian teaching and worship which the church has developed through its continuing reflection upon the definitive revelation it has received. In 1972 the International Theological Commission reminded Catholics that:

"Dogmatic formulations must be considered as responses to precise questions and it is in this sense that they remain always true. Their permanent interest depends on the lasting relevance of the questions with which they are concerned; at the same time it must not be forgotton that the successive questions which Christians ask themselves about the understanding of the divine word, as well as already-discovered solutions, grow out of one another so that today's answers already presuppose in some way those of yesterday, although they cannot be reduced to them ... Yet this revelation is always the same, not only in its substance, but also in its fundamental statements ..."[9]

A spirit of inquiry must characterise the Catholic church in New Zealand. There is evidence that inquiry is taking place. Maori theologians are making considerable advances in determining the traditional Maori precedents of Christian teaching and life. But much of their thinking is not yet expressed in written form.

Many concepts of a religious nature are also expressed in the living situation of the marae. From speeches given by elders on the marae younger Maoris are isolating the concepts of a Maori theology. At the same time study is taking place on Polynesian ritual, art, and architecture, with a view to their incorporation into Catholic liturgy. These are promising beginnings.

The theology of the young Catholic church in New Zealand must also be concerned with orthopraxis. That means that the systematic reflection on faith and the experience of the believing community is not merely an intellectual affirmation about purely spiritual matters. It must also take place in word and action.

The theology of orthopraxis has been described in the following way by one of the groups which has given it its greatest impetus:

> From a theology of supernatural values, super-imposed on natural ones, we shift to a theology in which the supernatural is integrated with the natural ...from a theology which separates soul and body to a theology of integrated man; from an abstract to a political theology in which the people participate in the development of society in its economic, political, and social areas.[10]

Hope for a future life also involves hope for liberation from unjust social and economic structures. And love is understood to include the solidarity of men and women struggling for a new and different future.

The aspirations to equality and self-indentity which are signs of the present times, are developments of the anthropology we find in the Bible. God is the God of all people. So the cultural change which equality and self-identity for all people requires, is itself a demand for catholicity.

Political Involvement and Social Change

Following the more open vision of the relations between the church and the world proposed by Vatican II it is no longer possible to confine the mission of the Catholic church to specifically religious activity. Specifically religious teaching, development and liberation are not simply juxtaposed activities: in the one mission of the Catholic church they are connected.

But, while Catholics stress the importance of development and liberation in the mission of the church, they do not believe that these are the specifically religious task or are adequate substitutes for it. Catholics cannot equate the Gospel message with the task of solving pressing social problems. That would not be authentic Christianity.

In Catholic teaching, liberation is, in its strictest sense, a freeing from sin. But this freeing also has consequences in the social and political arenas. It may involve criticism and opposition when the fundamental rights of men and women are not respected.

In recent years Catholics have begun to think in terms of liberation as well as development. The Catholic bishops of New Zealand, together with the Australian and Pacific bishops, have stated:

"We affirm that if the church, as the effective sign of Christ's saving presence in the world, is to be faithful to its mission, it must assume an active role in the process of liberation, both by striving for its own renewal and by working for the liberation of all men." [11]

The new way of thinking has wide-ranging implications. More and more Catholics in New Zealand are beginning to realise that established social and political structures do not have to be accepted as part of man's inevitable lot. They can be transformed. When they are unjust they must be changed to make it possible for all people to live in freedom and dignity.

One writer describes the implications in this way:

"The process of development that aims to bring liberation for those who suffer injustice will involve radical changes in society. It will require bold transformations, innovations that run deep, in fact, revolutionary changes. The shift of power that must accompany such a movement will certainly involve some form of conflict. So Christians who are committed to the development of peoples in solidarity with the poor and oppressed, will have to reflect on the theological questions about violence and social change." [12]

Ecumenism

Vatican II's *Decree on Ecumenism* has moved Catholics to closer relationships with other Christian and non-Christian churches. Now the times are favourable and there is a welcome atmosphere of goodwill. There is a conscious desire for unity on the part of Christians. So New Zealand Catholics are encouraged to find ways of proclaiming with other Christians the common deposit of Christian faith. They are invited to search for contemporary expressions of faith which reflect common witness rather than controversy.

Ecumenical activity is carried on at many levels. Official discussions take place through joint working committees. Through these the National Council of Churches and the Roman Catholic Church in New Zealand have come to some common theological understandings in doctrinal matters and more recently, to common undertakings on development. Possibly even more extensive discussion and action takes place at local parish levels, often initiated by ministers' fraternal groups.

The Catholic Church in New Zealand is becoming more aware that if it is to take the contextual nature of its mission seriously, it must know what is happening in other Christian and non-Christian communities. So must the contributions of social sciences be respected and used. Their findings must be taken into account by those responsible for decision-making in the Church; in their programmes of action and in their statements.

Conclusion

The changes which have taken place in the Catholic church in recent years on a widespread scale and at an accelerated pace have been accompanied by uncertainty, confusion, doubt, and even panic. Some have looked for extremist answers, either conservative or progressive. Others have over-simplified the complexity of the situation in which the changes are taking place.

In spite of all the attendant dangers the Church must change if it is to live and grow. Only by continuing its quest for a truly distinctive New Zealand Christianity will the Catholic Church in New Zealand reach its fulfillment. In that quest it will be making its contribution to an indigenous New Zealand religion.

Notes:
1. VATICAN Council, 2nd, 1962-65. Dogmatic constitution on divine revelation, article 4. *In The documents of Vatican II.* Abbott, W.M., ed. London, Chapman, 1966. p. 111-128.
2. VATICAN Council, 2nd, 1962-65. Dogmatic constitution on the Church, article 18; Dogmatic constitution on divine regulation, article 12; Decree on ecumenism, article 21. *Ibid.*
3. LARACY, H. M. Pompallier. *New Zealand's heritage.* Wellington, Paul Hamlyn, 1971. vol 1. part 12, p. 329.

4. LARACY, H. M. Bishop Moran; Irish politics and Catholicism in New Zealand, p. 62. *The journal of religious history 6:* 62-76, 1970.
5. VATICAN Council, 2nd, 1962-65. Dogmatic constitution on divine revelation, article 8; Decree on the Church's missionary activity, article 22. *In The documents of Vatican II, op. cit.*
6. VATICAN Council, 2nd, 1962-65. Pastoral constitution on the Church in the modern world, article 40; Dogmatic constitution on the Church, article 16; Declaration on the relationship of the Church to non-christian religions, article 1; Decree on the Church's missionary activity, article 8. *In The documents of Vatican II, op. cit.*
7. VATICAN Council, 2nd, 1962-65. Pastoral constitution on the Church in the modern world, article 62. *In The documents of Vatican II. op. cit.*
8. VATICAN Council, 2nd, 1962-65. Decree on the Church's missionary activity, article 22. *In The documents of Vatican II. op. cit.*
9. INTERNATIONAL Theological Commission. Theological pluralism. *African ecclesiastical review 15;* 367-370, 1973.
10. RUETHER, R. *Liberation theology: human hope confronts Christian history and American power.* New York, Paulist Press, 1972.
11. *The CATHOLIC Church and the development of peoples in the South Pacific: Conference held in Suva, Fiji, August, 1972.* Wellington, Episcopal Conference of the Pacific in conjunction with Corso, 1973. (5 booklets)
12. CURNOW, E. J. *Human development — a Christian response,* p. 14. Booklet 5 of *The Catholic Church and the development of peoples in the South Pacific. ibid.*

The Protestant Contribution

HAVE THE MAINLINE PROTESTANT CHURCHES MOVED OUT OF THEIR COLONIAL STATUS?
Ian Breward

'Colonial status' implies a combination of dependence and exploitation which is normally understood in political, cultural and economic terms, even after legal independence has been granted. In a former British colony like New Zealand when there was substantial migration from the United Kingdom, 'colonial' has a very different meaning than in Ghana, where the indigenous population remained a vast majority. It was entirely natural that settlers should establish churches with which they were already familiar. Indeed they were mostly so involved with conviction about the superiority of white Protestant civilization, that they did not think any other form of Christianity was possible.

The result was a 'provincialism' of the spirit, rather than the imposition of alien standards by a colonial elite, though that deeply affected Maori Christianity. Such dependence could be even more limiting than colonialist exploitation, because Britain was not seen as the oppressor, (unless by the Roman Catholic Irish) but as the source of religious enlightenment and culture, scholarship and spiritual leadership. Though New Zealand was fortunate in the high quality of some of the pioneer clergy, like Bishop Selwyn (Anglican) or Rev. Thomas Burns (Presbyterian), the desperate and continuing shortage of clergy meant that men with limited education and modest social status often found their way into the clergy, achieving a distinction and position which would have been much less easily attainable in Britain. One of the most remarkable examples of this was Rev. C. Scrimgeour (Uncle Scrim), one of the most influential Methodist ministers New Zealand has seen. Such clergy were often very dependent on the patterns of parent churches and disinclined to depart from the religious environment they remembered there.

The independence of Selwyn and his friends in creating a substantiallydifferent form of church government, which allowed the laity a real voice in the affairs of the Church of the Province of New Zealand was quite unusual. Ministers and members alike depended heavily on the latest mail and imported books or periodicals like *The Evangelical Magazine* or *The British Weekly* for inspiration and solace against the spiritual loneliness that could depress the strongest spirits, deprived of the customary institutional and cultural support that British Christians took for granted. Alexander Don delicately hints at the source of desolation the cultured Rev. J. M. Smith and his wife felt when they arrived at the raw mining town of Naseby in 1871. The letters of Bishop Selwyn's wife show the eagerness with which home mails were awaited. George Hepburn, a leading Dunedin citizen, recorded his disgust at a consignment of newspapers being ruined on the voyage out.[1]

The most visible sign of dependence can be seen in the buildings the settlers erected for worship. Though some of the materials would never have been used in Britian and the proportions were frequently grotesque, the styles were variations on Victorian Gothic or Neo-Classical. Though some of the original wooden churches have remained and have a pleasing simplicity, touched with real beauty in the Selwyn churches or Old St. Pauls in Wellington, most eventually succumbed to borer and rot, or else were deliberately torn down to make way for brick, and plaster, or even stone. Only occasionally in some of the Maori churches were there signs of a different architectural idiom and decoration, as in Rangiatea Church at Otaki.

Some of the later churches built in the 19th Century like R.A. Lawson's Knox Church in Dunedin, had real distinction, but they could have been built anywhere in Britain.[2] Indeed a country which has yet to develop an indigenous architecture in which use\of local material and style mix in such a way that one could not envisage them outside New Zealand, can hardly be expected to do more than repeat overseas patterns of church architecture and furnishing, especially in an era of increasingly international bad taste.

Though isolated individuals made valiant attempts to think through theologically the purposes a church building ought to serve, groups like the Church Architecture Committee of the Presbyterian Assembly set up in 1937 had a difficult task moving congregations and architects to think of new patterns of building that were both functional and beautiful.[3] The waters of traditional prejudice run very deep and strong and only a few churches stand out from a very traditional style.[4] Traditional and familiar names were given to church buildings: St Pauls Cathedral in Wellington (Anglican), the Baptist Tabernacle in Auckland, St Andrew's Presbyterian Church in Auckland, Wesley Church in Wellington, or more recently Aldersgate in Christchurch (added to Durham Street Methodist Church). Methodists and Baptists are sparing on the use of saints' names! Ministerial and priestly dwellings received the familiar names of manse, parsonage, and vicarage, even if their appearance, size, and amenities differed from their British prototypes.

New Zealanders have likewise made very traditional use of their churches. Anglican liturgy made no concessions to the local environment, even though one suspects that vestments partly designed to keep clergy warm in medieval churches might well have been adapted for our more subtropical climate. It was not until the 1960's that Anglicans here reluctantly joined the ranks of the revisionists, appointing a Commission to produce a new liturgy, which was approved for general use in 1970. While not strikingly different from other Anglican liturgies, even this modest degree of change would have been unlikely without the example of change in mother churches in Britain and Europe. Presbyterians have been equally dependent on the work of the Scottish Church Service Society and its successive editions of the *Book of Common Order* to supplement the Westminster *Directory,* though the local Church Service Society has had an important influence through annual lectures published since 1941 and some very articulate members, like D.M. Hercus and C.I.L. Dixon. The Methodist Church approved a Communion Service in 1969 and the Presbyterian Church authorized experimental use of a new form of Communion Service in 1978. Where congregations have been fed a diet of extempore prayers, there is no way of recovering their style and fervour, though study of the occasional British Free Churchmen like John Hunter who produced collections of prayers suggests that there was a good deal of Biblical quotation and local application. For a historian, these lost prayers would be the most interesting, for they could give some clues about the changing ethos of Presbyterian, Methodist, and Baptist congregations in New Zealand.

Worship and spirituality have not been areas in which New Zealand Christians have excelled. The flat colourless language which passes for a means of communication among many Pakeha is unlikely to provide a basis for beauty of language in worship. No noteworthy collection of prayers has yet been produced by a New Zealander and devotional books likewise yield little sign of profound commitment.[5] The New Zealand Liturgy of the Anglican Church

(1970), contains some optional Maori sections, but little use is made of Maori in the vast majority of Churches. The Presbyterian Maori Synod produced a very comprehensive service book in Maori in 1933, but it is basically a translation from European sources. Despite the importance of religious orders in the Anglican tradition, only one local Anglican religious order has survived – the Community of the Sacred Name in Christchurch, which was founded in 1893. Important personal contributions to worship and spirituality have been made by members of the other numerous British Anglican orders, but any writing here, mapping the passionate personal search for God has been rare. Indeed, only James K. Baxter, a Catholic convert, has been able to articulate this. The Methodist inspired Riverside Community near Motueka is one of the few examples of an attempt to give salvation an economic and social framework.

Music and hymnology reflect the same reliance on the world church. Apart from the Anglican's *New Zealand Hymnal,* which was soon superseded by the cheaper and more comprehensive *Hymns Ancient and Modern,* all major denominations used British or American hymnaries and the Presbyterian *Church Hymnary* was not untypical in that it had one hymn by an Antipodean–'God of eternity and Lord of the ages', written by Dr. E.N. Merrington, Master of Knox College. The various songbooks used in the charismatic movement of the seventies, like *Songs of Praise,* show a similar dependence on overseas models. Methodists in Australia and New Zealand were the first to produce a local hymnbook, containing a few hymns written in this part of the world. [6] The last few years have seen a number of congregations produce their own supplements, but the only writer and composer of any significance is Dr. Colin Gibson, a Methodist from Dunedin. The success of the N.Z.B.C.'s 'Sing a New Song' indicates that New Zealanders can write hymns, given some incentive. The fairly lively tradition of musical performance has not yet spilled over into much song composition, secular or religious, though these *signs of change* are an indication that our excessive provincialism is waning. As yet, however, there is little sign that the considerable talents of New Zealand poets have been used to explore religious themes that could be set to music. The very secularity of New Zealand society, which is indigenous, reinforces the reliance on overseas spirituality, liturgy, and music. Though attempts have been made to produce a N.Z. hymnal under the auspices of the National Council of Churches, the economics of publishing make its appearance unlikely, especially since the appearance of an excellent Australian Hymnal in 1977. The only significant local product is the Pacific Islanders Church Hymnary.

The sermons preached in the last century have largely perished. The historian has a difficult task in trying to reconstruct what the people heard and an impossible one to discover what they understood and built into the fabric of their lives, because there are very few records of the piety of ordinary church members.[7] There were a surprising number of sermons published and reported in the 19th century and, before the days of T.V., public speakers and lecturers attracted very large audiences. Yet examination of published sermons does not reveal any significant attention to local issues or even national ones. Collections like Rutherford Waddell's *Behold the Lamb of God* (1903) could have been preached in Britain, or anywhere else in the Empire. Ministerial training in homiletics was heavily influenced by British models, and the situation of dependence has not changed now that North American influences are strong.[8]

One promising area for research would be to discover what kind of sermons Maori ministers preached. Contemporary Maori preaching can be an interesting blend of European style with the style of Maori oratory and a fondness for allusion, illustration, and vivid pictorial imagery; it may lack the formal and logical structure of a Pakeha sermon, but it can have considerable emotional impact.[9] Pacific Islanders' sermons have similar qualities. Until fairly recently, one could not even be sure of hearing a New Zealand accent in the pulpit. Irish accents in Roman Catholic Churches, upper-class English accents in Anglican churches, Scots/Irish accents in Presbyterian pulpits still have a certain cachet and respectability, especially among those born before1945.[10] The impact of popular religious broadcasters like Father Leo Close's Irish accent or the mellifluous tones of Canon Bob Lowe shows that the way things are said is still important to significant parts of the audience.

In terms of leadership the churches have only moved away slowly from those born in Britain. The Anglican episcopal bench has become entirely Antipodean only since 1973 with the consecration of Bishop Norman. A study of Presbyterian Moderators or Baptist and Methodist Presidents shows that those of British birth dominated until well into this century. The same can be said for theological college staff. At the Theological Hall, Knox College, there was a majority of expatriate staff until 1960 when the appointment of Professor L.G. Geering tipped the balance in a New Zealand direction. With the exception of Professor D. Glenny (1977) all the present staff have had British or European post-graduate study, so that the ties with the mother churches are still strong and students are likely to be better informed about the theological debates of Britain or Europe than about the beliefs of the culture in which they will minister. At St. John's College in Auckland there has not yet been a New Zealand born and trained Warden, though the defunct College House in

Christchurch has had two local Principals, the Rev. S. Parr and the Rev. Martin Sullivan. Trinity College and Baptist College have had largely local staff, though the Congregational College was staffed by British men until its closure. (Holy Cross College in Mosgiel, the National Catholic Seminary, had its first New Zealand Rector in 1978; the majority of its staff are Australian Vincentians and Jesuits).

Theological scholarship has been slight, though not negligible. Few clergy had the depth of training which British theological students of comparable ability could take for granted. There were always too many other urgent things to be done and the culturally impoverished and intensely practical backgrounds from which most theological students have come ensured that very few either had the interest or ability to play a significant part in shaping local culture.

Where parish ministers have produced substantial books, like James MacGregor's Trilogy on Apologetics, they were usually extraordinary men.[11] Where theological teachers have produced substantial books, they have usually been addressed to an international rather than a local audience, for the simple reason that the market for such books in New Zealand is very small.[12] *The New Zealand Journal of Theology*, edited by J.M. Bates and J. T. V. Steele lasted from 1932-35 and contained mostly articles on overseas problems and issues. *The New Zealand Theological Review* (1964-) provided more of a forum for the serious discussion of local theological issues, though it began to show signs of being an Australian rather than a New Zealand journal, when it changed its name to *Colloquium* in 1967. At another level, the dependence of local Evangelicals on overseas ideas can be seen in *The Reaper* and *The Evangelical Presbyterian*, which are largely reprints of British and American articles, as is *Reach Out*, the latest attempt to produce a youth periodical.

There have been many popular books and booklets, but it was not until the Geering controversy that New Zealanders had a really significant theological debate which attracted national interest and resulted in the publication of several substantial books, not least two by laymen.[13] Though it can scarcely be claimed that the result was an addition of a new dimension to the worldwide debate on the nature of the Christian hope, it has been the first time that a major debate has been conducted at a level which would be normal in Britain or North America.

New Zealand's small size means that discussions of ethical issues such as sexuality, temperance, gambling, and race relations show a similar dependence on overseas discussions. Local Christians do not appear to have the energy, expertise, and passion which British, American, and European scholars bring to ethical issues[14] When one compares the originality and boldness of local technology and scientific research, the historian needs to ask why it is that the New Zealand churches do not have any ethical achievements or discussions comparable to the innovation in the Hamilton jet boat. Ecclesiastical thinking and action on race relations, for example, is very insular, with a strong flavour of smugness and an almost complete lack of the depth or urgency which characterises discussions and action in Britain and North America, or South Africa.[15]

Does this sampling of New Zealand Protestantism's colonial dependence lead to the conclusion that it simply reflects the dependence of our society as a whole and the lack of interest in our own environment which characterizes communities that rely on metropolitan inspiration for initiative in cultural and spiritual matters? Little has happened since the rather wry comments of Dr. John Harré about the failure of the churches to take root in New Zealand society.[16]

The answer should not be given before one further cluster of evidence is examined. Mission churches' freedom from colonial dependence has been partly judged by ability to support themselves financially, to govern themselves, and to propagate themselves. Though it is generally recognised now that these tests are altogether too crude, they cannot be ignored in a rounded study. Here the situation of New Zealand Protestantism is strikingly different from sister churches of similar age in Asian and African or Latin American countries. Financially, settler churches here were expected to support themselves from the beginning, though Anglicans continued to seek help overseas for the building of cathedrals long after other churches were completely solvent financially. Methods of financing the church have usually been copied from overseas, but the course of the Stewardship Movement in the Presbyterian Church during the 1950's was marked by a wider vision than raising congregational income. Ideas and experience from here were taken back to the Church of Scotland by Professor G.A.F. Knight and the Rev. J.G. Matheson, the latter of whom became Secretary of the Committee of Stewardship. This is one of the few examples I have been able to discover of the daughter church actually influencing the practice of the mother church. The history of the Melanesian Mission is another example involving partnership in mission.[17]

Congregationalists and Baptists were best equipped for immediate self-government, but both Presbyterians and Anglicans were quickly to adapt to life in the colony. The Presbytery of Auckland was founded in 1856, followed a year later by the Presbytery of Wellington. Bishop Selwyn and the formidable group of laymen with which he was associated drafted a Constitution for the Church of the Province of New Zealand in 1857, which owed something to North American precedents, but was the most radical in the Empire and gave laity participation to an extent which has only recently been attained in England - an interesting example of the daughter leaving the mother far behind.[18]

Nor were the colonial churches slow to share the task of proclaiming the gospel to the heathen. It could be argued that this was simply a reflection of the colonialist mentality of the British settlers, but it has frequently been seen as a sign that a church has become indigenous. The fact that New Zealand included a large part of the Pacific, in the diocesan boundaries assigned to Selwyn, meant that the Church of the Province was in the position of being both a mission and also involved in mission. New Zealand Methodists were early involved in Tonga and Fiji and Presbyterians began work in the New Hebrides along with their co-religionists from Scotland and Nova Scotia. Since then, New Zealand participation in missions overseas has become literally world wide, extending far beyond the neighbouring Pacific Islands to South America, China, India, Pakistan, Malaysia, Singapore, Indonesia, and East Africa.[19] Some very distinguished missionaries have emerged, who have exerted an influence out of all proportion to the size of our involvement, making a contribution to the world church as a result. J.W. Burton, W.M. Ryburn, C. Fox, and J.O. Sanders are names that spring most readily to mind.

Transmission of spiritual and ethical values to the rising generation is another area deserving of historical analysis. The churches began by seeking to play the leading role in education to which they had been accustomed in Britain. Geography, poverty, and shortage of teachers made their efforts quite inadequate and by the 1860's, a significant group of thoughtful Christians were beginning to feel their way towards a state system of education which was free, secular, and compulsory. This was not unique to New Zealand, but the discussions showed that New Zealanders were capable of drastically modifying their heritage when circumstances justified it. Though a significant group of clergy never accepted the 1877 Education Act, the bill could not have been passed without the support of a large group of churchmen who were fed up with sectarian strife and convinced that a combination of public and voluntary efforts would ensure the moral welfare of the rising generations. The Nelson system which emerged in the 1920's and 1930's as a serious alternative to the campaign to modify the Education Act by making Bible reading and worship possible was a compromise unique to New Zealand. It was far from ideal, but it worked and was finally given legal recognition in 1962, by which time the concern of

Protestants for education had substantially diminished from that of three decades before.[20]

Another interesting example of New Zealand adaptation of an *imported institution* can be seen in the foundation and growth of the Bible Class movement in the Presbyterian Church from 1888 on and its spread to the other mainline Protestant Churches.[21] Begun in Wellington by a talented immigrant Scot, George Troup, the movement provided a social and spiritual home for the young men and women who were no longer content to be organised by their elders and wished to make their own way in the world. Run on co-operative lines, with a strong emphasis on discussion, self-improvement and sport as well as more overtly religious activities like evangelism, the movement caused considerable ministerial unease, because it almost seemed to be a church within a church. Though the movement reached its zenith in the early 1920's it continued to play an important role and many distinguished New Zealanders like Sir James Hay and Sir John Marshall were decisively influenced by it, until it disappeared nationally in the 1960's. In addition, other groups were introduced to New Zealand without any modification - Christian Endeavour, Boys' & Girls' Brigades, Y.M.C.A., Y.W.C.A., Scouts, Guides, Tertiary Students Christian Fellowship, S.C.M., Scripture Union, Youth for Christ, Y.W.A.M., Navigators.

The role of women in colonial societies is ambivalent. In some respects, they were freed from British social conventions and restraints. They received the vote in 1893. Otago Girls' High School, founded in 1871, was the first of its kind in the Empire. Traditional roles and taboos still remained unchanged until very recently. Women were not permitted to be meat packers until 1956, on the ground that menstruating women would contaminate meat. Women's role in marriage and the family was very strongly reinforced by all the churches and organisations like the League of Mothers and the Anglican Mothers Union, but the combination of employment opportunities and philosophies of women's liberation have begun to work far reaching changes in community perceptions about the role of women.

Women's organisations like the Aglow Fellowship are a contemporary example of the way that churches still segregate sexes for teaching and edification. Groups like the Baptist Women's Fellowship, or the Association of Presbyterian Women have important social, educational, financial and community service functions (Ladies a plate please!) while overseas mission and many New Zealand charities depend almost entirely on the voluntary services of Christian women. Such organisations closely resemble British or American counterparts and do not indicate religious innovation. Nevertheless, there are some differences, for Methodist (1959), Presbyterian (1966), and Anglican (1977) churches have all ordained women to their ministry before their British counterparts, as well as permitting participation in local, regional, and national church government, though by no means in the proportions of actual female membership and activity. Paradoxically, the growth of the charismatic movement may strengthen traditional attitudes, because of the literalness with which Biblical teaching on women's roles is taken.

These examples of practical adaptation are perhaps our most significant clue to the slow emergence of a New Zealand religious ethos. They were not startlingly original. They began in a small way and won their position by hard work. Where imported institutions performed with reasonable adequacy, they were left alone. But when placed in a situation of pressure, the New Zealander showed himself surprisingly resourceful in a quiet way. The radical courses of the 1890's and the 1930's were another reminder of that. Perhaps it can be suggested that the churches of New Zealand will not really throw off their dependence on Britain and North America until they are really threatened with disaster. Or to use another model, New Zealand industry was not able to develop without a tariff barrier. Perhaps the same may prove to be true in matters of the spirit for what remains of the 20th century.

Notes:
1. DON, A. *Memories of the golden road; a history of the Presbyterian Church in Central Otago.* Dunedin, Reed, 1936, p. 311.
   STEWART, W. D., (ed) *The journal of George Hepburn on his voyage from Scotland to Otago in 1850 ...* Dunedin, C.S.W., 1934, p. 132.
2. KNIGHT, C. R. *The Selwyn churches of Auckland.* Wellington, Reed, 1972.
   STACPOOLE, J. and Beavan, P. *N.Z. art: architecture 1820-1970.* Wellington, Reed, 1972.
   HISLOP, J. *History of Knox Church, Dunedin.* Dunedin, J. Wilkie, 1892.
3. Minutes are deposited in the Knox Church Library. See also:
   HERCUS, D. M. *The building of churches.* Christchurch/Dunedin, Presbyterian Bookroom, 1945.
4. BRUGGINK, D. J. and Droppers, G. H. *Christ and architecture: building Presbyterian/Reformed churches.* Grand Rapids, Eerdmans, 1965. Gives illustrations of the international trends which have affected New Zealand. See also:
   SMITH, P. F. *Third millennium churches.* London, Galliard, 1973.

5. RITA Snowden is probably the most widely published devotional writer and J. K. Baxter the most profound.
BAXTER, J. K. *The flowering cross.* Dunedin, N.Z. Tablet, 1969, is a landmark in the genre. More ephemeral types can be seen in:
MILLER, G. *For pilgrims only.* 1939.
J. H. Deane of the Bible Training Institute wrote prolifically.

6. *Sing a new song,* 1970. The Joint Board of Christian Education has also produced two interesting collections *Songs of faith,* 1966, and *Songs for worship,* 1968. No serious analysis has been made of Ratana hymns or the Ringatu chants.

7. LAIDLAW, R. A. *The reason why.* Auckland, Auckland Bible House, *c* 1925. This tract is possibly the most notable example. It has circulated in millions. More sophisticated lay versions of Christianity can be seen in:
WALSH, J. *Living with uncertainty.* 1968.
SHOVE, H. W. (A. Colquhoun) *John Brown's soul goes marching.* London, Epworth Press, 1964.
DON, A. *Memories of the golden road. op. cit.,* offers some useful portraits of Presbyterians.

8. For examples of different styles of preaching see:
SERMONS for lay readers
SPROTT, T. W. *Redeeming the time; a selection of sermons and addresses.* Wellington, Reed, 1948.
BLACK, W. B. *I travel the road.* Christchurch, Presbyterian Bookroom, 1947.

9. KOHERE, R. T. *The autobiography of a Maori.* Wellington, Reed, 1951, is one of the few accounts of a Maori minister. Mr J. Rangihau of Waikato University is editing and publishing a collection of Ringatu prophecies which may totally alter estimates of Ringatu worship.

10. More research is needed on the extent to which British styles of ministry dominated parish life, even after New Zealand trained ministers were in the majority.
KEMP, W. *Joseph W. Kemp.* London/Edinburgh, Marshall, Morgan and Scott, 1936. Gives useful insights into the work of a notable Baptist minister, who worked in New Zealand and overseas.

11. MacGregor had been a professor at New College, Edinburgh, until he came to New Zealand for health reasons and played an important part in the Synod of Otago and Southland from his pulpit at Columba Church, Oamaru. Notable examples of what can be done are:
GIBSON SMITH, J. *The Christ of the Cross, or, the death of Jesus Christ in its relation to forgiveness and judgement.* Wellington, Gordon and Gotch, 1908.

BURTON, O. E. *The conflict of the Cross.*

DAVIES, W. M. *An introduction to F. D. Maurice's theology.* 1964.

12. DICKIE, J. *The organism of Christian truth: a modern positive dogmatic.* London, Clarke, 1931.

RANSTON, H. *Ecclesiastes and the early Greek wisdom literature.* London, Epworth/Sharp, 1925.

KNIGHT, G. A. F. *From Moses to Paul: a Christological study in the light of our Hebraic heritage.* London, Lutterworth, 1949.

KNIGHT, G. A. F. *A Christian theology of the Old Testament.* London, S.C.M., 1959.

NICHOLAS, H.G. *The story of salvation: a series of biblical essays.* Auckland, Congregational Union of New Zealand, 1962.

13. GEERING, L. G. *God in the new world.* London, Hodder and Stoughton, 1968.

GEERING, L. G. *Resurrection – a symbol of hope.* London, Hodder and Stoughton, 1971.

REX, H. H. *Did Jesus rise from the dead?* Auckland, Blackwood and Janet Paul, 1967.

BURTON, O. E. *To whom shall we go?* Auckland, Forward Books, 1973.

BLAIKIE, R. J. *'Secular Christianity' and God who acts.* London, Hodder & Stoughton, 1971.

The lay contributions were:

BLAIKLOCK, E. M. *Layman's answer: an examination of the new theology.* London, Hodder & Stoughton, 1968.

MORTON, J. *Man, science and God.* London, Collins, 1972.

14. Contrast:

SALMOND, J. D. *Cult of the Golden Kiwi: a plea for concern for our young New Zealanders, pakehas and Maoris.* Christchurch, Presbyterian Bookroom, 1962, and

GREEN, P. *Betting and gambling.* 1935.

Despite the intensity of the abortion debate up till 1978, the only local book was:

O'NEILL, J. S. *Fetus-in-law.* Dunedin, Independent Publishing, 1976. Note also:

YULE, R. M. (ed) *Christian responsibility in society.* Wellington, Tertiary Christian Studies Programme, 1977.

15. Contrast:

MOL, H. *Religion and race in New Zealand.* Christchurch, National Council of Churches, 1966, and:

THOMPSON, R. *Race relations in New Zealand: a review of the literature.* Christchurch, National Council of Churches, 1963, with:

CAWOOD, L. *The churches and race relations in South Africa.* 1964.
NGK Report. *Human relations in South Africa.* 1966.
16. Landfall 20: 37, 1966.

> "Religion has several key functions in society. It assists in the physical integration of the group (that is, by assembling the members it makes them aware of their group affiliations). It provides a symbolic expression of group identity. It is the most potent means of controlling the actions of group members within an accepted system of morality and values. For the individual, religion provides a measure of psychological integration — it gives him confidence and enables him to explain his failures. It is my contention that in all these fields Christian religion in New Zealand is a failure. In some respects this is a comment on the Christian church as a whole — in others it is related more specifically to New Zealand. To some extent it is the system which is at fault, but most of the problems are accentuated by a lack of realization of social factors on the part of the clergy and a lack of any real dedication amongst all but a few of the laity."

17. ARMSTRONG, E.S. *The Melanesian Mission.* London, Isbister, 1900.
MORRELL, W. P. *The Anglican Church in New Zealand: a history.* Dunedin, McIndoe for the Anglican Church of the Province of New Zealand, 1973.
18. MORRELL, W. P. *ibid.* gives the most authoritative account, p. 49-71.
19. CARTER, G. *A family affair: a brief summary of New Zealand Methodism's involvement in mission overseas, 1822-1972.* Auckland, Wesley Historical Society, 1973.
GREGORY, K. S. *Stretching out continually: "whaatoro tonu atu": a history of the New Zealand Church Missionary Society, 1892-1972.* Christchurch, the author, 1972.
MURRAY, J. S. *A century of growth: Presbyterian overseas mission work, 1869-1969.* Christchurch, Presbyterian Bookroom, 1969.
MacDIARMID, D. N. *Tales of the Sudan.* Melbourne, Sudan United Mission, 1934.
LOANE, M. *The story of the C.I.M. in Australia and New Zealand.* 1965.
20. MACKEY, J. *The making of a state education system: the passing of the New Zealand Education Act, 1877.* London, Chapman, 1967.
BREWARD, I. *Godless schools? A study in Protestant reactions to the Education Act of 1877.* Christchurch, Presbyterian Bookroom, 1967.
21. ELDER, J. *History of the Presbyterian Church of New Zealand, 1840-1940.* Christchurch, Presbyterian Bookroom, 1939.
SAGE, C. *Jubilee history of the YMBC Union* (MSS)

ALLAN, A. *Life upon life: a history of the Presbyterian Young Women's Bible Class Union.* Christchurch, Presbyterian Bookroom, 1954.

The forthcoming study of the Boy's Brigade by M. Hoare will be a valuable study of one of the Church-related organisations.

The Ecumenical Contribution

ECUMENISM IN NEW ZEALAND: SUCCESS OR FAILURE?[1]
Colin Brown.

In 1828 Thomas Poynton and his wife, devout Irish Catholics. settled at Hokianga where he established himself as a timber merchant and on his property the first Roman Catholic missionaries settled after their arrival on January 10, 1838. Not long after this event a group of twenty or thirty Maoris, converted to Wesleyan Methodism, having performed their Sunday religious duties, appeared in front of Bishop Pompallier's temporary residence and in no uncertain fashion indicated their hostility to him and all that he represented. When Thomas Poynton, who had vacated his house for the Bishop's benefit, had calmed them, he went at once to call on the local Wesleyan missionary, a Mr Turner.

> Both men became rather heated. "You know that we call all those who adhere to the Roman Catholic religion, idolaters?" said Turner. "Well there is no cause of quarrel on that point, for you know that we are not idolaters, but you *are* heretics," replied Poynton, determined to make things perfectly clear.[2]

New Zealanders may think that they have come a long way since then and the funeral ceremonies for the late Norman Kirk in September 1974 might seem to bear this out. On all three occasions, in the Anglican Cathedral Wellington, in the Christchurch Town Hall, and at the graveside in Waimate, Roman Catholic clergy participated in the rites along with Protestants and Anglicans. It was, it might be claimed, a fine demonstration of ecumenical fellowship, of a unity in Christ which waits only for some tinkering with the ecclesiastical machinery to find visible expression in organic reunion. But, apart altogether from the matter of reunion schemes, their fate and present condition (more will be said of these later), at least two things should be said about the contrast between the heated exchange of 1838 and the amicable display of ecumenical fellowship in connection with the late Prime Minister's funeral.

It took Christians a long while to reach this latter state of affairs. The attitudes expressed by Poynton and Turner did not pass quickly or easily: this is made clear, if nowhere else, in Professor Breward's history of the controversies over religious education in schools.[3] Nor, to take a second point, have such attitudes altogether vanished from the New Zealand scene. It is well worth remembering that there are 'exclusivist' sects in our midst and that they will have no truck with ecumenism in any shape or form. Whatever their numbers and whatever some of us may think of their views they constitute part of the total religious spectrum. Even within the mainline churches suspicions linger although religious rhetoric may have abated somewhat; in setting up the Joint Working Committee with the Roman Catholics the National Council of Churches proceeded with circumspection because of unease in some quarters especially among Baptists.[4]

So far I have been discussing ecumenism as an attitude: changing attitudes between churches and Christians have found expression in various ways: in agencies for inter-denominational co-operation, in schemes for organic reunion, and in movements cutting across denominational lines. There are a good many examples of most of these but for our purpose three contemporary instances, an example of each type, deserve attention - the National Council of Churches, the current reunion negotiations involving Anglicans, Presbyterians, Methodists, Congregationalists and the Associated Churches of Christ, and the 'Charismatic Renewal' movement.

The National Council of Churches

The National Council of Churches is not, of course, the only agency created by churches to further their co-operation but it is certainly the most prominent, to date probably the most important of such agencies, and its origins, achievements, and present difficulties all merit some attention. The National Council of Churches came into existence on July 23, 1941 at a meeting presided over by Bishop (late Archbishop) West-Watson in Christchurch. At that stage the Anglican, Presbyterian, Methodist and Baptist Churches, together with the Associated Churches of Christ, the Congregational Church, and Quakers, comprised the Council. The Salvation Army joined in 1944; the Greek Orthodox

Church in 1947 and the Cook Islands Christian Church in 1959. In 1965 Roman Catholic observers first appeared at a meeting of the Council; since 1969 the Roman Catholic Church in New Zealand and the National Council of Churches have participated in a Joint Working Committee discussing a range of issues such as conscience and authority; education, inter-faith marriages, the Eucharist, marriage and the family, the ministry of the Church, and the character of Christian morality. Besides the Joint Working Committee there are contracts at other levels: on local councils of churches, in local branches of the N.C.C. committees and commissions. In 1975 the N.C.C. and the Roman Catholic Church set up a joint secretariat on 'development' and co-operation on immigration and the re-settlement of refugees has, since 1970, been formalised in the Inter-Church Committee on Immigration. All this amounts to a good deal in the way of quite close co-operation but there are no clear indications that the Roman Catholic Church is particularly anxious to secure full membership of the N.C.C.[5] In addition, the Council has varying degrees of contact with Lutherans, the Ratana and Ringatu movements, and, from time to time, with Seventh Day Adventism and the Pentecostal Churches.

From its foundation the National Council of Churches has maintained a double emphasis corresponding to the 'Faith and Order' and 'Life and Work' emphasis of the world-wide Ecumenical Movement which gathered force from about 1910 onwards and with which some New Zealand church leaders were in close touch. The passion of such men for the reunion of the churches was accompanied by a deep conviction that Christianity has something to say about the whole of human life and must say it. Indeed the first major activity of the N.C.C. was the Campaign for Christian Order in 1943 followed up by a conference on 'Christian Order' in 1945.[6]

The N.C.C. has had a good deal to do with conferences, committees, and commissions; some critics would say that too much of its energy has gone into such activities. This is arguable but certainly its list of activities is impressive, including negotiations to obtain degrees in theology at the University of Otago, conferences for theological students, the resettlement of refugees in New Zealand, a major part in establishing prison, university and industrial chaplaincies in this country, representations to the government on a host of issues, the organising of ecumenical and nation-wide study programmes, the facilitation of discussions with the Roman Catholics and, best-known of all, Inter-Church Aid (now Christian World Service), its Christmas appeal and the more controversial Programme to Combat Racism. If it is asked, "What has all this activity achieved?" or more vulgarly in these inflationary days, "Are the churches getting value for their money?" one can point to certain tangible achievements - so many refugees settled, so much money raised and sent overseas, so many chaplaincies of various kinds established, and so on. But while it is hard to see how the churches could now operate without some such agency it is much more difficult to frame a balance-sheet of its activities partly because, to the best of my knowledge, little if any careful analysis has been carried out in an attempt to assess the extent and depth of the Council's influence. Some like to think that it has helped to awaken New Zealanders to their responsibility in Asia or to direct attention to the evils of the war in Vietnam or racism in South Africa but the plain truth appears to be that we just do not have the data available at present on which confident claims can be securely based. [7]

In the meantime, however, the N.C.C. has been overtaken by problems not all of its own making; its 1974 annual report began: "This has been a year of increasing crisis for the Council". This has, of course, its obvious financial aspect: in 1973 the deficit (met by dipping into the Reserves Fund), was $6,338, in 1974 it was $8,910 and the N.C.C appealed to the churches to increase their grants to the Council substantially. But the Churches, like everyone else, are hit by inflation and at a time when other challenges confront them. The N.C.C. is troubled by controversy over the World Council of Churches' Programme to Combat Racism but this is only one expression of a quite widespread controversy about the content of Christian salvation and the manner in which it is to be realized (social or individual, political or spiritual?), a controversy moreover which goes well beyond the N.C.C. and the W.C.C. and cuts across denominations. Then too, there is declining interest in and support for ecclesiastical institutions and, perhaps, for voluntary institutions generally.[8] This declining interest is suggested, as far as the N.C.C. is concerned, by the present age-structure of its annual meeting. Looks can be deceptive but a casual glance over attendance in recent years suggested that there were few under 40 years of age present: by contrast those under 40 years of age are strongly represented in the 'Charismatic Renewal' at least in the Anglican and Roman Catholic Churches. Incidentally the Youth Council of the National Council of Churches went out of existence a few years ago, in 1972; it was, among other activities, an important recruiting base for the parent body.

In short then, the N.C.C. has a multitude of activities to its credit, some easily identifiable and solid achievements, much that awaits further investigation and assessment and - it has an uncertain future. There are even whispers, in some quarters, that euthanasia should be sanctioned, although with the hope that sooner or later, the Council or some equivalent body, will rise again with clearer vision and renewed energies.

In the event the Council has survived thus far; in most cases, the churches have increased their grants but, even so, inflation has continued to wreak havoc and the Council now ekes out a somewhat restricted existence deprived of the resources for any expansion of its activities. Moreover, a continuing tendency is to separate off specific areas from the N.C.C. and to allow the bodies concerned a semi-autonomous existence. This has happened with industrial chaplaincies, education, and most recently, where immigration and re-settlement are concerned. Amidst this proliferation of semi-independent commissions the N.C.C. seems destined to become, in large measure, a clearing-course not only for concerns common to the churches but also for the work of a series of ecumenical commissions and committees.

Plans for Union

Nor has the recent attempt at achieving organic union between some, at least, of the major churches, been attended by unqualified success. Concern for such union is no new thing on the ecclesiastical scene in New Zealand. It is often said that the Ecumenical Movement is the child of the Missionary Movement and, although the scandal of disunity took longer to become apparent in New Zealand than in, say, India and China, where Christianity was a tiny minority, concern for Christian unity in New Zealand and for its visible, organic expression, dates from the latter part of the 19th century.[9] Divisions which had at least a historical justification in Britain had less point in the colony; by 1901 the Presbyterian Church in New Zealand was a united body although the arrangements for this were long delayed; the first move seems to have come from the Auckland Presbytery on January 4, 1861. Likewise by 1913 the Wesleyans, Primitive Methodists, Free Methodists, and Bible Christians had joined to form the Methodist Church in New Zealand.[10]

The Presbyterians were barely united when, in 1902, their General Assembly acceded to an 'overture' which created a committee for discussions with the Methodist and Congregational Churches. Two years later the discussions were abandoned when it became clear that, in the event of any such union, there would be a substantial continuing Presbyterian Church. In succeeding years similar moves were made; from 1907-19 the Baptists also were involved in such discussions. What one Presbyterian participant in such discussion called "a dramatic change" took place in 1964 when the Anglican Church in New Zealand entered into negotiations which were already going on between the Presbyterian, Methodist and Congregational Churches and the Associated Churches of Christ. A 'Joint Commission' on Church Union was established by the churches concerned, they proceeded to a formal "Act of Commitment" in the Anglican Cathedral, Wellington on May 10 1967, and, in September 1969 a "Plan of Union" was published. It was widely discussed and, when reissued in 1971, had, according to one commentator, "been revised in a generally Anglican direction in the sections on worship, sacraments, and ministry, and in a generally Presbyterian direction in the sections on government."[11] The Associated Churches of Christ, the Presbyterian and Methodist Churches all voted in favour of the Plan as a basis for proceeding to union. Of eight continuing Congregational churches, two were in favour and six against the Plan while the Anglican General Synod in 1974, voting according to 'houses' (i.e. bishops, clergy, and laity), failed by two clerical votes to secure the two-thirds majority for the Plan agreed on by the Synod in advance as appropriate.[12] Nevertheless by vote of the General Synod, the Anglican Church was committed to continuing membership of the Joint Commission and to reconsideration of the existing plan at the General Synod to be held in 1976.

By 1976, when the Anglican General Synod met again, the dioceses of Auckland, Waikato, Waiapu, and Christchurch had accepted the Plan as a basis for union; Nelson, Wellington and Dunedin had refused assent. The General Synod, noting the fact that three dioceses were opposed to further moves on the basis of the Plan, resolved against proceeding further on this basis. Instead, however, the Synod supported moves towards the 'unification' or 'reconciliation' of the ordained ministries of the respective churches, declared this to be "a preliminary step towards the organic union of the negotiating churches", and expressed willingness to enter into a covenant to this effect. If these moves are successful the result will be that the five churches will retain their independence but ministers already ordained could serve in any one of the churches and ordinations in the future would involve the participation of representatives of all the negotiating churches. The complicated legal and theological issues involved in this tactic are still being thrashed out at the levels of commissions, committees, and local representative assemblies of the churches concerned. Among Anglicans there does seem to be a slightly greater degree of support for this piecemeal approach, as distinct from organic union in one stage, but present indications are that bishops of Wellington and Nelson will oppose this development as they did the Plan also.

Just why opposition to the Plan should have crystallized in Dunedin, Wellington and Nelson is not altogether easy to determine and merits further investigation. Some of the most highly articulate opponents of the Plan emerged in these dioceses; many but not all of the authors of pamphlets issued by the 'Selwyn Society', which opposed the Plan, were from Wellington.[13] Opposition to the Plan may well have been one aspect of the provincialism which survives quite strongly in New Zealand life generally, heightened in the case of Nelson and Dunedin, by relative geographical isolation from the main centres of population. Ecclesiastically both Dunedin and Nelson have had a long history of comparative isolation from the life of the Anglican Church generally in New Zealand while theologically Dunedin has been notable for a rather rigid Anglo-Catholicism whereas Nelson has had a markedly Evangelical emphasis nourished by bishops imported from Australia and clergy either from there also or trained there in theological colleges of an Evangelical character. In the case of Dunedin there was a fairly general fear that Anglicanism would be swamped by the numerically dominant and generally more vigorous Presbyterianism which forms a sort of local 'establishment'. The bishops of Nelson and Wellington, especially the former, took a strong stand against the Plan: this may have influenced voting by both clergy and laity. Thus, after the 1974 General Synod, when the Plan was sent to diocesan synods for re-consideration and four dioceses voted for its adoption and three against, only in the diocese of Dunedin did clergy and laity diverge from the stand taken by the bishop concerned. In Nelson and Wellington, bishops, clergy and laity voted against; in Auckland, Waikato, Waipau and Christchurch all three 'houses' voted the other way but in Dunedin the bishop (at the time a recent appointee and rather more 'liberal' than many of his clergy and laity), voted for the Plan whereas both clergy and laity rejected it. When the matter came to General Synod in 1976 it seems clear that very few, if any, were prepared to force the issue and opponents of the Plan had long threatened to create a 'continuing' Anglican Church in the event of the Plan being carried. Whether or not these threats will materialise again if plans for unifying the ministries of the churches go forward, yet remains to be seen.

In the meantime, however, union schemes of various kinds are going ahead on the local level with varying degrees of participation by the churches concerned. In 1968 there were 47 such co-operative ventures operating; by January 1973 there were 56 union parishes and 25 'Joint-Use' agreements. "By the end of 1973", says a report of the Joint Commission, "33 Anglican, 9 Congregational, 9 Associated Churches of Christ, 108 Methodist, and 100 Presbyterian 'units' were involved in co-operative ventures . . . it is now inconceivable that the Churches could return to anything akin to denominational isolation."[14] This process has continued and, at September 1, 1978, there were 63 'union' parishes, 34 'co-operating' parishes and another 20 under special agreements of various kinds.[15] Heartening though such developments may be to ecumenical planners, the ecclesiastical situation is now thoroughly untidy and, without reunion at the 'top' between the churches concerned, all sorts of ecclesiastical and legal anomalies are surfacing. Moreover, as soon as one asks about the meaning of all that has happened one is up against some interesting questions. In the absence of detailed study of union parishes (and I do not know of any such study), it is perhaps hazardous to generalise but it is quite possibly true that, in many cases, economic and other exigencies have as much to do with the burgeoning of such union schemes as theological conviction and religious feeling. (Of course if a Christian believer wishes to interpret economic and other pressures as 'God's way of doing things' that is another matter!) It would be interesting to know if the history of such ventures justified Bryan Wilson's by now well-known comment that "Ecumenism may be a policy not only induced by decline, but one encouraging decline."[16]

The slowing-up of negotiations for organic reunion may belong to a more general trend and, in any case, the negotiations in New Zealand do not yet involve the Baptists and the Roman Catholics not to speak of other although smaller Christian bodies. There is some awareness within the Joint Commission itself (like the N.C.C. a body with a predominantly 'older' membership), that conditions are changing beyond those in which moves began. Archbishop Johnston, then chairman of the Commission, said at its May 1973 meeting:

> It may be that the very historical conditions within which our negotiations began have changed and we have not been sufficiently aware of this .... It might be a useful exercise to consider some of these changes since negotiation between our churches first began. I do not propose to attempt this now but only to say that we are not in the same situation as we were, say, seven years ago. Take the institutional life of our Churches as one example. I think there has been a profound change, of which all may not be aware, in all of our churches. Today, both from within and without the membership of the Churches, there is a different attitude towards the institutional Church ... When I first entered into the conversations with other Churches communicant figures and other statistical data in my Church were still increasing. New Churches were being built in many places, and there was still a feeling of security and maybe complacency that the institution as such was not in such bad shape.[17]

Archbishop Johnston's further comments indicated that, for himself, he thought that the situation called, not for abandonment of the Plan, so much as for a realistic assessment of the perspective in which it must now be viewed.

Commentators on the world-wide ecumenical scene vary a good deal in their assessment. S.M. Cavert observes that "Those who expect 'instant ecumenicity' and are discouraged when they do not see it have little understanding of the way in which meaningful social advance is made." He adds:

All in all, then, in spite of a slackening of popular interest in some quarters, there is solid ground for believing that the ecumenical movement is just at the beginning of its long-range influence.

But Cavert, and with respect, Archbishop Johnston, also both belong to an older generation. Wherever the younger generation of church leaders are, they are not especially evident in ecumenical leadership at the top levels in this country. Barry Till believes, indeed, that many such, sense that a change of course in the life of the churches may be imminent, although in just which direction is, he considers, far from clear at present.[19]

The Charismatic Renewal

For some of course, this direction is already charted in the movement for 'charismatic renewal' which it is important to discuss both as an expression of ecumenism and one, so far anyway, not so much opposed to plans for organic union of churches, as disinterested in them because its focus of real interest lies elsewhere.[20] It is not, of course, the first movement among Christians in New Zealand to cut across denominational boundaries and to engender a certain lack of concern for organic union largely because participants believe that an infinitely precious spiritual union exists already and suffices. But the 'Charismatic Renewal' movement is certainly worth attention partly because all too little is known of it, partly because it involves Roman Catholics also.

Among Roman Catholics in New Zealand it seems to have appeared first in Christchurch about 1969; by May 1974 fourteen charismatic prayer meetings existed among Roman Catholics in this area. The movement is firmly established in Auckland also; less so elsewhere as in, e.g. Wellington, Dunedin, Hamilton, Invercargill and Nelson. The question of participating in the Communion services of other churches has been raised in some Roman Catholic groups which are open, in varying degrees, to non-Catholics, but the bishops appear to be adamant against any relaxation and there has been tension in some groups over the issue because such rules seem petty by comparison with a felt spiritual unity with other charismatic Christians. Just where this movement will go and how it will affect other ecumenical endeavours remains to be seen; certainly in theUnited States its leaders are strenuously active to keep the movement within the Church and to insist, at least to some degree, on the place of visible expressions of unity.[21]

As far as the growth of the movement among Anglicans is concerned there were certain contacts with Pentecostalists back in the early 1950's but a more obvious place to begin the history of the movement as it affects Anglicans, is in 1965 with a small group, mostly students, associated with a Wellington Presbyterian congregation. In touch with this group was the Reverend R.J. Muller then an assistant-curate at All Saints' Church in Palmerston North and a university chaplain. Indeed Palmerston North has become a veritable centre for the movement; in 1972 Muller became full-time director of Christian Advance Ministries which held the first of a series of notable 'summer schools' at Massey University in January 1973 characterised by a strong emphasis on containing the renewal within the Church; the 1978-9 'School' attracted a capacity enrolment of 1300. The renewal early won an important supporter in Professor John Morton, a professor of zoology at the University of Auckland and well-known as an Anglican layman, a supporter of the Plan for Union as of the ordination of women although, in other ways, relatively conservative theologically. Vigorous groups and centres have emerged in Auckland and Christchurch also, and some elsewhere too.

But the role which 'charismatics' will play within the Anglican Church where moves for organic union are concerned is uncertain although clergy and laity affected by the movement co-operate readily enough with fellow-charismatics in other churches. In Christchurch at least, of clergy known to be affected by the Charismatic Renewal, some were opposed to the Plan for Union while others were amongst its supporters. On the other hand, there is little or no overlap of personnel between leaders in the Renewal and top-level negotiators for church union. In part this appears to be an age difference; there is some evidence to indicate that those under 40 are more heavily represented in the circles of the Renewal than in the population at large; the negotiators for church union or for that matter, representatives of the churches on the National Council of Churches, tend to be drawn from older age-groups. Two other general factors may be involved. In some quarters of the Charismatic Renewal there is a degree of anti-intellectualism and a certain amount of prejudice against theology and theologians which do not fit easily with the theological concerns and intricacies entailed in church union negotiations. Secondly, there is the simple matter of time: not even a clergyman, aided by supernatural grace, has more than twenty-four hours in each day, and anyone affected by the Renewal and active within a parish and more generally, probably has little time for other concerns which, in any case, will come well down on his or her scale of priorities. But, when all this has been said, it remains true that, where organic union and the institutional structures of the churches are concerned, the Charismatic Renewal presents a variegated picture. For some, especially laity, it intensifies impatience with such things as restrictions on sharing in the communion services of other churches but, on the other hand, the clerical leaders of the movement are often intensely loyal, if not to their denomination specifically (and this is true in some cases), at least to the institutional church in general. Just how far all this will affect reunion moves remains to be seen. It depends, in part, on the extent of the continued growth of the Charismatic Renewal both in sheer numbers and on whether its converts come to include a larger number in 'leadership' positions and such growth, in turn, depends on factors both internal and external to the Charismatic Renewal.[22]

The National Council of Churches, the current reunion moves between the 'negotiating churches', and the Charismatic Renewal, constitute three contemporary aspects of 'ecumenism'. In any longer survey other quite important developments could be reviewed: the growth of contact between the National Council of Churches and bodies such as the Ratana Church, Seventh Day Adventism and the churches of 'classical' Pentecostalism; the long-continued existence of an 'evangelical ecumenism' which has found expression in such bodies as the British and Foreign Bible Society, and the emergence of bodies loosely linked with the N.C.C. such as the Churches' Commission on Education. In addition, even for the movements considered, analysis 'at depth' needs to be done; thus, only for the Methodists do we have a detailed picture of how the vote for the Plan for Union went and what influence education, occupational and other differences may have had. These other topics would have to be included in any fuller survey of 'ecumenism' in New Zealand, its past history, present state, and future development.

A New Zealand 'Civil Religion'?

In all this the focus of interest is on ecclesiastical or at least religious developments but the term 'ecumenism' is, after all, derived from the Greek *oikoumene,* meaning 'the whole inhabited world'. This suggests a final comment which brings the discussion back to Mr. Kirk's funeral again. What united many of the population on that occasion was national rather than religious in the narrower sense of that word; the nation generally and perhaps some churchmen too, were not united on the basis of religious belief at all. Thus, in Christchurch anyway, there was some criticism of the fact that the address at the service in the Town Hall, while treating the occasion as commemorative of the achievememt of Mr. Kirk, interpreted it also as a time of rejoicing for the power of Christ's resurrection. By contrast, Archbishop Johnston's address was more favourably received in the same quarters, because, at least as reported, it avoided such specifically Christian themes and dwelt on Mr. Kirk's commitment to justice and humanitarian principles generally. By some, then, the first speaker was felt to have misjudged the occasion whereas the Archbishop acquitted himself somewhat better. All of this prompts two further reflections. If the uniting symbols for New Zealanders are what Mr. Kirk's funeral suggests they are, then, this may indicate that the Christian belief of quite a few New Zealanders ranges from the non-existent to the tenuous and vacuous. This is not to say that such persons have no system of 'ultimate values' - a religion even, in some sense; part of Mr. Kirk's 'magic' may have lain in his ability to activate such 'value-systems' for quite a proportion of the population. Further, this indication that the uniting symbols and beliefs of many New Zealanders are no longer, perhaps, religious in the narrower sense, raises the whole question of 'civil religion'.[23] This is too large a subject to enter in detail upon here, but it is worth referring to in this connection partly because in his article "Church and Nation," W. Merlin Davies argued that "religious influence and national life generally have both suffered for lack of any national church."[24] He adds:

> New Zealand culture, the New Zealand way of life, has been coming to birth without very much religious influence .... Religion has conserved some values from the past and contributed to little in shaping things to come .... The best hope for the Christian future of New Zealand's national life and culture lies in the modern Christian Unity Movement with which all the major Churches in New Zealand have become intimately involved.[25]

Archdeacon (now Canon) Davies went on to add that he believed that "within a short period of years there will be a 'Church of New Zealand',... embracing I am told, 60% to 70% of the New Zealand population according to census figures."[26] But this judgement has now to be qualified; it is doubtful whether the reunion which Canon Davies envisaged will be consummated as soon as he believed it would be, if at all, and if it is, that it will include as many as 60% to 70% of the population. Moreover it is questionable too whether all those who may be involved formally, at least by virtue of their present membership in the 'negotiating churches', will regard themselves as committed to the sort of mission to the nation which Canon Davies envisaged. Many people, including some politicians, just do not see Christianity that way at all. And, to return to Mr. Kirk's funeral once again, it is worth reiterating that what took place there suggests that a substantial proportion of the population can be activated by symbols and causes although probably not by specifically Christian ones. Perhaps then, a wider ecumenism is called for.[27] Instead of asking how Christians can create a national Church to influence the nation *perhaps* the question for Christians and churches is: How can they contribute to the creation of a 'civil religion' in a religiously pluralistic society, and assist in guarding against its prostitution by politicians and others? [28] Some, of course, may want to ask the further question as to whether a society must have a 'civil religion' as its highest unifying factor but this issue, interesting although it is, cannot be pursued here.

Notes:

1. This essay is a substantial revision of a paper first presented at a seminar organised by the Extension Studies Dept., Victoria University of Wellington in October, 1974. I am especially indebted to Ken Booth and Ian Breward for their comments on my earlier paper.
2. KEYS, L. G. *The life and times of Bishop Pompallier.* Christchurch, Pegasus Press, 1967, p. 96.
3. BREWARD, Ian *Godless schools? A study of Protestant reactions to the Education Act of 1877.* Christchurch, Presbyterian Bookroom, 1967. See also:

   O'CONNOR, P. S. Storm over the clergy − New Zealand 1917. *Journal of religious history 4:* 128-48, 1966.

   −−−−−−. Sectarian conflicts in New Zealand, 1911-20. *Political Science 19:* 3-16, 1967.

   −−−−−−. 'Protestants,' Catholics and the New Zealand Government, 1916-18. *In W. P. Morrell: a tribute; essays in modern and early history ...* Wood, G. A. and O'Connor, P. S. eds. Dunedin, University of Otago Press, 1973. p. 185-202.
4. See, e.g. annual reports of the N.C.C. for 1965 and 1967 and the annual general meeting minutes for 1967. The grounds for Baptist hesitation were two-fold: some Baptists had theological reservations about co-operation with Roman Catholics and Baptist polity, congregational in character, imposed a lengthy process of consultation.
5. It is understood that within the Roman Catholic Church there is some quite vocal support for an application for membership but reservations at the episcopal level. As things are the N.C.C. would probably stand to gain more from Roman Catholic membership than would that Church itself.

6. W. M. Davies says: "It is significant ... that the N.C.C.'s first major project was a Campaign for Christian Order in 1943. Almost as soon as they were brought together, awareness of their marginal influence upon the life of the nation as a whole moved the Churches first to 'restudy the total life of the New Zealand community and to restudy the contribution of the Churches to that total life'." (Church and Nation, *Landfall 20:* 22, 1966)
   In interviewing some of the founding figures of the N.C.C., I was more impressed by the extent to which the experience of the depression years of the thirties weighed with them, pushing them, without too pronounced a sense of the weakness of the Church's impact, to move in directions already suggested by the 'Life and Work' aspect of the world-wide 'Ecumenical Movement' with which they were in close touch. For a study of the impact of the depression years on New Zealand church leaders especially in the Roman Catholic and Methodist Churches see, K. Clements. The religious variable; dependent, independent or interdependent? *In A sociological yearbook of religion in Britain,* no. 4 ed. M. Hill. London, S.C.M., 1971. I am indebted to Kevin Clements for several suggestions relating to the topic of this paper.

7. One attempt at assessment on a specific issue is M. McKessar, 'An introduction to and discussion about the National Council of Churches in New Zealand and its reaction to the Vietnam War, an example of New Zealand value-oriented pressure group' unpublished Sociology III project, University of Canterbury.

8. On this, and on the charge of 'bureaucratization' in relation to the World Council of Churches, see, eg.
   VISSER 'T HOOFT, W. A. Is the ecumenical movement suffering from institutional paralysis? *Ecumenical review 25:* 295-309, 1973. See also:
   GOODALL, N. *Ecumenical progress: a decade of change in the ecumenical movement, 1961-1971.* London, Oxford University Press, 1972. esp. p. 122-33.
   On withdrawal from voluntary associations generally, see the brief comment in:
   MARTIN, D. *The religious and the secular: studies in secularization.* London, Routledge and Kegan Paul, 1969, p. 16.

9. GEERING, L. G. The Church in the new world. *Landfall 20:* 26, 1966.

10. On Presbyterian developments see:
    ELDER, J. R. *The history of the Presbyterian Church of New Zealand, 1840-1940.* Christchurch, Presbyterian Bookroom, 1940, Ch. 9.
    On Methodism see:
    BROOKES, N. E. *New Zealand methodists and church union: an historical and sociological survey.* Thesis, M.A. University of Canterbury, 1976.

11. STUART, P.A. in *Church and people,* Sept 20, 1971 and cited in:
    MORRELL, W. P. *The Anglican Church in New Zealand: a history.*
    Dunedin, Anglican Church of the Province of New Zealand, 1973. p. 239.
12. At the General Synod Anglicans voted as follows for the Plan: bishops 6/2,
    clergy 12/9 and laity 21/7. Overall voting figures were:

	For	Against
	%	%
Anglicans	58.06	41.94
Assoc. Churches of Christ	55	45
Congregational	54	46
Methodist	86	14
Presbyterian	69.7	30.3

(Percentages taken from *Background,* 10 January, 1973)

The referendum was illuminating in other ways, e.g. as to the real rather
than the numerical strength of the Churches according to the census figures.
Thus it was calculated that there were 604,746 nominal Anglicans entitled
to register and vote but only 61,438 - 10.16% - did so. The voting figures
merit analysis in other ways also. As far as Anglicanism is concerned the
heaviest votes against acceptance of the Plan were recorded in
well-established city parishes especially where the vicar or other clergy threw
their weight against the Plan. e.g. In Christchurch – S. Michael's, Merivale,
S. Albans, and Woolston. Examination of the voting figures from other
dioceses supports this conclusion. The voting figures for individual parishes
were published in *Church and people 32*(9): 3, 1972. Only the Methodist
vote – interestingly much the strongest – has been subjected to detailed
analysis: See Brookes, *Op. cit.*
13. The Selwyn Society emerged first in Auckland but gathered most strength in
    the dioceses of Nelson and Wellington: its pamphlets were issued from
    November 1971 onwards. Some controversial literature emerged in other
    churches also: see, e.g. I. Breward, *Unity and Reunion* Dunedin: published
    privately, 1972; issues of the *Evangelical Presbyterian* and *The continuing
    Presbyterian* together with the newspapers of the denominations concerned
    esp. *Church and people* (Anglican), *Outlook* Presbyterian), and *New citizen*
    (Methodist), formerly *New Zealand Methodist* and, earlier, *New Zealand
    Methodist times.*
14. *Background,* 13 June, 1974.
15. JOINT Commission on Church Union in New Zealand. *Report to the
    negotiating churches, 14th.* Wellington, Office of the Joint Commission,
    1978, p. 19.

16. WILSON, B. R. *Religion in secular society: sociological comment.* Harmondsworth, Penguin, 1966, p. 203.

    MEHL, R. *The sociology of Protestantism.* London, S.C.M., 1970, argues that ecumenism is born out of a certain sense of weakness and cites Crespy: 'When churches proudly think that they hold a truth which puts them out of reach of all difficulty, there is no ecumenism (this is the case for the fundamentalists; not long ago it was still the case for the Roman Church)' (p. 195) For some comments on Wilson's thesis see:

    TOWLER, R. *Homo religiosus; sociological problems in the study of religion.* London, Constable, 1974.

    BROOKES, N. E. *op. cit.*

    BLACK, A. An analysis of theories of ecumenism, with particular reference to the formation of the United Church of Canada. Unpublished paper, American Society for the Study of Religion Conference, August, 1976.

17. *Background, 11* June 1973.

18. Is the ecumenical movement slowing down? *Christian century* May 1, 1974: 476-77. See also:

    LANGE, E. The malaise in the ecumenical movement; notes on the present situation. *Ecumenical review 23:* 1-8, 1971.

19. TILL, B. *The churches search for unity.* Harmondsworth, Penguin, 1972, p. 516.

20. The earlier version of this paper included some details about the origins, growth, and present general condition of the Charismatic Renewal but these have been largely omitted here since they can now be found, with references to the relevant literature, in my article, How significant is the charismatic movement, re-printed in this volume.

21. See, e.g. S. Clark, *Where are we headed? Guidelines for the Catholic Charismatic Renewal,* Notre Dame, Indiana, Charistmatic Renewal Services Inc., 1973. In Appendix 9 of his unpublished S. Th. thesis, 'Institutional Churches and the Charismatic Renewal', Allen Neil reprints a statement from the (American) Catholic Charismatic Renewal Service Committee which insists; "We recognise that, as Catholics, we are called to work for a unity among the followers of Christ – a visible unity which the world can see . . . We are called to this commitment because we realise that the renewal of the Church will not be complete until a full and visible unity among Christians has been restored".

22. For discussion of the factors and the possible future impact, see my article reprinted in this volume.

23. A pivotal essay, relating to the scene in the United States but capable of more general application, is

    Bellah, R.N. Civil religion in America, Ch. 9 *In* his *Beyond belief: essays on religion in a post-traditional world.* N.Y. Harper & Row, 1970. Reprinted most recently in *American civil religion.* Richey, R. E. and Jones, D. G. eds. N.Y., Harper & Row, 1974, with other contributions to the debate and a useful bibliography.

24. *Op. cit.,* p21.
25. *Ibid.* p. 22.
26. *Ibid.,* p. 23.
27. One New Zealand churchman who sensed something of this is the Rev. R. M. O'Grady, formerly Associate General Secretary of the N.C.C. See his: The National Council; where to from here. *Church and community 24* (6): 8-9, 1967.
28. I am thinking here of the debate caused by HERBERG, W. *Protestant, Catholic, Jew.* Garden, City, N.Y., Doubleday, 1955, and his claim that what religions — Christian and Jewish — in the United States 'celebrate' is not so much the Christian or Jewish faith but a bland version of the 'American way of life.'

The Charismatic Contribution

HOW SIGNIFICANT IS THE CHARISMATIC MOVEMENT?[1]
Colin Brown

A paper by a young Anglican clergyman begins:

> Over the past fifteen years there has appeared within the historic churches in New Zealand a movement of spiritual renewal which has had some critics prophesying its rapid demise and others claiming that it is God's answer to the spiritual and moral bankruptcy of our nation. The charismatic renewal has risen from obscurity to a recognisable force within contemporary New Zealand Christianity.[2]

The movement to which he refers has affinities and links with Pentecostalist churches such as the Assemblies of God; both are characterised by such features as 'baptism in the Spirit', 'gifts' of healing, and 'speaking in tongues'. Both, too, are still very much movements in flux and research is largely lacking concerning many of their aspects; e.g. the sources of recruitment both in general and of ministers in particular, the social and political attitudes of those involved, and their religious outlook as expressed in both formal statements and the songs which have become so characteristic and pervasive. At this stage, then, any assessment must be imprecise and may be rendered inaccurate by increased knowledge and the turn of events. But the Charismatic Renewal has been around a while now and 'classical Pentecostalism' is certainly no newcomer to New Zealand; in both cases it is appropriate to attempt a general assessment. Within the limits indicated this essay aims to sketch the growth of classical Pentecostalism and the Charismatic Renewal in New Zealand, to suggest causes for their appeal, and to indicate ways in which both may be expected to have long-term effects on the New Zealand religious scene.

DEFINITIONS:

In order to clarify usage I have employed the following terms:

1. "Pentecostal Churches" or "classical Pentecostalism" refers to the movement outside the larger Christian denominations, to, e.g. the Assemblies of God as contrasted with the Anglican or Methodist Churches. The use of "Pentecostal" in this context is based on the fact that such churches seek to reproduce the type of Christian experience described in Acts 2.

2. "Charismatic Renewal" refers to the current movement within the larger denominations. The term "charismatic" is derived from the Greek word "charisma", signifiying, in the New Testament, a 'gift' given by the grace of God; as used in this context it often highlights particular 'gifts', notably 'glossolalia' (popularly called 'speaking in tongues'), and 'spiritual healing'.

3. "Pentecostalism" refers to the movement as a whole; it embraces (1) and (2). By some within the movement this term is regarded as derogatory but, like terms such as 'sect' it is used here for convenience and, hopefully, not pejoratively.

Pentecostal Churches in New Zealand: History and Growth

The beginnings of the Pentecostal Churches in New Zealand lie in the 1920's and, generally speaking, especially in the period of origins and earlier development, these churches owed more to Great Britain than the United States. The Pentecostal Church was legally incorporated in 1925; in 1953 after a complex transmutation which need not concern us here, it changed its name to the Elim Church. Today it is still a relatively small denomination with, when Worsfold wrote, only four full-time ministers.[3] It was in Palmerston North on 27 February 1927 that a congregation was organised as the "Assemblies of God in New Zealand" and was soon strengthened by secession from the Pentecostal Church. At the end of 1978 the Assemblies of God claimed 104 full-time ministers and 78 churches.[4] As far as the Apostolic Church in New Zealand is concerned its beginnings can be dated from 1925 when 12 New Zealanders chose to identify themselves as members, although the first organised congregation was not formed until 1934.[5]

In addition to these Pentecostal Churches there are a number of small bodies which should be reckoned among the churches of classical Pentecostalism. They include the Christian (or National) Revival Crusade which now has 8 congregations throughout New Zealand, 6 Commonwealth Covenant churches, the Church of Christ (N.Z.) (Foursquare Gospel), and some congregations quite independent of any grouping at all.[6] Some of these groups have grown strikingly in recent years; most notable, perhaps, is the growth of congregations known by place-names (Christchurch, Auckland, etc.) and the designation 'Christian Fellowship' or 'New Life Centre'. At last count about 60 congregations came into this grouping; some degree of formal association has developed at least at ministerial level and whereas this grouping originated in points of difference with classical Pentecostalism, relationships are now harmonious as is signified by this group's membership of the Associated Pentecostal Churches of New Zealand.

In general terms the history of classical Pentecostalism can be summed up as one of growth in four main directions. Before discussing numerical growth two points are worth making. The 1976 census figures show that numerical growth has been sustained by most of the churches commonly labelled 'Pentecostal'. Secondly the figures used in this essay are based on the self-identification offered by those who completed census papers but they are probably fairly accurate where the churches concerned are not of high social status and expect a high level of commitment. Moreover it should be remembered that such groups probably have a larger fringe membership than is suggested by these figures.[7]

The figures as given by the 1975 issue of the *New Zealand Official Year Book* and the Census and Statistics Department's publication (1974) on religious professions in New Zealand are as follows (preliminary figures for 1976 census added):

	Number of Adherents			Percentage		
Religious Profession	*1966*	*1971*	*1976*	*1966*	*1971*	*1976*
Assemblies of God	2,028	3,599	5,581	0.1	0.1	0.2
Apostolic Church	1,841	2,361	2,693	0.1	0.1	0.1
Pentecostal	1,110	1,859	4,846		0.1	0.2
Church of Christ (N.Z.)	610	1,085	835		0.1	
Commonwealth Covenant	506	385	361			
Elim Church	169	101	259			
Christian Revival Crusade		30	75			

Several points are interesting about these figures:

1. There is a higher proportion of Maoris in classical Pentecostalism than in the general population. This may be because, as compared with the major

denominations, such forms of Christianity provide freer forms of worship, more intimate community, and are closer in social composition to that position in the social scale where many Maoris find themselves. This may be taken with the point that until relatively recently classical Pentecostalism had grown more in urban areas where conditions of employment and large residential conglomerates create circumstances in which fellowship in smaller communities, whether religious or otherwise, is welcome. Interesting parallels are provided by the growth of sects and cults among blacks when they moved into urban areas in the United States from c. 1918 onwards and by the 'New Religions' of Japan in the years after the Second World War.

2. Classical Pentecostalism has not grown as fast as some other groups, e.g. and especially, Mormons and Jehovah's Witnesses.[8] But certainly classical Pentecostalism has not lost ground as have all the larger denominations. Classical Pentecostalism has grown, slowly and unevenly it is true, not just in sheer numbers but in terms of a proportion of the total population.[9] In the table above this is especially clear in the case of the Assemblies of God and 'Pentecostal'.

In detail classical Pentecostalism, after a period of initial growth, grew only slowly until about the late 1950's and 1960's when the rate of growth quickened especially among the Assemblies of God and with the emergence of groups independent of the then existing churches of classical Pentecostalism. It should not escape notice that this period of quickened growth coincided with the rise of the Charismatic Renewal in the larger Churches; this suggests that both were a response to changes in society in general at that time. (It is worth noting, also, that similar growth occurred about the same time in many other countries.) By contrast the picture in recent years of the major denominations is as follows:

Religious Profession	*1956*	*1961*	*1966*	*1971*	*1976*
Anglican	35.9%	34.6%	33.7%	31.3%	29.2%
Presbyterian	22.3	22.3	21.8	20.4	18.1
Roman Catholic (inc. Catholic undefined)	14.3	15.1	15.9	15.7	15.3
Methodist	7.4	7.2	7.0	6.4	5.5

3. It may be, of course, that some of the growth in classical Pentecostalism is related to erosion of the traditional denominations but this would not

account for much of the loss. Nor have groups such as Baptists, Brethren, Salvation Army, and the Church of Christ registered gains in proportion to the growth of the population. Some sectarian groups have increased proportionately to the total population, e.g. Ratana, Mormons, Seventh Day Adventists, Jehovah's Witness; but the big leakage appears to be into the categories listed in the following table:

	Number of Adherents			Percentage		
	1966	*1971*	*1976*	*1966*	*1971*	*19⁻6*
Christian (undefined)	21,548	33,187	52,478	0.8	1.2	1.7
Agnostic	4,960	9,481	14,136	0.2	0.3	0.5
Atheist	5,474	9,291	14,283	0.2	0.3	0.5
No religion (so returned)	32,780	57,485	101,211	1.2	2.0	3.2
Not specified	19,300	103,533	39,380	0.7	3.6	1.3
Object to state	210,851	247,019	438,511	7.9	8.6	14.0

The second area in which growth has taken place is in the development of organisation. Thus the Assemblies of God has developed an overseas missionary interest (it now supports 38 missionaries), publishes religious literature, and has an active religious education programme. Organisationally they now have a General Council meeting biennially with ministerial and lay membership and an Executive Council which meets between gatherings of the General Council. By contrast, however, the Apostolic Church has simplified its structure to give more responsibility to local churches. But this development too is related to growth in numbers and seems to have been motivated, in part, by the feeling that the structure of the Assemblies of God was a factor in their faster growth rate.

A particular aspect of this growth in organisation is the recent tendency to play down differences between the Pentecostal churches and to formalise co-operation. Such moves go back to 1928 although it was not until 1964 that the Apostolic Church, the Elim Church, the Assemblies of God, and the National Revival Crusade, formed the New Zealand Pentecostal Fellowship with both a National Executive and local chapters. But such moves have been subjected to some strain partly because some classical Pentecostalists have little interest in a doctrine of the visible church and its practical consequences. There is now in existence, however, the "Associated Pentecostal Churches of New Zealand"; it has a co-ordinating secretary and has recently begun publication of the *New*

Zealand Times. This paper provides evidence of some social concern on the part of the leadership for, in the second issue (May 1976), abortion, pornography, sports tours of South Africa, and New Zealand political life and economic conditions come under review. The positions taken up are, for want of a better word, 'conservative'. e.g. South Africa should be left to shape its own destiny; the Halt-All-Racist Tours organisation and the Citizens' Association for Racial Equality both come under criticism.

A fourth area in which change has occurred in classical Pentecostalism is in the direction of what can best be called 'respectability' or, looked at from another angle, 'acceptability'. It is clear that some of the leaders of classical Pentecostalism have made strenuous efforts to change the popular image of the movement. Thus the Apostolic Church has been willing to encourage its younger ministers to take advantage of the opportunities offered for theological education at St. John's – Trinity College, Auckland and at Knox College and the University of Otago. More generally the New Zealand Pentecostal Fellowship and its successor have not been averse to contact with the National Council of Churches. Other instances could be cited, Sir John Marshall contributed to the second issue of the *New Zealand Times;* Worsfold lists (p. 291), the occasions on which Governors General, Prime Ministers and other public figures have attended services in the Apostolic Church. Moreover the second issue of the *New Zealand Times* carried a photograph of a well-known Pentecostal minister playing cricket for a team of clergy against members of Parliament! Participation in cricket and acceptance by one's fellow-ministers are evident signs of 'respectability' if anything is! Finally: at an Extension Studies' seminar at Victoria University in July 1976 a spokesman for classical Pentecostalism took strong exception to the designation 'sect' as applied to Pentecostalist churches and it was quite clear that it was the pejorative associations of the term which troubled him.

Classical Pentecostalism is, then, growing in 'respectability' and acceptability. This is due partly to deliberate efforts by some of its leaders and such efforts may well have helped to win wider acceptability for it, hence acting as a cause of its uneven but real growth in numbers. Moreover, in some respects classical Pentecostalism has changed in ways which facilitate conversion to it by demanding less of a break with normal social life. The hard lines of a 'Puritanical' ethic concerning activities such as attendance at the theatre and films have been eroded in recent years.

The Charismatic Renewal: History and Growth
Both as to origins and present condition there are some important differences

between the major Christian denominations where the movement of Charismatic Renewal is concerned. With Anglicanism the beginnings are usually dated from 1965 when, at Palmerston North, both in All Saints' parish and at Massey University, and associated especially with the Rev. R. J. Muller, the movement surfaced and included instances of glossolalia. Partly because bishops, clergy and laity were sometimes hostile Anglican charismatics developed, if they did not already possess, links with classical Pentecostalism: if anything this influence has probably diminished more recently. No independent figures of growth are available but sources sympathetic to the movement estimate that, "by November 1974 between 40% and 50% of the clergy in the Auckland diocese were either participants in the renewal or were open to the possibility of a charistmatic experience. In at least one third of Auckland parishes there are lay people who claim to be 'baptised in the Spirit'."[10] According to the same source 30% of Anglican clergy in the diocese of Christchurch were, at about the same time, either participants in the Renewal or sympathetically interested; in most, perhaps all parishes there were (and are) 'charismatic' Christians; in earlier years a diocesan prayer meeting provided fellowship and teaching but regional groups, some of which are ecumenical in composition, are now the pattern. Although Christchurch and Auckland are the main centres where Anglicanism is concerned there appear to be groups and individuals involved with the Renewal throughout the Anglican Church in New Zealand. "Overall", however, "the increase in the number of participants in the movement appears to be levelling out and in some areas even declining."[11]

In the Roman Catholic Church the movement can be clearly identified from 1971 onwards and there, curiously enough, by contrast with Anglicanism, there is more lay leadership including that of women; in Anglicanism the movement has tended to be clerically dominated.[12] As with Anglicanism Auckland and Christchurch appear to be the centres of greatest activity but there are groups in Wellington, Dunedin, Invercargill, and Hamilton together with smaller groups elsewhere. Within such groups there has been tension over issues such as intercommunion. Biblical interpretation, organisational structures for the movement, and the role of the hierarchy, the attitude of which has ranged from extreme caution to sympathetic and judicious pastoral concern. In August 1973 the leaders of the movement in Auckland surveyed charismatic groups throughout the Roman Catholic Church in New Zealand and discovered that of 1,001 active in 23 prayer-groups, 880 attended regularly. Of these 118 were 'Religious' (33 priests, 27 brothers, and 58 nuns); in comparison with the distribution of the population generally those over 60 were under-represented whereas those under 40 were heavily represented.[13] Laity provided most of the leaders and women participated on an equal basis. This, and the fact that parochial links were sometimes loose, contrasts with the movement in the Anglican Church. But the similarities are, of course, basic; in both churches, as more generally also, the movement is serviced and buttressed by visits from overseas speakers, literature mostly imported but some local, tapes and all the related paraphenalia now available for the propagation and maintenance of any movement, secular or religious.[14]

Details of the Charistmatic Renewal movement as it affects other churches are less readily available. In Methodism few churches were seriously affected in the earlier years of the movement; Mangere was a notable exception. Some idea of the relatively slight impact can be gauged from the fact that only 17 Methodists were present at the Christian Advance Summer School in 1974.[15] Since then, however, there has been significant and widespread growth, notably in Christchurch. The annual Conference of the Methodist Church in 1975 received, from its Development Division, a relatively brief report sympathetic to the Renewal and the substance of this was conveyed to the church at large by a pastoral letter from the Methodist President for that year. As far as Presbyterianism is concerned Christchurch in general and Leeston particularly emerged as early as 1968 as centres of the Charismatic Renewal in that Church. The Presbyterian Church was early concerned about the movement and in 1973 its General Assembly received two reports on the subject; in general these took up a more sympathetic stance than a report presented in 1967 but this may say as much about changes within the movement as within the Presbyterian Church itself. By now the movement is fairly widespread in the Presbyterian Church but, although it has affected perhaps 20% of the parishes, few are dominantly 'charismatic'. The movement is, perhaps, strongest in Auckland but Presbyterians are active in prayer groups (many of them ecumenical in character), scattered throughout the country and produce a regular newsletter.

In smaller Protestant bodies, e.g. the Associated Churches of Christ, the Congregational Church, and the Baptist Union, the Charismatic Renewal has made itself felt, sometimes disruptively. e.g. In 1965 the Awapuni Baptist Church withdrew from the Baptist Union. Despite this, and a cautious report on the movement presented to the annual meeting of the Baptist Union in 1970, the movement surfaces rapidly in widely divergent places. It has been claimed that by February 1975 25% of Baptist ministers had been 'baptised in the Spirit' (the figure would be about the same in 1978), that many Baptist theological students were products of the Renewal, and that congregations favourably disposed to it were growing faster than those critical of it.[16] The main centres of the Renewal where the Baptists are concerned are in the Waikato, in Christchurch, and in Auckland to some extent, with sparse representation in Dunedin and Wellington. The most recent 'official' statement, by the general secretary of the Baptist Union (July 1, 1976), notes the presence of charismatic Christians in "practically every church" and expresses reservations about some aspects of the movement.

Where Closed and Open Brethren are concerned the pattern at first was for those affected by the Renewal to leave Brethren fellowship voluntarily or to be expelled although this did not happen in all cases where the Renewal manifested itself. [17] This represented a rather different pattern to that followed by the major churches which have sought to contain the movement and have sometimes gone to considerable lengths to do so. More recently among Open Brethren at least there has been some 'softening' of attitudes; among Open Brethren no assemblies are preponderantly charismatic in character, the movement is tolerated without being encouraged and the strategy among the leadership seems to be that of circumventing the Renewal rather than opposing it directly. The virtual absence of the Renewal movement from the Salvation Army is interesting; is this related to more adequate opportunities for the release and expression of the emotions, to relatively strict disciplinary patterns, or what?

Suggested Causes for the Growth of Pentecostalism

Before offering some suggestions as to the causes of such growth as has occurred a few preliminaries are necessary:

1. Knowledge in this area is sparse; this is true in two senses. Psychological and sociological studies of Pentecostalism and associated phenomena such as glossolalia have not yet provided a body of assured generalisations on a wide range of issues.[18] Secondly, as far as I am aware, few detailed studies exist of either classical Pentecostalism or the Charismatic Renewal in New Zealand.[19] We do not have, for instance, any full-scale study of the sources of recruitment for the Renewal in New Zealand.

2. At one level it is possible to make much of external influences such as the continued presence of classical Pentecostalism, the visits of overseas speakers, and the 'Jesus marches' of 1972 which brought together, sometimes for the first time, 'evangelical' Protestants and Roman Catholics united in their opposition to what they regarded as the two-headed monster of permissive morality and liberalising theology. But when one seeks to go behind such 'causes', to ask why such influences should have evoked a favourable

reception (after all classical Pentecostalism had been on the New Zealand scene since the 1920's), the picture is, in the absence of reliable research, much less clear.

3. What does seem clear, however, is that the growth of Pentecostalism may be related to a variety of needs; it does not have to be confined to one and only one set of social circumstances, cultural pattern or type of personal need. In some cases, perhaps not directly in the New Zealand context, its emergence may be related to economic and social deprivation; in other instances more general social and cultural disorientation may be operative; with others (especially clergy), it may be a matter of reaction to a confused theological scene or lack of evident success; in yet other situations its emergence may have to do with protest against the ossification of institutionalised Christianity . . . and so on.

It is important to remember, too, that factors important in the genesis of a movement may not necessarily explain its continued growth which may come to owe more to the 'internal dynamics' of the movement concerned.[20] Thus, where it has been available, wise and judicious leadership has been a factor in retaining those influenced by the Charismatic Renewal in the larger Christian denominations and in increasing their numbers. But – I repeat – generalisations about the role of psychological and sociological factors in relation to the Charismatic Renewal and the growth of Pentecostalism generally are, in the present state of our knowledge, more easily made than established.

4. Finally: it is important to avoid misunderstanding and to make clear what is being said here. Some within Pentecostalism deprecate the search for psychological and sociological causes and see it as one more attempt to deny that the current revival is genuinely a work of the Holy Spirit. That claim is neither being denied nor affirmed here; the problem as to how natural and supernatural causes are to be related is an issue for the believer and the theologian, not for the historian, sociologist, or psychologist.

All this said, however, and as a personal observation more than anything else, I suggest that the following factors may have been especially important on the New Zealand scene:[21]

1. There is a general tendency, especially among younger age-groups, towards a much freer expression of emotions in all sorts of situations, not merely in words but in gestures also. This is closely related to the tendency to prefer immediate experience to rational reflection and to denigrate the role of the intellect whether in religious matters or more generally.[22] At least among the 'middle' classes and possibly more widely also, greater frankness, fewer

inhibitions, and increased demonstrativeness are more common than in the immediate past at least. If this supposition is correct it supplies one suggested cause for the growth of the Charismatic Renewal in churches with a fixed liturgy and a high degree of institutionalization generally. But it is probably going too far to talk in terms of 'counter-cultural' religion in this context because the changes referred to have taken place over quite large areas of society.

2. Religiously and socially the pace of change has been rapid and continues. In such a situation the cautious, the liberal, and the temperate tend to be upstaged by those with clear and unequivocal answers. Even although some of those within classical Pentecostalism and the Charismatic Renewal disavow Biblical fundamentalism and occupy a variety of positions, the general stance is that of clear-cut conservatism on theological and moral issues. Such views may be heard not just because they are conservative in content but also because they provide clearer answers in uncertain times — and this is what some at least seek from religion.[23]

3. Reference was made earlier to the growth of classical Pentecostalism in urban areas and this suggests that desire for more intimate forms of community may be a factor. This is a fairly general tendency today; it is expressed in various ways and is accentuated by certain of the conditions of urban life. Moreover, as was suggested earlier, it may be especially important where Maoris are concerned. There is another aspect of this more intimate community life which may be significant at the present time. The level of pastoral care and mutual support in Pentecostalist circles is often quite high; this and the security of religious values generally, probably appeals to some of those who find that economic circumstances have added to the strains and stresses of marital relationships and family life.

4. Where clergy are concerned special factors may well be operative. Many clergy have been nurtured on success and experienced the more ebullient church-life of the 1950's and 1960's. Confronted by static situations or even by decline, and so by claims that the Charismatic Renewal does 'renew', there must be a strong inclination to go along with it. The confusion of theological scene and uncertainty over the role of clergy (pastoral counsellor, social activist or what?) may well operate in the same direction. It is, perhaps, significant in this connection that, at least among Anglicans and Presbyterians (I have less information on others), clerical participation in the Charismatic Renewal in Auckland is quite high. Have urbanisation and other factors gone further in Auckland in exacerbating the difficulties of exercising the Christian ministry at least in its accustomed forms?

But in this matter, and more generally, I am offering hunches rather than informed generalisations based on the interpretation of data as 'hard' as can be mined by questionnaires and related techniques.[24]

The Impact of Pentecostalism

If it is hard to answer questions about the causes of the growth of Pentecostalism in the absence of anything like precise data, it is harder still to predict the future. The immediate effect of the Charismatic Renewal has been and continues to be a degree of polarisation and this stage is not yet over.[25] In the longer term just what emerges will depend largely on two factors. Clearly the character, quality and outlook of the leadership whether in classical Pentecostalism, the Charismatic Renewal, or the larger denominations will be important. This is especially so in churches such as the Roman Catholic and Anglican where hierarchical authority still exists in name and, to some extent, in fact also. The general cultural context is important too; changes there will obviously affect the forms of religious expression. What results might possibly follow?

1. By bringing together Christians from across the denominations the Charismatic Renewal may aid the cause of reunion. But at least two other factors may come into play and affect the result. Whether Christians who have experienced a 'spiritual unity' cutting across denominational boundaries press on from that experience in organic unity will depend, in part, on the importance they attach to the expression of this inward unity in organisational forms. Moreover some may have been drawn into Pentecostalism out of a desire to find smaller, warmer forms of Christian unity in preference to the 'big organisation' type of church. The impact on the moves towards organic reunion is, then, not all that easy to predict.

2. Much the same is true of social concern. There is a tendency among some — but only some — leaders of Pentecostalism to play down such 'gifts' as glossolalia and 'spiritual healing' (which remain important to others and one of their bases of appeal), and to stress the outworking of the charismatic experience in attitudes and actions of loving and caring. Whether this will lead to social concern of the 'ambulance' variety only or to criticism of the 'structures' of society remains to be seen.[26]

3. Liturgically there are already signs of the impact of the movement on the larger denominations. It is hard to avoid the conclusion that the greater informality and emotional warmth of at least some liturgical occasions in the Roman Catholic and Anglican Churches owe something to the Charismatic

Renewal. At the least it represents a change on the part of 'establishment' churches anxious to retain their 'clientele'.

4. Theologically Pentecostalism is one element in the 'move to the right' which is a feature of the current scene. Indeed it is possible to interpret a good deal of what has happened within Christianity in New Zealand in recent years as a contest between 'conservatives' or 'evangelicals', and liberals for position and power. Just how far there is a swing to the 'right', and how far it has gone are, again, questions to which there are few precise answers. Certainly the Pentecostalist 'right' is where many theological students are at least when they enter their respective colleges. Another related development which may yet have important educational and social consequences and in which 'charismatic' Christians are very much to the fore is the move to found 'Christian schools where children can be educated away from the humanism and permissiveness that some feel increasingly pervade the public schools.

But just what long-term effect all this will have on religious patterns in New Zealand is arguable. More significant, perhaps, than the slow growth of classical Pentecostalism, more significant than the growth of the Charismatic Renewal, are other trends working towards a greater degree of religious pluralism. My own guess is that, at least at present, the tides of social change are in favour of a still greater extent of religious pluralism rather than a wholesale return to evangelical Christianity even when warmed up by classical Pentecostalism and the Charismatic Renewal.[27] To specify just what social changes are edging us towards a still greater degree of religious pluralism is another subject for another occasion.

Notes:

1. This essay is a revised version of a paper published under the same title in *Dialogue on religion: New Zealand viewpoints 1977.* P. Davis and J. Hinchcliff, eds. Auckland, Printed at the University of Auckland Bindery, 1977, and republished here by permission. Among those who offered suggestions for revision I am especially indebted to Ian Breward, Ken Booth, Allen Neil and James Worsfold.

2. NEIL, A. G. The charismatic renewal in New Zealand: Observations from an historical perspective. Unpublished paper presented at a colloquium in May 1976, organised in connection with the centenary of the Theological Hall, Knox College, Dunedin.

3. WORSFOLD, J. E. *A history of the charismatic movements in New Zealand.* Bradford, Julian Literature Trust, 1974, p. 196.

4. Information supplied by Pastor Jim Williams, General Superintendent of the Assemblies of God in New Zealand. In 1976, according to information supplied by James Worsfold, this group had 45 full-time ministers and 65 congregations or churches.
5. *Ibid,* p. 237.
6. Details in *ibid,* chs. 25-7 but developments since 1974 need to be taken into account. My main source of such information has been James Worsfold and representative figures in the various groups as suggested to me by him and by Allen Neil also.
7. Much the same point is made, in a sociologically sophisticated manner, by Michael Hill in 'Do sects thrive while churches languish' which appears as a chapter of this volume.
   CHAPPLE, G. When the spirit moves. *Listener 82:* 24-5, 1976, claims a membership of 16,000 for classical Pentecostalism and 20,000 for the Charismatic Renewal. The basis for and the sources of these figures are not given. The article adds: 'Both estimates are conservative'.
8. The comparative figures for these groups are:

Religious Profession	Number of Adherents			Percentage		
	1966	*1971*	*1976*	*1966*	*1971*	*1976*
Latter Day Saints	25,564	29,785	36,130	1.0	1.0	1.2
Jehovah's Witness	7,455	10,318	13,392	0.3	0.4	0.4

The growth of sectarian movements in New Zealand is described and analysed in Michael Hill's paper to which reference has been made in n. 7 above.
9. I have been greatly assisted by a statistical survey supplied by James Worsfold and prepared by the secretary of the Associated Pentecostal Churches of New Zealand.
10. CHURCH of England in New Zealand. Commission on the Charismatic Movement. *Report. In* General Synod of the Church of the Province of New Zealand, 42nd, Christchurch, 1976. Proceedings, p. 33.
11. *Ibid,* p. 34. Allen Neil, on whose work the Commission leaned heavily at this point, now feels that this statement is less than accurate and that while there has been "levelling out" there has hardly been "decline".
12. NEIL, A. G. *The origins, development and present extent of the charismatic renewal in New Zealand.* Unpublished paper submitted to the Anglican Provincial Commission on the Charismatic Renewal, 1975, p. 14-15.
13. *Ibid,* p. 33. For details and analysis see also:
    MYERS, Michael *Ideological and organizational change in the Auckland*

Catholic charismatic movement. Unpublished paper presented to the Conference of the N.Z. Association of Social Anthropologists, August 1976. REIDY, M.T.V. and Richardson, J. T. Roman Catholic neo-Pentecostalism: The New Zealand experience. *Australian and New Zealand journal of sociology 14:* 222-230, 1978.

14. Overseas speakers have included Dennis Bennett, Terry Fulham, Michael Harper, Graham Pulkingham, Kevin Ranaghan, Tom Smail, and Colin Urquhart – some of whom have visited New Zealand more than once. Periodicals include *Renewal* (England), *New Covenant, Pastoral renewal, New wine* (all U.S.A.), and *Restore* (Australian). Within New Zealand there are *The Paraclete* (Presbyterian) and the Christian Advance Ministries newsletter.

15. NEIL, A. G. 'The origins, development and present extent of the charismatic renewal in New Zealand'. p. 72, Christian Advance Ministries was formed in 1972 with strong but not exclusive Anglican participation. It has sought to produce 'balance' within the Renewal notably by arranging national 'Summer Schools' and local seminars. Small Methodist participation may be explained by the fact that the Methodists felt that such 'schools' were rather dominated by Anglicans and Roman Catholics.

16. *Ibid.,* p. 81. Clearly at this and other points the sociologist and historian cry out for more and harder data, e.g. Where comparisons between parishes are in question a knowledge of *all* the relevant factors including age structure and population changes is essential for valid conclusions. The figures for the Baptist Union are disputed by some Baptist leaders.

17 According to Neil (*ibid,* p. 82), the theological reason for Brethren hostility from their 'Dispensationalism' on the basis of which they insist that 'gifts' such as healing and glossolalia must come from sources other than God. My informants among Open Brethren preferred to base their criticism on the ground that 'charismatics' tend to begin from their 'own' experience rather than from the Biblical revelation as such.

18. Some of the work in this area is surveyed in my paper, Pentecostalism, neo-Pentecostalism and naturalistic explanation, *The religious dimension.* J. Hinchcliff, ed. Auckland, Rep Prep, 1976, p. 55-7, but see now esp. McDONNELL, K. *Charismatic renewal and the churches.* N.Y., Seabury Press, 1976.

19. To the best of my knowledge the only studies based on research in New Zealand are those by C. T. Waldegrave, M. Myers, and M. T. V. Reidy and J. T. Richardson. For details see bibliography.

20. See esp.
GERLACH, F. P. and Hine, V. H. Five factors crucial to the growth and spread of a modern religious movement. *Journal for the scientific study of religion 7:* 23-40, 1968.

21. REIDY, M.T.V. and Richardson, J. T. *op. cit.* offer some suggestions as to causes and consider the movement to be "a conservative reaction to a rapid social and cultural change."

22. Bryan Wilson's point is a related one. He remarks that "Spontaneity and subjectivism have become powerful elements in contemporary culture. Inner feeling has been widely hailed as more *authentic* than intellectual knowledge" (*Contemporary transformations of religion.* London, Oxford University press, 1976, p. 37) In Wilson's view the Charismatic Renewal is one more sign of the decline of the traditional churches, and, hence, evidence of 'secularization,' at least as he interprets that protean term.

23. See eg.
KELLEY, D. M. *Why conservative churches are growing; a study in sociology of religion.* N.Y. Harper & Row, 1972. For comment on Kelley's views, including his rejoinders, see *Theology today 30:* 43-55, 1973-4, and *Journal for the scientific study of religion 17:* 129-37, and 165-72, 1978.

24. NEIL, A. G. *op. cit.* no. 2, attempts to relate the emergence of the Charismatic Renewal to conditions in the churches and society generally.

25. The visit to Auckland in 1976 of Archbishop Bill Burnett (Capetown) a selfconfessed 'charismatic', helped re-kindle tensions between 'charismatic' and 'non-charismatic' clergy.

26. BORCH, R. J. and Faulkner, J. E. Religiosity and secular attitudes; the case of Catholic Pentecostals. *Journal for the scientific study of religion 14:* 257-70, 1975, suggest that in the United States some Roman Catholic Pentecostals hold quite 'liberal' attitudes on at least some social and political issues extending to a concern for "the structural nature of social problems" (p. 259).

27. It would be interesting to know in this connection what proportion of those involved in Pentecostalism have come from quite beyond Christianity. Within the movement opinion varies on this question. Allen Neil has suggested to me that, of those affected by the Charismatic Renewal in two Anglican congregations of which he has personal knowledge, about half have been non-Anglicans and, of these, about half again had no real, prior contact with church life. An informant from the Assemblies of God suggested that, in the last 10-15 years 80% of their members have been from the 'unchurched'; he added that this applied especially to Samoans. But this, again, is an area on which we need much more information for firmer conclusions together with precise definitions of 'unchurched' and similar terms.

The Sectarian Contribution

DO SECTS THRIVE WHILE CHURCHES LANGUISH?
Michael Hill

The main source of data used in this paper is the published statistical information on religious preferences of the New Zealand census. The relevant item on the census form simply asks the respondent to state his 'Religion' and allows for respondents who object to state (in 1926, 4.7% of the total population so objected, while in 1976 it was 14%). Though the paper includes little direct observation of religious groups in New Zealand, relevant material of this sort has been included from other social contexts in order to suggest ways in which sectarian groups develop and the sorts of functions they fulfil. Because the topic belongs to another section, I have not looked at predominantly Maori religions such as Ratana and Ringatu. On the other hand, where Maori membership has been significant in the growth of inter-ethnic groups, as it has in the example of the Mormons, this factor is discussed. Religious professions such as Hindu and Buddhist, which probably contain a sectarian fringe but which are more likely to be predominantly ethnic, are also omitted, and the paper focusses on minority Christian and inter-ethnic groups. It should be noted that, in an attempt to indicate some recent changes in smaller religious groups, a different scale has been used on each of the graphs (in one case running from 0-40% of the total population and at the other extreme from 0.00-0.06%). As a result, the profiles are not intended to be comparable but rather are intended to portray the particular 'experience' of each group. For instance, the Pentecostal group shown in table 4 increased from 0.04 to 0.06 of the population between 1966 and 1971, which represents a tiny fraction in overall terms. However, for the adherents concerned (assuming their religious profession related to distinct groups rather than to more diffuse styles of religious expression) an increase of 749 members from 1,110 to 1,859 in the space of five years represented a 68% addition and must have been experienced as significant growth.

The question remains of how reliable census data is in the area of religious adherence; indeed, to what extent does any large-scale statistical study get beyond a superficial assessment of the religious situation? We are all familiar with the accusation that statistics can be used to prove anything: a more charitable version of this would be the statement that statistics need to be *interpreted* before they can be meaningful, and most sociologists would fully agree with it (I quote no percentages!). I interpret the census data on religious adherence as follows. The respondent who calls himself 'Anglican', 'Presbyterian', 'Roman Catholic' or 'Methodist' may signify by that designation a general assent to the church's beliefs, a transient (even unremembered, as in infant baptism) encounter with the church in the form of what sociologists like to call a 'rite of passage' and laymen more expressively refer to as 'hatch, match and despatch', or perhaps an allegiance to some broad ethnic identity such as an Irish or Scottish ancestry; *or* the respondent may signify a considered and firm commitment to and involvement in the claimed religious group. If I assume that the latter type of commitment is a proportion, sometimes a small proportion, of the total stated adherence, the reason is simply that when these religious bodies publish statistics of what *they* consider to be their membership (on criteria which may vary from Easter communicants to 'ticket' holders) the figures are smaller than those for expressed adherence. The classic case is that of England, where in national surveys some two-thirds of the population profess their allegiance to the Church of England, a proportion which coincides almost exactly with the proportion of the population which has been baptized in that church. At this point, the church's own statistics take over and tell a rather different story: 24% of the population are confirmed Anglicans; only 6% make their Easter communion and 5% their Christmas communion. To generalize from these figures, it is the pattern for large religious bodies to attract a substantial group of residual — or perhaps more accurately, recumbent — religionists.

For reasons which will become apparent later in this paper, the interpretation which can be given to minority and sectarian religious groups, as represented in census data, is somewhat different. The census respondent who states 'Jehovah's Witness', 'Christadelphian' or 'Society of Friends' on his form is, I suggest, more likely to be found deeply committed to and involved in the beliefs and practices of those groups. This is in no way meant to imply that he or she is any more *truthful* than the average Anglican or Roman Catholic, but that he *means* something different by his designation. Furthermore, it has been true, at least until fairly recently, that the larger religious bodies have been more or less tolerant of recumbent religionists: sects, by contrast, insist on a committed clientele.

Sociologists and Sects

A brief statement of the sociological approach to religion, which includes as one of its most productive areas the study of sects, may help to clarify the scope and, more importantly, the limitations of this paper. It was one of the founding fathers of the discipline, not one of his critics, who confessed that his readers might find him writing 'soullessly of the soul, and unspiritually of spiritual things.' One of the best known of the early sociologists who devoted a large part of his work to the study of religion, Max Weber, in a similar way admitted that he was 'religiously unmusical'. Is religious belief necessary before the study of religion can begin? I would argue not, as long as sociologists are prepared to agree that in studying religion they are studying only one *aspect* of it, what might be called the 'outward and visible form' of the religious group in question. Included in this aspect of religion would be the socially significant features of the history, organization and practices of those who share its beliefs. In these terms, the solitary mysticism of the *guru* might appear to be of marginal importance, but if the *guru* were to attract disciples or take the model of other *gurus* as something to emulate, this would be of social significance.

It is, in addition, possible to discuss beliefs which we do not necessarily share, as long as they are taken 'as given' rather than as statements whose truth or falsity has to be arbitrated. It is especially in the study of sectarian groups, which have had an equivalent status in the sociology of religion to the tribe in anthropology, that problems in the interpretation of beliefs have arisen most clearly. This is not surprising, since sectarian beliefs tend to be both clear-cut and distinct from other, more widely-held beliefs. Thus one observer, noting that the belief in direct inspiration and a rejection of 'bookish' religion (both common beliefs in sects) were frequently found among culturally deprived social groups, labels the phenomenon a 'philosophy of sour grapes' and seems to dismiss sectarianism as a misguided and disreputable religious response. This is bad sociology. Rather more acceptable is the approach which sees sectarian responses as providing for their membership just as meaningful an authentic a set of beliefs as do the more socially acceptable religious groups for their members. This latter approach has occasionally led sociologists to defend sectarian groups which have found themselves the target of newspaper, television and even parliamentary attacks, as happened in Britain to the Exclusive Brethren in 1964. A recurring theme in sociology, and one of its more humane elements, has been concern for the 'underdog', whether in the shape of factory worker, political dissident, or coloured immigrant, and the extensive literature on minority religions belongs for the most part in the same category.

At the beginning of this century sociologists began to study what they saw as two prevailing tendencies within Christianity, and they borrowed from the religious vocabulary the terms 'church' and 'sect' to label these tendencies. Whereas the terms had previously been used in theological debate ('church' = 'the established religion to which I belong', 'sect' = 'the rest'), they were given a more neutral connotation by defining them in terms of features of organization and belief which could be traced in the development of Christianity. Thus the church broadly accepts, and is accepted by, society and is in principle universalistic; sects, on the other hand, avoid or attack society and are small and exclusive. The church tends to have an upper-class connection and a conservative stance while the sect caters for the lower classes and is radical. Although Christianity had for several centuries sought to contain both elements (the sectarian in the form of monasticism) the Reformation had seen a considerable fission of groups, with established churches confronting dissident sects. The possibility that contemporary churches may still retain sectarian 'colonies' is one to which I will return.

A professional characteristic which sociologists share with theologians is a concern for detail and an insistence on precision. Hence, while they have avoided such dubious quantification as the number of angels that can be got on the head of a pin, there has been a steady stream of literature on, for instance, the number of characteristics needed to define some group as a sect: a conservative estimate of the major literature in the field gives over one hundred items. Avoiding too much casuistry, I will summarize one of the most useful working definitions of a sect before going on to examine the variety of sectarian responses. In this way I hope to address the question in a more precise form by showing *which* sects thrive and which do not. If a definition has any purpose it is, hopefully, to provide the type of cutting edge which can dissect an irregular segment of reality.

One of the features which sects often emphasize in their beliefs and seek to ensure through their organization is their voluntary nature. Individuals choose to join particular sects and sects choose whom they will accept or reject, frequently requiring that full membership can only be given on the basis of conscious adult choice. For this reason, census declarations are more likely to be representative in the case of sects, where a clear definition of member/non-member is maintained. Furthermore, a sect will normally impose some well-defined criterion of 'merit' on the part of the intending member before membership is offered: the strong sense of sectarian self-identity which this engenders might similarly be expected to lead to greater precision in census responses. Reinforcing this tendency is a characteristic of sects towards a monopoly of their members' allegiance, overriding other political, social and even close kinship allegiances. Unlike most large groups in contemporary Western societies, sects have a tendency towards exclusiveness and elitism, especially when membership is believed to bring with it some special guarantee of salvation or spiritual benefit. Elitism of this type usually involves a separation of the group from other religious and secular organizations, so that one would assume that few Christadelphians or Jehovah's Witnesses, for instance, would be found among census respondents listing themselves as 'Protestant', 'Christian', or 'Undenominational'. A related feature, and one which stands in marked contrast with broader church-type groups in a contemporary context, is the sectarian practice of expelling wayward or heterodox members, with the effect once more of strengthening in-group definitions of the sect and generating conscientiousness.

Compared with the majority religious culture of most Western societies, sects clearly represent *deviant* responses. In particular, they reject what might from their viewpoint be called the 'low-key', secularized idiom of the major religious groups in favour of some more enthusiastic, spontaneous, stringent, or esoteric conception of religion. But as I hinted earlier, the initial statement of the church-sect dichotomy offered the contrast as two complementary *strains* within Christianity which had not always implied separate organization. Is it possible to approach the contemporary religious situation with the dual perspective in mind? Peter Berger is one writer who thinks it is. If we look at the sect as a group whose members believe that the spirit is immediately present and the church as a group whose members believe the spirit is remote (I prefer the word 'mediated') then we can begin to talk in terms of an 'ecology of the sacred'. While the traditional structure of the church has involved 'hedging in' or 'reserving' the sacred behind altar rails or in tabernacles, the sect views the sacred as immediately present in the group of devotees. Sectarian movements are thus 'island formations' which may exist independently but which may also interpenetrate church organization in the form of 'ginger groups' or 'turbulent conventicles' (depending on the observer's point of reference).

One of the often-cited components of secularization is the loss of by religion of its public function, either as society's moral arbiter or as the ideological expression of particular groups within society. Is the corollary also true? — that as the public role diminishes, the possibility opens up for religion to perform more effectively the function of articulating and responding to the more personal concerns of individual members? If so, we are correct in not restricting our interest to distinct sectarian groups alone. Substantial changes may simultaneously be in progress among the larger, more institutionalized religious groups. As evidence for this one could point to the growing importance of fundamentalist and pentecostal groups in the Church of England, Roman Catholicism and Nonconformity. At the same time, it is clear that the Church of England has begun to insist on 'tighter' criteria of membership, such as a restriction of Electoral Roll members to active church attenders and a revised attitude to infant baptism and the marriage of non-attenders. The loss of a 'public' role has been followed by a greater concentration on the religious needs of committed adherents; and to the extent that this movement represents a break in the church's universalistic aims, a heightened insistence on conscious choice of membership, a weakening in traditional conceptions of hierarchy (perhaps the prophet can once more claim an edge over the priest) and a less mediated conception of the sacred, it would be correct to state that the sectarian strain in institutional Christianity is thriving quite apart from any developments among minority religious groups. Above all, recent developments highlight the tensions which exist in any group within Christianity. For the church, the dilemma is one of continuity at the expense of spontaneity; for the sect, of spontaneity at the expense of continuity.

Sects in Finer Focus

Any attempt to study the dynamics of sect development must sooner or later face the problem that there is an immense variety among such groups. As a crude indicator of this, in the 1971 New Zealand census there were well over 100 categories of religious profession which were conceivably sectarian (and I use this word carefully, since some are obscure in the extreme — one wonders, for instance, how the 8 'Builders of the Adytum' have fared under the National Government's housing policy). Whereas in 1966 the Government Statistician was able to include professions with only one claimant, in 1971 the minimum number for separate reference was five. Projecting forward, it could reasonably be expected that the results of the 1981 census will reveal yet another expansion of the list of 'minor religious professions', and that sometime in the not-too-distant future we will witness demands by aggrieved sectarians that they be removed from that limbo of the Department of Statistics, the 'Facetious' category.

One sociologist who has attempted to create order out of the apparent chaos of sectarian groups, and who has strongly influenced other sociologists in the field, is Bryan Wilson. I will outline his typology and relate it to the New Zealand material. The first type of sect considered by Wilson is the one which is most commonly associated with this form of religious response to the world, the *conversionist* sect. Sects of this general category are those which devote their resources to proselytizing with the goal of eliciting from new members a definite 'proof' of conversion experience, often of an emotionally charged kind. Such experience is interpreted as a direct encounter with God by contrast with the more attenuated conversion process and mediated concept of salvation among institutionalized church-type organizations. This sectarian response shades off almost imperceptibly into the fundamentalist denomination so that it becomes very much an academic exercise in demarcation to trace the limits of the sect. An excellent historical example of this is Methodism which, originating within the Church of England as an 'island formation', had by the beginning of the nineteenth century evolved a stable, institutional structure as far as its Wesleyan branch was concerned. However, shortly after Wesley's death in 1791 the Methodist New Connexion ('Kilhamites') were established (1798), followed by the Primitive Methodists (1811) and Bible Christians (1815) — all of the latter being located on the radical sectarian fringe of Methodism.

In the New Zealand census data the group which fits most clearly into this pattern is the collectively-styled 'Brethren' — a label which includes a range of responses from relatively open membership to the much-publicized closed nature of the Exclusive Brethren. As a percentage of the total population this group has remained relatively stable over the past 50 years at around 1% of the total population, just as the response rate for Baptists has remained around 1.6% over the same period. No indication can be given of the relative 'mix' within the overall group of Open and Exclusive professions, but some remarks can be made about the intensification of beliefs among the exclusive wing. A fundamentalist group which preaches a literal interpretation of the Bible and which also resists the formation of a separate ministry is likely to experience more strongly the influence of 'informal' local leaders, and in the case of the Brethren — a movement which, paradoxically, arose to promote Christian unity but which has experienced several schisms — the informal leader who put forward a more explicit interpretation of Biblical injunctions was Jim Taylor Jnr., a member who belonged very much to the tradition of John Darby, the early 'exclusive' leader. What seems to have prompted most public antagonism is the way in which the injunction to 'be separate' has been interpreted to mean the 'disfellowshipping' of non-member kin and friends. The rejection of widely-held social values such as support for the family is a sure source of social tension *unless* some means can be found of isolating or insulating the group against everyday social contacts: even this is likely to be a source of conflict, as the Exclusive Brethren have found when trying to move *en bloc* into residential areas. Monastic groups, practising an ideal of celibacy which is very much against the norm, have either isolated themselves physically in enclosed communities, or at least signified their commitment by wearing special dress, just as the early Quakers and contemporary communities such as the Amish adopted distinct styles of dress.

This is an important insulating feature of another fairly large conversionist group in New Zealand, the Salvation Army. The rationale behind the distinctive uniform is not only its function in symbolizing the group's quasi-military organization but also its practical value in gaining the group access to otherwise potentially threatening situations. The non-uniformed seller of the *Socialist Action* in a central Wellington pub on a Friday evening adopts a more exposed social role than do the *War Cry* salesmen. The military style does seem to have been important in a different form of insulation, namely the insulation of the Salvation Army as a conversionist group against the frequent tendency to adopt a religious style which is little distinguishable from that of other conversionist groups. Despite a small dip in percentage membership around 1960, the Salvation Army now has the same level of adherence as it had in 1950 (see Table 2). By contrast, the Church of Christ – also a conversionist group and, like the Brethren who were mentioned earlier, dedicated originally to the task of healing Christian divisions – has steadily declined since the war. Although recent membership figures have apparently been influenced by mergers, the downward trend cannot be attributed to that alone: the very fact of amalgamation signifies a loss of sectarian exclusiveness and the type of 'merging with the landscape' often associated with secularization.

A major area of growth among conversionist sects has its parallels in other larger churches. Pentecostalism, in the form of the Apostolic Church, the Assemblies of God or the Pentecost Church, showed an accelerated growth in the 1960's (Tables 3 and 4) and might well be expected to reveal a similar trend in the 1981 census. The large part played by Maori membership in recent growth is worth noting: for instance, between 1961 and 1966 there was a 141% increase in the number of Maori adherents to the Apostolic Church and a 190% increase in the Pentecost Church. Although Maori growth rates for these groups were much lower between 1966 and 1971, they were large compared with growth rates for other groups. Factors which might help account for Maori pentecostalism are the appeal of a spontaneous style of worship, the intense concern for fellowship among members and the compensation offered within the group for social stresses and some of the tensions of urban life. These factors, together with the possibility of enjoying within the group a spiritual status which may often be much higher than members' social status in the wider society, have always been associated with the growth of conversionist sects, especially in periods of rapid social change.

The sectarian response which appears to show considerable resilience and in some cases massive growth in New Zealand belongs to the second of Wilson's categories, the *revolutionist* sect. The Jehovah's Witnesses, the Seventh Day Adventists, and the Christadelphians all eagerly expect a millennial transformation of the existing world and characteristically draw attention to its imminence by reading the 'signs of the times'. Because membership of such groups is only possible after their doctrines have been thoroughly learned, and because this is a more efficient 'filter' than subjective experience in terms both of identifying full commitment *and* preventing the process of 'merging with the landscape' which conversionist groups tend to experience, revolutionist sects generally have a hard-core quality about them. Since millennial sects frequently hold the belief that only those who are fully members will enjoy the new order, there is strong in-group identification.

Numerically, the Seventh Day Adventists and the Jehovah's Witnesses, both with over 10,000 adherents in 1971 (Table 5) are the most significant sectarian groups of this type in New Zealand. However, while the Seventh Day Adventists had some 6,000 adherents in 1951, the Jehovah's Witnesses had less than 2,000 and have increased rapidly. Again, the growth in the percentage of Maori adherents is an important influence. Between 1966 and 1971, for example, the Jehovah's Witnesses showed an increase of 40% in Maori adherence compared with 8% for the Seventh Day Adventists. On a world-wide scale the Witnesses have grown more quickly than any other Christian sect over the past 40 years, but it is interesting to note that the colonial connection of the movement has been of particular importance. Apart from North America and certain European countries, the Witnesses have been most numerous among Africans. One explanation for this has been that the egalitarian beliefs and practices of the movement are attractive to ethnic groups which find themselves in an underprivileged position, and the doctrine of an imminent transformation of the world has obvious appeal for such groups. Whether this explanation is adequate in the case of Maoris is uncertain, but the widespread belief that Black and White share an equal place in American society, the home of the Witnesses, may well have some influence. Such a belief has been associated with recent Melanesian cults (including the President Johnson cult on the island of New Hanover) and a similar explanation has been offered for the enormous increase in Maori membership of the Mormon Church, from 6,551 in 1945 to 17,301 in 1971. The Mormons, though a rather more complex group than the type we have labelled a conversionist sect (Wilson himself refers to Mormonism as 'the many-sided sect'), have a strong millennial strain together with an ideology which offers a substantial appeal to ethnic minorities. The growth of this group in New Zealand, especially since the war, has been marked (Table 2).

The Christadelphians are a sect with a notable political emphasis. Their literature combines Biblical exegesis with diagnoses of the 'signs of the times' in world affairs, and they have a close identification with the Jews — an identification which is made by a number of religious movements including Hau-Hau, British Israel, and Ras Tafari. Thus for Christadelphians the development of Zionism and the establishment of the State of Israel are matters of great concern. Another revolutionist sect with a strong political component which appears for the first time in the 1976 census is the Unification Church. This group, which attracted newspaper attention after a non-member attempted to 'reclaim' one of his family, originated in 1936 with Mr Sun-myung Moon, a Korean who is now in his mid-50's. It is strongly millennial and virulently anti-communist, as demonstrated by a recent march in Wellington which was organized by the sect. Its amalgam of adventism and prophecies of communist advance led one observer to dub it 'the doomsday cult'.

If revolutionist sects adopt a fairly aggressive stance towards 'the world', the alternative is to seek salvation in the community of believers. The *introversionist* response is perhaps represented best by the Society of Friends, which has maintained a small but stable proportion of adherents over the last two decades (Table 4). The introversionist response avoids active proselytizing and seeks a moral transformation within the group of adherents. For this reason it is a response which may find expression in communitarian styles of organization. The recent growth in the commune movement in Britain and the United States has produced a number of religiously orientated communities which would come into this general category. Some of these groups, far from seeking to proselytize, prefer to maintain a 'hidden' existence, and as an example of this one might cite

'Commune Y' — a group of people interested in the charismatic renewal of Christianity — described by Tim Jones and Ian Baker (*A Hard-Won Freedom,* Hodder and Stoughton, 1975, pp. 99-103). The commune, in Christchurch, is described as being modelled on the church of the first century and sounds — with its well-equipped suburban home and respectable members — like a kiwi Little Gidding. Perhaps because of this reluctance to 'open up' for fear of eroding the inner life of the group, it is possible that this is precisely the form of religious response which is least likely to emerge in statistics; and certainly it is a response which could most readily be accommodated within broader denominational groups.

The last type of sect outlined by Wilson is the *manipulationist* sect. In many respects the groups which would come under this general heading are the most contemporary, and often the most transient, of all. The response they have in common is less one of avoidance of 'the world' than of manipulating it by means of some esoteric technique. In an important way, such movements represent a well-developed form of religious individualism, since they reject both the universalism of the church and the tightly-knit fellowship of the sect: the one-to-one relationship of the guru/disciple epitomizes this type of group, in which the deity is hardly a redeemer but more an abstract idea of spiritual power. Christian Science, Theosophy, Spiritualism, and Scientology are all examples of this last type of sect (or, as some purists would argue, cult). None of them preaches a rejection of the world — instead they offer a new means of coping with one's environment. Thus, it has been found that some groups of this type play an important role in resocializing drug-users, and this may well be a valuable selling-point in the group's public relations exercise. Both Scientology and the smartly-dressed admen of the Maharishi Yogi, for example, sell their esoteric product in much the same way as the advertisers of built-up shoes and acne cures in the personal columns of newspapers. To give a flavour of their message, the following is an extract from the glossy publication 'Successes of Scientology':

'As a concert pianist and former child prodigy, I used to be afflicted with stage-fright which would grow worse as the performance continued. I also used to have unstable moods ranging from enthusiasm to grief. Now I have an inner calm. Through Scientology training and processing, I have been able to achieve a high degree of musical communication with the audiences . . .'

Similar testimonies abound in the publications of these groups; indeed, publications are one of the main forms of communication within the cultic fringe. And in case it should be thought that my choice of the word 'sell' in the case of a religious product is inappropriate, it is worth noting that the cost of some of these techniques and panaceas can often be considerable. One estimate of the complete cost of a course of Scientology 'auditing', for instance, put the figure at between $3,000 and $6,000, and there has been recent controversy among transcendental meditators on the question of fees. I think of this type of religion in contemporary society through the image of a supernatural supermarket: its patrons 'shop around', selecting components of their 'world-view' from among the variety of products on sale, each one having a different mixture in their trolley. It is this 'shopping around', best defined in the concept of 'seekership', that most characterizes the contemporary urban middle-class sectarian scene: individualistic conceptions of membership, frequently of a tangential kind, combined with urban anonymity, support the growth of these esoteric products.

Of the three groups shown here, Christian Science, with its older, female-dominated memberships, has declined markedly in recent years (Table 3); so has the original 'light from the east', Theosophy (Table 4)*; whereas Spiritualism, again with an older, majority female membership, has shown some resistance to erosion (Table 4). In view of my earlier remarks, it might seem paradoxical that these groups have declined, but in fact they are the older, more institutionalized representatives of esoteric cults. They now have to compete for their potential clientele with a rich array of newer groups offering more sophisticated techniques. Most manipulationist groups frequently draw on scientific thought for their amalgam of ideas (it is worth noting that the theory of Dianetics which lies behind Scientology first appeared in a science fiction magazine, and that research on altered brain-wave states has been carried out for certain techniques of meditation). As science changes, so does the scientific content of manipulationist theories. Novelty is a well-tried technique of marketing.

A Brief Conclusion

From this superficial survey of statistical data it appears that sectarianism is in a thriving condition in contemporary society. To the extent that this

---

*Note, however, that many members of the Theosophical Society do not see Theosophy as their personal religion and in a census might well declare allegiance to the Church of England or some other denomination (including the so-called Liberal Catholic Church, which is allied to the Theosophical Society).

represents a radical movement within Christianity, we must not overlook the important role played by radical movements *within* larger, institutional churches in the last decade. Modern cities tend to be anonymous places where religious experimentation can be tolerated because it is invisible — although if it intrudes, as in the example of Hare Krishna, it can be condoned because it is colourful; but this very anonymity encourages the growth of small, face-to-face sectarian groups within which members can find a new fellowship and often a heightened sense of personal identity. One reason given for the popularity of Mormonism among Maoris is the personal, face-to-face approach in the initial proselytizing stage. Sectarian groups occasionally offer more than psychological support by providing economic and welfare services.

In short, sectarian groups have a strong resonance with certain aspects of modern society, though this is perhaps rarely an intended consequence of the groups' beliefs and activities. Membership of a sect may, for instance, be the means by which the newcomer to a city becomes socially integrated and economically established. Participation in the spontaneous worship of a fundamentalist sect may be one solution to economic or cultural deprivation, just as radical Methodism has been seen as a form of psychological release for the industrial working class of the late 18th and early 19th centuries. Increasingly in modern society, with its goals of success and material wellbeing, manipulationist groups offer an alternative route for those who have been unsuccessful through the conventional channels of education and career. It is among this group of sects that I would expect most development to occur, thus confirming a prediction made as long ago as 1912 by Ernst Troeltsch. Describing the residual Christianity which he saw developing in his own day he thought that 'all that is left is voluntary association with like-minded people . . .' The end product, he thought, was 'simply a parallelism of spontaenous religious personalities'.

Table 1

Reported adherence to selected religious groups (N.Z. Census)

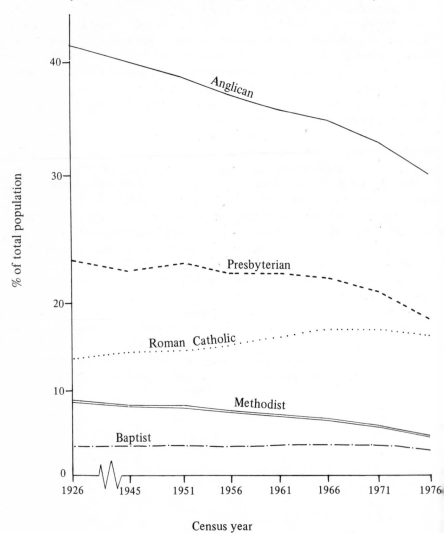

Census year

Table 2

Reported adherence to selected religious groups (N.Z. Census)

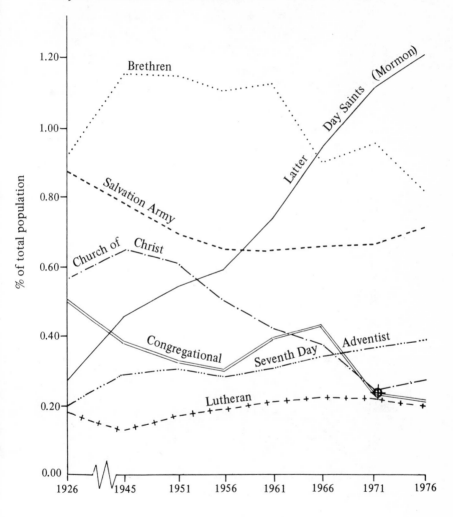

Census year

⊕   amalgamations influence figures

Table 3

Reported adherence to selected religious groups (N.Z. Census)

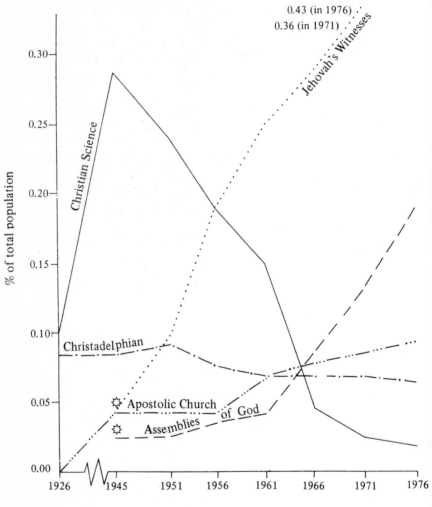

Census year

☆　　excluding Maoris (but numbers minimal)

Table 4

Reported adherence to selected religious groups (N.Z. Census)

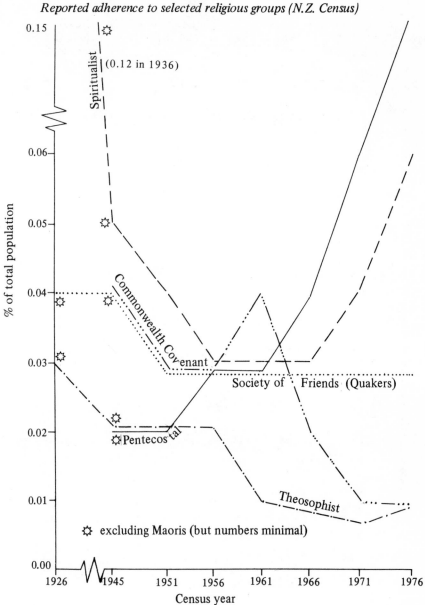

Table 5

MAJOR RELIGIOUS PROFESSIONS BY NUMBERS AND PERCENTAGES, 1926 AND 1956 TO 1976

Religious Profession	1926 Number	1926 Percent	1956 Number	1956 Percent	1961 Number	1961 Percent	1966 Number	1966 Percent	1971 Number	1971 Percent	1976 Number	1976 Percent
Anglican (Church of England)	575,731	40.9	780,999	35.9	835,434	34.6	901,701	33.7	895,839	31.3	915,202	29.2
Presbyterian	331,369	23.5	483,884	22.3	539,459	22.3	582,976	21.8	583,701	20.4	566,569	18.1
Roman Catholic (including Catholic undefined)	181,922	12.9	310,723	14.3	364,098	15.1	425,280	15.9	449,974	15.7	478,530	15.3
Methodist	125,278	8.9	161,823	7.4	173,838	7.2	186,260	7.0	182,727	6.4	173,526	5.5
Christian n.o.d.	1,110	0.1	7,662	0.4	12,130	0.5	21,548	0.8	33,187	1.2	52,478	1.7
Baptist	21,979	1.6	33,910	1.6	40,886	1.7	46,748	1.7	47,350	1.7	49,442	1.6
Latter Day Saints (Mormon)	4,060	0.3	13,133	0.6	17,978	0.8	25,564	1.0	29,785	1.0	36,130	1.2
Ratana	11,760	0.8	19,570	0.9	23,126	1.0	27,570	1.0	30,156	1.1	35,062	1.1
Protestant n.o.d.	3,789	0.3	47,999	2.2	45,100	1.9	46,090	1.7	37,475	1.3	33,309	1.1
Brethren	12,980	0.9	22,444	1.0	25,764	1.1	23,139	0.9	25,768	0.9	24,414	0.8
Salvation Army	12,284	0.9	14,122	0.6	15,454	0.6	17,737	0.7	19,371	0.7	22,019	0.7
Atheist	1,079	0.1	2,977	0.1	3,359	0.1	5,474	0.2	9,291	0.3	14,283	0.5
Agnostic	804	0.1	1,748	0.1	2,288	0.1	4,960	0.2	9,481	0.3	14,136	0.5
Jehovah's Witness			3,844	0.2	5,944	0.2	7,455	0.3	10,318	0.4	13,392	0.4
Seventh Day Adventist	2,957	0.2	7,219	0.3	8,220	0.3	9,551	0.4	10,477	0.4	11,958	0.4
Church of Christ	8,011	0.6	10,852	0.5	10,485	0.4	10,301	0.4	8,930	0.3	8,087	0.3
Congregational	7,288	0.5	7,448	0.3	9,377	0.4	12,101	0.4	7,704	0.3	6,600	0.2
Lutheran	2,531	0.2	4,012	0.2	4,817	0.2	5,730	0.2	5,930	0.2	6,297	0.2
Ringatu	3,872	0.3	5,092	0.2	5,377	0.2	5,605	0.2	5,635	0.2	6,230	0.2
Assemblies of God(1)			747		1,060		2,028	0.1	3,599	0.1	5,581	0.2
Hindu	353		1,597	0.1	2,074	0.1	3,599	0.1	3,845	0.1	5,203	0.2
Pentecostal(1)	726		567		659		1,110		1,859	0.1	4,846	0.2
Undenominational	984	0.1	2,062	0.1	1,514	0.1	3,069	0.1	3,709	0.1	4,222	0.1
Eastern Orthodox	268		2,728	0.1	3,328	0.1	3,605	0.1	4,319	0.2	4,153	0.1
Hebrew	2,602	0.2	3,823	0.2	4,006	0.2	4,104	0.2	3,803	0.1	3,921	0.1
Union Church					193		279		1,154		3,045	0.1
Apostolic(1)	12		969		1,399	0.1	1,841	0.1	2,361	0.1	2,693	0.1
Undenominational Christian	1,365	0.1	1,765	0.1	2,170	0.1	1,968	0.1	1,903	0.1	2,554	0.1
Buddhist	160		111		350		652		1,370		2,382	0.1
Spiritualist	1,271	0.1	748		683		843		1,015		1,731	
Christadelphian	1,079	0.1	1,459	0.1	1,498	0.1	1,628	0.1	1,667	0.1	1,686	0.1
Mohammedan	76		200		260		551		779		1,415	
Reformed Church of N.Z.			60		787		1,242		1,628	0.1	1,358	0.1
Society of Friends	449		721		790		887		966		1,074	
Humanitarian	12		25		90		241		510		1,060	
Orthodox			33		104		1,100		580		1,047	
Uncertain	224		243		447		364		353		1,029	
No religion (so returned)	3,217	0.2	12,651	0.6	17,486	0.7	32,780	1.2	57,485	2.0	101,211	3.2
All other religious professions(2)	13,087	1.0	14,271	0.7	14,698	0.6	19,087	0.7	16,075	0.6	33,597	1.1
Object to state	65,778	4.7	173,569	8.0	204,056	8.4	210,851	7.9	247,019	8.6	438,511	14.0
Not specified	7,672	0.5	16,252	0.7	14,198	0.6	19,300	0.7	103,533	3.6	39,380	1.3
Total	1,408,139	100.00	2,174,062	100.0	2,414,984	100.0	2,676,919	100.0	2,862,631	100.0	3,129,383	100.0

(1) Associated Pentecostal Churches of New Zealand group.
(2) Includes also some cases of facetious answers and those which were not specified in sufficient detail to allow precise classification.

The Judaic Contribution

THE JEWISH COMMUNITY IN NEW ZEALAND
David Pitt

There are currently two diametrically opposed models of the nature of contemporary Jewish communities. There is what might be called the traditional view in the social sciences of Jewish communities as 'unmeltable ethnics'[1] with 'the cohesion of an invincible national cultural solidarity'[2]. It is usually assumed that whatever may happen to other minorities in the flood tides of modernisation and its consequent social problems Jewish communities somehow survive and even flourish having an economic status and influence far beyond their numbers. The basic dynamic is assumed to be the strength of traditional institutions. This image which is also part of the academic view of the New Zealand community may be shared by some people[3] in the Jewish communities themselves but many (including many in the New Zealand community) currently have a much more pessimistic view. There have been, to quote the *New Zealand Jewish Chronicle* (1976, Vol. 32, No. 10, page 3) 'endless discussions about indifference, dwindling numbers, internecine strife, assimilation and bigotry'. The current New Zealand situation is compared unfavourably with the supposed strength of overseas communities, including Melbourne and Sydney or the greener pastures of previous periods in New Zealand Jewish history. Assimilation has of course been welcomed by some academics, notably the Marxists,[4] but most in the New Zealand communities regret the situation. The purpose of this brief paper is to examine the optimistic and pessimistic models against what we know about the history[5] and present situation of the New Zealand Jewish community. Our point is that the sociological picture is very much more complicated than either simplistic model. We would intend this as a contribution to growing comparative literature on Jewish communities and we would argue that the New Zealand case is quite different from many of the overseas studies.[6]

Let us take first of all the demographic dimension. The New Zealand Jewish community is very small — 3921 at the 1976 Census. Also compared to many other countries the proportion of the Jewish population to the total population is very small. At the 1971 Census 0.13% of the total population recorded themselves as Jewish. By comparison the Jewish community in Australia in the 1960's comprised approximately[7] 0.5%, 1.1% in Canada, 0.7% in Great Britain, 2.9% in the United States.

The Jewish population in New Zealand now appears to be declining. Between 1966 and 1971 a 1.4% annual decline was recorded in the census figures. (Of course there are difficulties in interpreting these census figures — some Jewish people who remember the abuse of documentation in Nazi Europe do not record their religion, taking advantage of the statutory provision to write 'object'.) There are now only 3 synagogues[8] (orthodox) in New Zealand: Auckland, Wellington and Christchurch and the first has considerable financial problems because of falling interest. However two new Liberal Temples were established in Auckland (1959) and Wellington (1960).

The decline is also reflected in synagogue memberships and participation generally and one can project an even greater future natural decline. The natural increase rate has varied at different periods of Jewish history in New Zealand and has been greatly affected by migration, both immigration and emigration. Some earlier increases in population were the result of successive waves of immigration in the mid nineteenth century from Britain and then the refugees from central Europe, at the end of the nineteenth century as a result of the pogroms in Russia and in the 'thirties and 'forties from the Nazi persecutions. But migration did not necessarily have a permanent demographic effect. Had all those who arrived stayed, the community would have been very large. But many moved on and at any period of New Zealand history many in the community were newcomers. For example in the 1966 Census in the Auckland urban area only 765 out of the total of 1620 people were born in New Zealand (i.e. 47.2%), the proportions for Wellington (42.3%) and Christchurch (39.5%) were even less. It appears as if many Jewish people have regarded New Zealand as a temporary home before going on somewhere else. In the nineteenth century New Zealand was seen (and of course not only by Jewish migrants) as literally the end of the world, an extremely dangerous place. E. G. Wakefield apparently approached the Chief Rabbi[9] about sponsoring a settlement in the 1840s but that very

Reverend gentleman was not at all impressed with the prospect of a country thought to be inhabited by cannibals and the refuse of Europe and America. Even in the twentieth century when there was a search for settlement area for refugees[10] no South Pacific areas were considered suitable after investigation. From the 1930s also successive New Zealand governments were not sympathetic to large scale Jewish immigration. An historian of the community has talked of 'tremendous obstacles' and writes 'Many Jewish children and adults from Europe might have found a haven of refuge in New Zealand but for an adamant exclusive departmental policy which indeed reflected public opinion – a hatred of foreigners which included many traces of antisemitism.'[11]

There were also strong forces pulling people away from New Zealand. Emigration was partially economic. There were outflows of population particularly during the recessions of the later nineteenth century and the nineteen sixties reflected in intercensal decline. Kinship was also an important factor. Because the community was so small, many left to find marriage partners especially in Australia or North America. Status was important too. For many migrants America was the ultimate goal, a society in which it was believed social and economic mobility allowed minorities to flourish and in which of course there was an increasingly large Jewish community. After the establishment of the State of Israel there was also *aliyah*, the emigration based on a desire to participate in the life of the new nation. Recently however much of the *aliyah* has involved a short term movement to Israel with either a return to New Zealand or some other diaspora country, particularly Australia. In fact much of the youthful migration today is to the bright lights of fashionable Sydney or Melbourne. This applies even to the most religious. Evidence from the longitudinal studies of youth groups[12] shows how only 10% of 91 former *B'nei Akiva* (Religious) and *Habonim* (Zionist) members aged 20-24 were in Israel (and some of these intended to return) compared to 18% in other overseas countries.

Intermarriage also had an effect on the demographic picture. Many community leaders certainly have pointed to intermarriage as a cardinal sin and a major cause of communal decline. But there is doubt about this question. There are no firm figures on the rates of intermarriage[13] and the data on the supposed social problems consequent on intermarriage are all from overseas.[14] It appears that certainly in the early history of the community, intermarriage was offset by conversion. Goldman[15] comments that '. . . intermarriage became so frequent and so many families became involved, that it gradually lost a great deal of the distaste with which members of the community had previously regarded it'.

Those who had married out achieved the highest offices in the community. By the end of the nineteenth century conversions 'were carried out with the minimum of formality'.[16]

Intermarriage seemed in fact in the New Zealand setting to have played an important part in the vitality of the community. The general pattern was for males to marry out. Some leading families were founded by Jewish patriarchs and originally gentile matriarchs. Women converts played important roles in communal affairs as well as in the home, achieving high office in Jewish women's associations, even editing the community Journal, and gaining respect, sometimes grudgingly, for frumness (i.e. devoted religious observance). Men converts were much rarer but one case at least was exceedingly frum, insisting when his house was built on separating *milchig* and *fleishig* kitchens (i.e. one kitchen for milk and one for meat cooking so respecting the ritual prohibition on mixing the two). Some forms of recent intermarriage have not really affected the kinship or demographic nature of the community, e.g. when older men have divorced their Jewish wife after their families have grown up to take a second gentile wife.

In the views of many community leaders intermarriage was not only a sin in itself but led to the greater sin of assimilation. But this process was clearly taking place whether or not there was intermarriage. Our study of youth groups[17] showed 32% of former *B'nei Akiva* and *Habonim* members aged 20-24 had no contact with the community and presumably there was an even greater rate of assimilation amongst those who were less clearly identified with the community. Assimilation however took different forms and was not necessarily permanent. Intermarriage without conversion was one reason for drifting away from the community but surprisingly often there was some observance of Jewish customs in the Calendar (especially the Day of Atonement) and eventually there was often a return to the fold and possible conversion of the gentile partner, especially at ritually important times such as the *brith* (the circumcision of a son), *barmitzvah* (the confirmation of a son), etc. Those who had not married out were more likely to drift back at some point, or to become acculturated without being assimilated, to use Rosenthal's phrase, again at times of important rites-de-passage. More significantly, observance of customs showed a characteristic waxing and waning intensity, a constant to and froing across cultural boundaries.[18]

The complex nature of the assimilative process can be shown with regard to what are regarded as the fundamental pillars of Judaism, religious observance, especially *shul* (i.e. synagogue) involvement, and *Kashrut*, the observance of dietary laws. *Shul*, including *shabbat* (sabbath) attendance, has never been large in New Zealand and may be declining, though certain days, notably *Yom Kippur* (Day of Atonement), are exceptions. As noted above, there are fewer synagogues now than in the nineteenth century. Certainly there have been exceptional periods, when there were charismatic rabbis or active communal leaders. There have also been pockets of devotion. The frum even convened a *minyan* (the ten men needed for a religious service) in their own houses so that they could walk to worship as is ritually prescribed. There have also been kosher butchers in Auckland and Wellington although they are not well patronized, and in one case not even recognised by the Rabbinical authorities.

There is also a considerable involvement in the Christian world. Religious observance seems to involve similar boundary crossings. Most community members are in Church at some time and there is a considerable ecumenical feeling. This goes right back to the earliest days of when sternly orthodox men like Abraham Hort, who founded the Wellington community, consecrated the stones of a church. Children of leading members of the community attend Church schools or take Christian religious lessons in state schools though sometimes this leads to friction. Most people eat *trefa* (non-kosher) food at some time, and some regularly. To some degree, this attitude can be seen in much of the present drive in the Auckland community to establish a conservative rather than the present orthodox community.

But assimilation in matters of religious observance does not always produce any dilution of feeling. On certain occasions in New Zealand synagogues one might imagine oneself to be in Stamford Hill. We have already commented on the huge attendances during *Yom Kippur* in which the faithful return to the fold after a year of infidelity, as pious and repentant as the frum. Some returned only at death and the well-kept cemetery contains many names that are virtually unknown in the community, and there have been some very bitter disputes about the right of burial. This underlines the importance of keeping open the gate so that a return can be made across the boundary, even if only at the very last minute.

This same anxiety also sometimes spills over into communal affairs. The so called recent 'Auckland crisis'[19] is a case in point. The crisis arose when a Rabbi was appointed who tried to insist on the letter of *halacha* (the traditional law). There was some objection to the Rabbi's insistence on two sets of cookers, crockery, etc., in the synagogue, and to his attempt to improve *Kashrut* generally. There was a more general feeling of concern over what some people interpreted as his antigentilism, e.g. when he objected to food that had been prepared by gentiles, or when he upbraided the Jewish Church school boys for the crosses on their caps. But most concern was felt when attempts were made to further restrict (and make retroactive) the rights of those who had married out. A public meeting was called and for once in its history the hall was packed. In an electric atmosphere the offending clauses were rejected and there was even a challenge to the lay hierarchy of an upper class family who had held the Presidency since the foundation of the community. Subsequently there were resignations and a new committee of professional men (doctors, lawyer) took over the running of the community.

Some local critics have regarded the combination of assimilative processes and professions of orthodoxy simply as hypocrisy. However, to the sociologist the position appears more complicated. First there is the very small group who are orthodox. Secondly, as we have said, those people who do assimilate or acculturate often cross back over the boundary. In fact, there seems to be an inverse correlation between assimilation and orthodoxy. Some who have strayed sometimes seem to have a backlash of ultra-orthodoxy which may be also found amongst converts. The phenomenon is sometimes associated with age changes. Sociologists dealing with status change since van Gennep[20] have been aware of the antithetical nature often involved in rites-de-passage. In the New Zealand Jewish community the rebellious youth may become the orthodox man, or vice versa. Oppositions may be temporal for the whole community too and the history of New Zealand Jewry is marked by vacillations (sometimes extreme) between orthodoxy and liberalism in fact or theory. At many points in time or space too the fissiparous nature of the community, the family base, overrides other situations. For example families, or individuals within families, may identify themselves by being at one point or another on the assimilation scale, mainly it seems as a mode of identification. Many families, especially the larger older families had their *mesuga* frum, 'intensely (insanely) religious', or conversely their black sheep.

Again as in van Gennep's model of boundary crossing there are often marked periods of separation, marginality or liminality. The couple who have married out will suffer a period of ostracism if they stay in New Zealand but may opt to go abroad, or to emphasise other non-communal forms of Judaism such as Zionism. Deviations in belief may be marked by periods of isolation or alienation, for instance at the University. Even the phenomenon of eating out may be marked by separation symbols. For example, people may feel in one sense or another (as traditionally) unclean or impure for a period.

Another contributing factor to the difficulties of the Jewish community in

New Zealand and a major contributing factor to the demographic situation has been the decline of important institutions such as the family. Traditionally (including nineteenth century New Zealand) the large extended family, the *mishpocha,* was the key unit of Jewish society. Within both Jewish political and economic structures kinship has traditionally been a vital constituent. More significantly the family historically has been the ceremonial and ritual focus, as much as the synagogue, certainly for women and children whose role in public ceremonies was much less. Today in New Zealand as elsewhere this domestic significance is declining. Recent surveys have shown that fewer people celebrate in the home very important occasions like *Erev Shabat* or even *Seder* night.[21] Commensality rituals and their accompanying gastronomic symbols are also in decline.

It is the decline of these ceremonial activities rather than strictly religious observance which is primarily important, for home ceremonials greatly affect the roles of women and children. Women no longer have a satisfying role in the kitchen and around the house and so go out to work which then effectively prevents them from participating fully in home activities. One might add here that there seems from the Census evidence to be very little economic reason for women in the Jewish community to go out to work since the level of income in Jewish households is relatively higher. The decline of the domestic and particularly the culinary role of women is also being accentuated by the synagogue changes we have described. Because of the new rules on *Kashrut* in Auckland women no longer bring in cakes, dishes, etc., so removing an important arena and incentive for social life. This new situation may in fact explain the declining numbers at synagogue functions. If the women do not have to bring in a plate (and compete with others bringing in plates) they will not come. If the women do not come, they do not make the men go either. Children also find the home much less a centre of warmth and affection than other institutions in society. The home becomes then merely a place to sleep, to snatch a meal, to spend brief periods of time in between what are considered to be more important activities.

The social consequences of the decline of home and family can be very considerable. As families become smaller and interaction less, the unit becomes more brittle and unstable. The chances of divorce, separation and irreconciliable rifts become greater. The generation gap is magnified so that children are not socialised into traditional activities but are most influenced by peer groups. Often of course, these peer groups are beneficial influences, but sometimes Jewish young people become entangled in the net of the counterculture, the drug culture, the permissive culture, etc., and become social problems in the eyes of both the Jewish community and the community at large. Studies being carried out by the Hillel group at the University of Auckland are showing that these problems are increasing in Auckland.[22]

Young people and women are not the only people detrimentally affected by the new kind of family. Traditionally the extended family encompassed within its network other people who for one reason or another were less able to cope with life — particularly the sick, the handicapped, and the old. Within the domestic economy these people had useful functions to perform and especially the old, had a very real status. Today the trend is to institutionalise those who cannot play an active role (including an earning role) in the family, to put them in hospitals, or homes, even if they are Jewish homes. The result is to increase the loneliness and anomie of all concerned and to deprive the Jewish household of real assistance and guidance. How many young couples having to pay for babysitters, day nurseries, etc., wish they had their grandparents to relieve them of this burden.

But again the situation is not completely simple. Larger families are reappearing, at the top, socioeconomically, of the community rather than the bottom, a characteristic possibly shared with similar strata in New Zealand society. There is too even in some small families a *'mishpocha* of the mind', a surrogate extended family created through distant kinship ties or friendship patterns. The tremendous efflorescence of Jewish societies for a wide range of Zionist, philanthropic or other purposes is another symptom of this trend. Some small families have also a great vitality, and abound in the symbols and symbolic behaviour typical of the larger *mishpocha*. The nuclear family may even have advantages in terms of intracommunal conflict. For one thing they seem less prone to produce the kinds of feuds and vendettas that accompanied the clans of earlier periods.

Some critics have in fact argued that what appears to be ubiquitous conflict is the most important weakness of the Jewish community. There is certainly a good deal of evidence of conflict, which quickly surfaces at communal meetings, is readily apparent in the communal literature, and in everyday speech. Although much traditional conflict was along *mishpocha* lines, family conflict is less today. There is however a quite considerable generational conflict. Many young people are disillusioned with what they take to be the hypocritical attitude of their parents to Judaism and either proceed outside the community or adopt a life style based on a firmer commitment to Jewish values, either in religious or Zionist activities.

Religious, political and status rifts are probably more important than family conflicts. There is an important division between the Orthodox (or what is called Orthodox) and the Liberal movements. The majority of those who affiliate to any congregation are Orthodox and the Liberals have only two small temples. The Orthodox communities acknowledge the jurisdiction of the Chief Rabbi of the Commonwealth and his *Beth Din* (Rabbinical Court). The Chief Rabbi grew out of the Great Synagogue in London and its jurisdiction extended first to the *Ashkenazi*[23] synagogues of the British provinces and then to the British Empire from 1845. The New Zealand Orthodox communities follow this ritual, though there are very few other links apart from the occasional pastoral tour.[24] The Liberal communities were much later developing in New Zealand and have a loose affiliation with the Reform Temples of the United States. There have been many serious and some bitter arguments between the two elements in New Zealand over such matters as conversion, burial rights, etc. Generally there is little mobility from Liberal to Orthodox though some reverse movement, often associated with an Orthodox member marrying out. The Liberal Temple has also attracted a number of new migrant families from North America where Liberalism is very strong.

Political rifts centre on attitudes to Zionism. Before the emergence of the State of Israel the New Zealand Jewish communities contributed strongly to funds and then after 1948 there were many who went on *aliyah* (return to Israel). The successive wars in the Middle East (especially the 1967 War) attracted much support from the local communities. But there have always been some critical of what they thought was an excessive Jewish nationalism and after the 1973 War especially there were some who were reluctant to support what seemed to them to be a military state. There were a minority who even went along with the extremely anti-Zionistic positions of left wing ideologies, bordering on anti-Semitism.

Status conflicts and differences were somewhat less obvious but still of importance: In many popular mythologies Jewish communities are supposed to occupy high positions in the socioeconomic and even the power structure in the society at large. The New Zealand evidence, however, indicates that the Jewish community is spread in terms of stratification indicators across the spectrum.

There is very little evidence on how much the Jewish community affected the power structure. Certainly as we have said there are some rich families and there has of course been a Jewish Prime Minister (Vogel) though his affiliation was rather tenuous. Certainly an analysis of the current Who's Who turns up only about ten names, a ratio very similar to the general population. Moreover none of these eminent people occupy any very significant power positions. Recent research has also shown that compared to overseas countries there is only a small Jewish intelligentsia with little influence in the Universities, art or culture. This may reflect the working class nature and basic anti-intellectualism of New Zealand Judaism and society generally.[25]

Some indication of the status spread of the Jewish community can be gained from essentially stratification conflict within the community. We have already mentioned that the elite families send their children to the elite Church (Protestant) schools even though there is now in Auckland a Jewish Day School (though a majority of the students are not Jewish). Some of these families also keep back their children from *Cheder,* the general Sunday School, where all congregants may send their children. During the courtship period the wealthier children may go overseas and bring back 'superior' spouses.

However, like most other boundaries within the Jewish community these religious, political and status boundaries are crossed in many different kinds of ways. First in a definite sense difference is more important than conflict. Indeed conflict and argument are something of a cultural mode in the New Zealand as in other Jewish communities. Communal meetings usually develop into a dialectical discussion. The traditional opposition of the Hillelian versus the Shammaian[26] stances which permeates so much of Talmudic argument may well underlie those who champion or oppose religious orthodoxy, or the hawks and doves of the contemporary Middle East Wars. Conflict may also have significant democratising functions challenging the rights of individuals or groups to monopolise decision making, etc.

More significantly there are crosscutting links which may create new conflicts but often also serve to temper the edge of old swords. The voluntary organisations are probably the most important of these. The service brotherhood order of *B'nai Brith* for males founded in Auckland and Wellington in the 1960s and its female chapter, which are based on Hillel's precepts pull in all sectors and also have significant links into the outside community. But membership is not large (about 100 men in Auckland) and there is a high rate of backsliding and lapsing. Sporting ties and social clubs have also been important at different times and places. The Wellington Club, for example, has long served as a place for meals or cards. In Auckland recently a new organisation has been formed, the *Maccabis,* which organises a weekly sporting and leisure evening which is well patronised. There are the annual picnics in the main centres, and some dances. There are luncheons at the Auckland synagogue. Generally the young people have very much less rigid boundaries even in the Zionist and religious youth groups. The young are currently in fact producing a new very vital form of community spirit not only in sporting and social activities but also in new synagogue youth services and student societies at the universities, etc.[27] The boundary however at adulthood, when many migrate away overseas or into the anomie and isolation of suburbia, still remains an important barrier to a more effective community.

Although the crosscutting links of a variety of associations are significant in creating effective communal institutions, these associations do not seem to maintain their effectiveness unless there is also effective leadership. The golden periods of the Jewish past in New Zealand were those when and where the communities existed under very able Rabbinical patriarchs. In Auckland Rabbi Goldstein reigned from 1880 - 1935, and his successor Rabbi Astor for forty years as well. In Wellington Rabbis Van Staveren and Pitkowski ensured a period of stability from the late nineteenth century to 1930. The problems of both communities began when the great leaders left and the problems of many other smaller communities were closely related to the instability caused by the processions of reverend gentlemen who passed through, unable to stand the rigours of the Kiwi Jewish life. Other leaders in the communities were hard to find; some youth leaders emerged but they vanished as their youth receded. There were plenty to fill the seats of the lay boards which ran the synagogues but their achievements have not been great when there were not able Rabbis to point the way. One critic, a disillusioned Board member himself, commented: 'Apart from visible evidence of their presence in synagogue they are scarcely known and one rarely hears what they are up to. Experience on the Board over a long period of time has shown me that for the most part they are up to very little and achieve even less'.[28] Significantly the lay leadership did not encourage participation, for example by very able women, youth, or intellectual leaders. The results of this lack of leadership were very evident in key areas of synagogue, in the choice of Rabbis and in education, where classes in the *Cheder* (the Sunday School) were taught by very junior, and sometimes incompetent teachers, with a consequence that standards of both behaviour and learning were low. This was a particularly tragic situation when there was a willing galaxy of teaching talent available in the community.

A further factor affecting the intensity of communal feeling has been the perception of anti-semitism. Some have argued[29] that anti-semitism in New Zealand was largely the product of Nazi propaganda, a transient phenomenon of mild proportions compared to other countries. But again there appear to be changes both in the probable incidence of anti-semitism and the perceptions of it within the community. There were in the 1930s especially currents of anti-semitism in New Zealand[30] to which the community were very sensitive. After the war many community members felt the strength of anti-Nazi feeling meant a more positive attitude to the Jewish people though there were some who felt that Jewish people were less likely to get on in some occupations or were excluded from some schools, clubs or other social groups. The French sociologist, Georges Friedmann[31] has argued that anti-semitism is really the cement that keeps the Jewish people together and as it disappears so assimilation proceeds. Certainly in the New Zealand case there is some inverse correlation between anti-semitism and assimilation, although as we have said, assimilation was a complex phenomenon. More significantly some people's fears of anti-semitism were never completely allayed. Many now feel that as the memory of the holocaust fades, as Arab propaganda about Israeli militarism (with which the Diaspora is closely identified) increases, the supposedly conspiratorial roles of Zionism becomes widespread, as people fear unemployment, recession and an energy crisis for which Israel or the Diaspora are blamed, as a climate of international cynicism, immorality and war develop, a new form of anti-semitism is developing.[32]

Certainly there is the feeling that the new anti-semitism in New Zealand is covert rather than overt, and certainly many people believe that other more visible minorities, notably the Polynesians, deflect much prejudice and discrimination. But the fear still remains and has led to many Jewish people looking closely at their basic identity. Some have been pushed further away by the new anti-semitism although more often the effect has been to strengthen community institutions and involvement especially amongst young people and those involved in the Zionist movement. The manifold fund raising activities and functions of the Zionists, the large scale distribution of their publications, etc., have brought together many, although others have been alienated by the emphasis on nationalism, the extreme politicisation of the conflict with the Arabs or a feeling that the Jewish community in New Zealand should be the first concern.

In summary then what we have tried to show here is that the New Zealand Jewish community is really neither assimilated nor separate, neither harmonious nor conflict ridden. On the one hand there is fragmentation within the community in space and time and certainly constant flux and change. On the other hand the boundary between the community and the outside world is constantly being crossed and indeed defined and redefined. Most sociological models of communities are not really able to explain adequately this complexity and certainly if we are to take overseas models of Jewish communities at face value then New Zealand is quite exceptional. Like so many other parts of the rich tapestry of New Zealand society, the Jewish community awaits the detailed, intimate and understanding interpretation that the deterministic sociologists so rarely attempt, and in all probability the comparative studies of Jewish communities must also look beyond appearances towards deeper meanings and complexities.

Notes:
  1. NOVAK, M. The rise of the unmeltable ethnics. New York, Macmillan, 1972.
     Two good introductions to Judaism are:
     SHAROT, S. *Judaism – a sociology.* Newton Abbot, David & Charles, 1976, and
     EPSTEIN, I. *Judaism: a historical presentation.* Harmondsworth, Penguin, 1979, whilst
     GLAZER, N. *American Judaism.* Chicago, University of Chicago Press, 1957 is a standard work on American Judaism.
     The most comprehensive work on the Israeli experience is:
     EISENSTADT, S. N. *Israeli society.* London, Weidenfeld and Nicholson, 1967.
     STRIZOWER, S. *Exotic Jewish communities.* London, Yoseloff, 1962, has described the more exotic Jewish communities in the Middle East and Asia whilst closer to home there is:
     MEDDING, P. Y. *From assimilation to group survival.* Melbourne, Cheshire, 1968, and
     JEWS in Australian society. P. Medding, ed. Melbourne, Macmillan, 1973.
     For general reference there is the magnificent
     ENCYCLOPEDIA JUDAICA. Jerusalem, 1971, and recent studies are regularly reviewed in *Jewish journal of sociology.*
  2. SIMPSON, G. E. and Yinger, J. M. *Racial and cultural minorities: an analysis of prejudice and discrimination.* 3d ed. New York, Harper & Row, 1965, p. 199: Cf:
     The GHETTO and beyond. P.I. Rose, ed. N.Y., Random House, 1969, and
     RINGER, B. B. *The edge of friendliness; a study of Jewish-Gentile relations.* New York, Basic Books, 1967.
  3. GOLDMAN, L. M. *The history of the Jews in New Zealand.* Wellington, Reed, 1958: Cf:

COLLINS, P. R. *The Jewish community in New Zealand; a contribution to the study of assimilation.* Thesis, M.A., Massey University, 1971.

4. For a discussion of Marxism and Judaism generally see the *Wiener Library bulletin 28:* (35-36): 2-8, 1975.

5. Our comments are based on a study of the Jewish community in New Zealand supported by the Hillel and Nuffield Foundations and the B'nai Brith Australasian Youth Commission, to whom we are most grateful. We owe a special debt to Dr B. Shieff for continual support and guidance. The study which began in 1973 has attempted first to interview in depth 100 families and most community leaders to ascertain the current nature of the Jewish community within New Zealand society and secondly to gather together historical and other documentary data on the communities in Auckland and elsewhere in New Zealand. Much of the interviewing was carried out by Russell Jaffe who has concentrated on Youth problems.
(Jaffe, R. *Social problems of Jewish youth in New Zealand.* Dept of Sociology, University of Auckland, 1975. (Ethnic relation report no. 3) mimeo)
Special thanks are due to Mr M. S. Pitt (Wellington) and Mrs A. Brem (Secretary, Auckland Hebrew Congregation) for help with historical materials.

6. Cf:
SHAROT, S. *Judaism – a sociology.* op. cit. no. 1 above, and
LIPSET, S. M. The study of Jewish communities in a comparative context. *Jewish journal of sociology 5:* 157-166, 1963.

7. *The JEWISH yearbook.* London, Jewish Chronicle Publications, 1965.

8. There were earlier synagogues in Dunedin, Nelson, Hokitika and Timaru.

9. SINCLAIR, K. *A history of New Zealand.* Harmondsworth, Penguin, 1959, p. 88.

10. See:
GURAU, A. M. Jews in the Pacific Islands of the South Seas. *Australian Jewish Historical Society. Journal and proceedings 1*(8): 257-70, 1942.

11. PITT, M. S. Caring for the aged. *New Zealand Jewish chronicle.* December 1977; 15.

12. PITT, D. C. ed. *Workshop on social problems of Jewish communities. Dept of Sociology, University of Auckland, 1975. mimeo. Appendix 2.*
JAFFE, R. *Social problems of Jewish youth in New Zealand. op. cit.*

13. Figures of between 25-30% are given, cf. JAFFE, R. *Social problems of Jewish youth in New Zealand, op.cit.* but these figures are guestimates as there is no communal register and attempts recently to establish one in Auckland have met with great resistance.

14. Cf:

JAFFE, R. *Social problems of Jewish youth in New Zealand. op. cit.*

15. GOLDMAN, L. M. *History of the Jews in New Zealand. op. cit.* p. 135.Cf: BALKIND, V. *A contribution to the history of the Jews in New Zealand.* Thesis, M.A. Canterbury University, 1928.

16. GOLDMAN, I . M. *History of the Jews in New Zealand. op. cit.* p. 135

17. PITT, D. C. ed. *Workshop on social problems of Jewish communities. op. cit.* Cf: JAFFE, R. *Social problems of Jewish youth in New Zealand. op. cit.*

18. Elsewhere I have suggested that this boundary crossing is in fact an important means of establishing the perimeter of identity in a situation where there is extensive culture contact, social flux and social confusion. See: PITT, D. C. *Being Jewish and/or Gentile in New Zealand.* Paper presented to the Annual Meeting of the American Sociological Association, Montreal, 1974.

19. FISCHMAN, A. The religious crisis in Auckland. *New Zealand Jewish Chronicle 30*(17): 14, 1974.

20. GENNEP, Arnold Van *Les rites de passage.* Paris, Mouton, 1909.

21. ALFORD, M. and Jaffe, R. *Jewish social survey.* Ms. Habonim Youth Group, Auckland, 1973.

22. JAFFE, R. *Social problems of Jewish youth in New Zealand. op. cit.* p. 75.

23. The *Askhenazim* is the Biblical name of the people descended from the area of Asia Minor called Ish-kuza identified by the Talmud with the Roman Province of Asia. Later (in the 10th century) the German and North French Jews adopted a common ritual in contradistinction to the *Sephardi* Jews of South Europe. With the movement of the Jewish population to Germany and East Europe the Ashkenazim became associated with these areas, apart from the Chassidim who adopted the Sephardi ritual.

24. E.g. HERTZ, J. H. *The first pastoral tour to the Jewish communities of the British overseas dominions.* London, Milford, 1924.

25. See: OPPENHEIM, R. S. The Jews and arts in New Zealand. *New Zealand Jewish Chronicle.* June 1978.

26. Hillel and Shammai were two famous Rabbis who flourished in Jerusalem shortly before Christ's time and who founded two schools. Hillel and his followers (Bet Hillel) were ready in religious and political matters to seek milder, more lenient interpretations and peace whilst the Bet Shammai were rigid and fanatically patriotic. Although the Bet Shammai first held the ascendent, the Bet Hillel has gradually been accepted by the Rabbis as more of a solid base for *halacha.* The following story is told of the two. A man

came to Shammai and asked to be taught the Torah (Law) whilst standing on one leg. Shammai drove him away with a stick but Hillel said "It can be done. What is hateful to thyself do not to another. This is the whole Torah — the rest is commentary." It is also widely recognised now that the non-legalistic side of the Talmud (the heart not the brain) i.e. *haggada* is most significant. Cf. the comments of J. H. Hertz in the introduction to the Soncino Talmud, London, 1934.

27. SHENKEN, L. Communal leadership. *Alon Lanoar* 6 (55), 1976.
28. See no. 27.
29. E.g.
GOLDMAN, L. M. *History of the Jews in New Zealand. op. cit.*
30. Cf.
KNIGHT, G. A. F. *The Jews and New Zealand.* Christchurch, Presbyterian Bookroom, 1948.
The Depression particularly produced a number of anti-semitic tracts, e.g.
FIELD, A. *The truth about the slump: what the news never tells.* Nelson, the author, 1931.
31. See:
FRIEDMANN, G. *Fin du peuple juif.* Paris, Gallimard, 1971.
32. Cf.
FORSTER, A. and Epstein, B. *The new anti-Semitism.* New York, McGraw-Hill, 1974.

The Indian Contribution

RELIGIOUS MOVEMENTS OF INDIAN ORIGIN IN NEW ZEALAND
Kapil Tiwari

This essay summarizes a study the author has made of some major Indian religious movements in New Zealand. These movements are Ananda Marga, The Divine Light Mission, The Hare Krishna Movement (formerly known as the International Society for Krishna Consciousness), and Transcendental Meditation. The word 'major' is used here not in any evaluative sense; it simply seeks to convey the teachings and beliefs of the selected movements which have made their presence felt, either in terms of controversy or in terms of following and publicity. There are several other religious movements of Indian origin in New Zealand such as the Meher Baba Movement, Radha Soami Satsanga, Yoga, Theosophy, Tibetan Buddhism, and the movements dealing with the thoughts of Sai Baba, Krishnamurti, Ramana Maharshi, and many other gurus; but they could not be brought into the purview of this study because of the limitation of space, although the author is aware of their importance.

Having pointed out the reasons for their growth and the salient features of these major movements, we will turn to a closer examination of how the movements function for the individual in his social milieu, how they help the individual in overcoming his problems and to what extent they influence the religious and counter-cultural outlook of the New Zealand people. This brings us to the final point in respect of the purpose of the present essay: I personally believe that these controversial movements ought to be taken seriously, and I have approached this subject more as a sympathetic analyst than as a critic, a fact that owes much to my own cultural and religious conditionings.

Eastern Religions and the West

I shall endeavour to present reasons for the upsurge of interest in Eastern religions and religious movements and the extent to which they stand in opposition to the historically derived structure of the Western religious consciousness. There are two central problems to be discussed. The *first* problem is whether these movements are symptoms of cultural decadence in the West and therefore harbingers of a new cultural dimension paradigm; the *second* is whether (owing to the increased awareness of the significance of the exchange of ideas between the East and the West) the presence of these movements is considered desirable or even necessary for creating in the West a global religious consciousness.

The latter is certainly an important issue, and many Hindu and Western scholars have seriously recommended such a reconciliation. As regards the first question, there is a mixed opinion. Those who still entertain a strong optimistic belief in the glorious West sustain themselves with the pious hope that soon these Indian religious movements will go out of fashion like the Beatles and we shall again be able to devote our undivided attention to Christianity, which alone is capable of bringing salvation to the whole world. Peter Clecak visualizes this possibility when he asserts: 'At the very least, the recrudescence of Christianity testifies to its abundant resources — the continuing appeal of its evangelical message of salvation, the power of its experiential and charismatic dimension in the ministry of the Holy Spirit, and its continuing concern with social action.'[1]

By contrast, scholars like Robert N. Bellah, Theodore Roszak, J. Stillson Judah, Charles Reich, and to a lesser extent Philip Slater have argued that the revolt of the young in socio-religious matters is serious, important, and redemptive; while Herbert Marcuse and Norman Brown, Allen Ginsberg and Allan Watts, Timothy Leary and Paul Goodman have all drawn our attention to the modern crisis in the Western world. To a lesser or greater degree, all the above thinkers are critical of the Western world-view which is based on 'objective consciousness at the cost of the subjective, the symbolic and the organic'. Robert Bellah's piece will serve as a brief illustration of the main problems. He finds the major meaning of the 1960s in the 'erosion of the legitimacy of the Amercian way of life', 'utilitarian individualism', 'the principal secular faith', and 'biblical religion'.[2] Against this gloomy picture, Bellah sets the new consciousness, which in its high period during the 1960s pushed toward 'socialism in one direction, toward mysticism in the other'. Judah has found several good points in Indian religious movements and 'because of the mood of the people shifting, with different emotional, pyschological and social attitudes developing',[3] he accepts the certainty of their survival and influence on the Western mind.

Both of the above perspectives raise basic questions. Their arguments, I believe, strike deep into the nature and structure of religion and religious consciousness as viewed by two different religious traditions, namely the Semitic and the Indian. Bellah and Roszak and others suggest that people in the Western world have increasingly found established Christianity cold and unsatisfying because of its alliance with utilitarian individualism, a 'scientific' way of experiencing the world that involves a sharp separation between objective and subjective knowledge, an alienated detachment from other people, and the mechanization of knowledge and experience. Whether or not their findings are also based on the presence of Indian religious movements is a different matter, but these movements have certainly provided an alternative mode of religious experience, entirely new and predominantly opposed to the Western religious consciousness as viewed by sociologists, politicans, and theologians. Since this is an important issue and has much to say on the upsurge of interest in religious movements of Indian origin let us dwell on this topic a little further.

In the Western religious context, many sociologists have examined the relationship between theological beliefs, theological self-classification, and socio-political beliefs. The relationship has generally been explained along Max Weberian lines by arguing that conservative Protestant beliefs are largely responsible for the development of this-worldly ethics based on conservative socio-political beliefs and attitudes. As everyone knows, Weber was more interested in the religious forces which carried society forward and added considerably to the modification of cultural conditions. He was mainly concerned with the origin of modern rational culture, unique in the history of civilization. His work, *The Protestant Ethic and the Spirit of Capitalism* delved into the origin of the modern hardworking capitalistic world: the conclusion was that only Protestant worldly asceticism could have achieved such a miracle. He looked into the religious motivation for secularization, free enterprise in industry and commerce, the rapid growth in trade and production, social institutions, government, and above all politics. This religious motivation, according to Weber, assumed the form of *rationalization* by which society can be transformed.

The transformation which Weber envisaged has indeed taken place; but too much emphasis laid on the rationalization process resulted in a tragic principle of social change which eventually undermined the true dimensions of human life. Weber regarded bureaucracy and technology as the powerful institutional factors in the transformation of culture which in sociological terms involved a solidaristic view of society: saving of the society, social movements, and the evolution of society as against 'the saving of man, protecting his honour and dignity and adding to his spiritual consciousness'. His approach on the whole is critical of mystical experience, socialism, new self-awareness, or the new cultural consciousness. Religion became an ideology, and strangely enough he claimed to base his observation on his understanding of Christianity as a legitimizing factor for his ideological and pathological beliefs and doctrines.

Christianity thus turned into a philosophical form of progressivism or technically speaking 'secularized religion'. The secularization of the 'religious ideal' gave way to the lowering of standards of socio-political life. The synthesis of Biblical Christianity and modern progressivism effected the miracle of producing an amazingly lax morality. Weber, Hegel, and Marx tried to assure us that the secularized version of Christianity will naturally culminate in the establishment of the best and most harmonious universal social order. Structurally the various implications of modern revolution based on the efficacy of secularized Christianity resulted in the process of dislocation of social groups and created a series of cultural and structural discontinuities. There developed a strong dissociation between the scientific advance and the cultural and religious heritage. Man and God became mere intellectual belief, perhaps a 'hypothesis' but of no importance in the practical handling of human affairs. Put simply, the main current of the time did nothing about religion and man except to explain them away in preference to science, technology, society, and capitalism.

The glorification of machine and technology resulted in the dehumanization of many and above all eroded the very base of 'self-identity'. It has implications not only for the 'death of God' but also for the 'death of man'. J. Ellul[4] talks of madness and machine. Madness is the only escape: 'only madness is inaccessible to machine'. He further thinks that our civilization is unique in suppressing and constraining ecstasy. Before the rise of modern technological society, the form that society took expressed the psychology of the individual. This is no longer true. Modern men are trapped by a society they did not even will or invent. The invasion of 'technique' desacralizes the world in which man is called upon to live. For 'technique' nothing is sacred: there is no mystery, no taboo. Oswald Spengler,[5] like Ellul, denied the possibility of ecstasy in the advanced stages of technological civilization. His 'quiet engineer', 'the priest of the machine', is quiet, hard-working, self-controlled. Ellul and Spengler both agree that technology supports life but robs it of humanity.

In the light of the about analysis, it is perhaps no wonder that there has been such an astonishing following of sects, such an increase in their number, diversity, and popularity in the 1960s. One intriguing aspect of this phenomenon is the fascination which many Indian religious movements seem to have in New Zealand in an age of technological and scientific achievements unparalleled in the history of mankind. The psychologists explain their popularity in terms of man's reaction to the nuclear sword that hangs over us all, necessitating some kind of retreat into an esoteric world where salvation can be obtained by some magic formula or mystical device. The theologians, on the other hand, admit that the failure of the established religions to solve the fundamental issue of human life has emptied the churches and is driving people into these sects, which promise some relief in the modern times of storm and stress. Some sociologists argue that sects which guarantee salvation or ecstasy are almost a necessity when many find it increasingly difficult to cope with our complex reality. Others see the popularity of mystical cults as an escape from the materialistic rat-race of modern life. There are a few who find these movements completely absurd and think that people like them because they are antirational: 'credo quia impossible' (I believe because it is absurd).

The reasons for the shift of interest in these movements are complex, and to consider them fully would take us far afield. Most fundamentally, this shift is partly due to the symptom of a more general 'loss of faith' in the Western 'technism' accompanied by its inability to legitimize the cherished goal of 'self-identity', the breakdown of the romantic notion of life, increasing scepticism regarding the ultimate value of life, demythologizing of religion, cynicism, and ideological defeat. This was felt more strongly among men and women who came in contact with other religions and life-styles. One aspect of the new movements must therefore be seen as a result of people's contact with the concepts and issues of Oriental wisdom. Kenneth Leech remarks: 'There has been a revival of Eastern spiritual methods in the early years of the century when such movements as Vedanta (supported by Aldous Huxley, Gerald Heard and Christopher Isherwood), theosophy, anthroposophy, and the systems of Gurdjieff and Ouspensky became popular. Rudolf Steiner was writing about the mystical quest for self-transcendence.'[6] In contrast to the interests of the modern philosophers of the West, Oriental wisdom has always been concerned with transformation or a radical change of man's nature and therewith a renovation of his understanding about himself and the world. Its problem is directly a transmutation of the soul, realization of profound inner awareness, not through praise and submission to God, but through knowledge, through self-effort. This we recognize as a primarily non-theistic, humanitarian, and romantic version of Oriental wisdom. But in New Zealand, it must be noted, this response to Eastern wisdom has come after the devaluation of Christianity. To quote H. Zimmer:

> The Christian, as Nietzsche says, is one who behaves like everybody else. Our professions of faith have no longer any discernible bearing either on our public conduct or on our private state of hope. The sacraments do not work on many of us their spiritual transformation; we are bereft and at a loss where to turn. Meanwhile, our academic secular philosophers are concerned rather with information than with that redemptive transformation which our souls require. And this is the reason why a glance at the face of India may assist us to discover and recover something of ourselves.[7]

It should be added here that the redemptive transformation which Zimmer is pointing out has been emphasized by all Indian religious movements. Since many followers believe in the mystical and romantic quest for self-awareness with which many were already familiar by the help of psychedelic drugs, some scholars have suggested that the initial interest in Eastern religious movements grew out of the early drug culture in the arousal of spontaneous expansion of consciousness. But the closer examination suggested incompatability between the drug-induced experience and the unified experience which Indian religious thinkers were talking about. It was at this point that Eastern religious movements began to hit the western world and initiated a new phase in this direction. Consequently, it was thought that Eastern religious tradition had more to offer than Christianity.

Another factor responsible for their popularity in New Zealand is that these movements do not exhibit, at least not directly, any grievances against the spirit of the Semitic religions. They simply aim to experience religion amid the practical concerns of life, and for this purpose they emphasize one's own experimentation, which typically enough has very little to do with the prescriptions of traditional religionists, mystagogues, and theologians. It is true, however, that they have high reverence for gurus, but it must be remembered that gurus are an exemplary model rather than an ethical one. What I want to suggest is that gurus cannot guarantee peace or salvation; they can only tell the path for new forms of subjective interiority which they have realized for themselves. Such an experience has nothing to do with science and technology; they can neither create it nor take it away. The vast changes that have been brought into lives are appreciated as such, but they have not struck at the wisdom foundations which the Hindu or Buddhist is prone to regard as his religion. In other words, the growth of science and technology along with its material implications belong to the lower level of truth and as such it has nothing to do with religious experience, either positively or negatively. Secondly, the vision of religious consciousness which they claim to have preserved as unbroken tradition does not increase or diminish with the 'loss of faith' in supernaturalism, largely because it does not have any supernatural direction. Since all these movements concentrate on the individual's peace and tranquillity, the notion of 'mission' or 'making history' as an act of sanctification seems quite extraneous to them although some might see a necessity for it, particularly because of their popularity in Western culture. In fact, all these movements derive a form of contemplation of the external within man from the ancient Hindu tradition in order to escape from the anxiety-laden world.

Ananda Marga

From this point onwards we will take up some of the Indian religious movements for a closer examination of their salient features in the light of the above discussion. First let us have a religious sect which has aroused a considerable amount of controversy in New Zealand. Ananda Marga, founded in India by Prabhat Ranjan Sarkar on 9 January 1955, attracted an enthusiastic following in New Zealand in 1973. The *Ananda Marga Pracaraka Samgha Inc.* made application for registration as an incorporated society in February 1974 on the basis of consent obtained from members at a general meeting of the society on 21 October 1973. At this stage the group was small - the list of active participants for 1974-75 quoted in the articles of incorporation totalled thirty three, which consisted of a spiritual director, namely Acarya Sunitananda Avadhuta, a President, Vice-President, Secretary, Treasurer, Publications Officer, Publicity Officer, Belief and Welfare Officer, and twenty-five members. The original headquarters of the group was a flat in Brooklyn, Wellington, but members were scattered all over New Zealand - in Auckland, Palmerston North, Porirua, and Invercargill.

Ananda Marga (The Path of Bliss) is, it claims, a non-political movement hoping to realize its ideals through spiritual revolution under the leadership of its founder, Mr Sarkar, affectionately known as Baba Anandamurti. Described in the literature as 'an ideology with which society itself can be constructively changed', it concentrates on the quest for social justice for all and more importantly the transformation of character among the followers. These two elements of its philosophy are embodied in its socio-economic theory, 'PROUT' (Progressive Utilization Theory), sometimes called 'spiritual socialism'. Its tenets are:

1. No individual should be allowed to accumulate any physical wealth without the clear permission of the collective body.
2. There should be maximum utilization and rational distribution of all mundane, supra-mundane, and spiritual potentialities of the universe.
3. There should be maximum utilization of all physical, metaphysical, and spiritual potentialities of the unit and collective body.
4. There should be a proper adjustment amongst these physical, metaphysical, mundane, and supra-mundane physical and spiritual potentialities.
5. The method of utilization should vary in accordance with time, place, and person, and is to be of a progressive nature.

Progressive utilization theory advocates 'Moral Government': the government by the most spiritual persons. It calls for the necessity of a World Government. Apart from the explicit formulation of universal social organization the philosophy of Ananda Marga demands a strict moral and spiritual discipline on the part of its followers. The ideals such as 'The Chosen Goal' *(Ishta)* and 'Moral Means' *(Adarsha)* have been consistently emphasized. The Ananda Marga ethical code reads as follows:

> One is to observe non-compromising strickness and faith regarding the sanctity of *Ishta* the chosen ideal. *Ishta* is the goal towards which we are moving the personalized aspect of the Absolute best suited to us, i.e. *Baba, Paramapurush* (God).

> This goal must never be lost sight of or sacrificed for any reason since our *Ishta* is the sacred thing to us. Ananda Margis should defend their chosen ideal against any sort of attack and must not attack any one else's *Ishta*[8]

Section eleven of the same ethical code states:

> 'one is to observe non-compromising strictness and faith regarding the sanctity of *Adarsha*. . . We practice meditation along with service to humanity. This ideology and our spritual practices have come from an intelligence far behond our own and comprise the means by which we hope to attain our goal in life; therefore to the best of our ability, we should not alter or compromise these things, nor allow others to ridicule them...'[19]

It should be noted that the attitude enjoined here is one of commitment, an unbending rule fostering a firmness of intent (non-compromising strictness), a rigidity of mind, and dedication to the spiritual welfare of society. Such an emphasis on commitment, together with Ananda Marga's implied belief in the corrupt state of the world would provide a greater impetus to its followers to have recourse to ideological activism. This call for spiritual direction of society entails major socio-political changes. Thus an article in the New Zealand newsheet *AEON* suggests the following desirable developments for New Zealand's future: a regeneration of leadership, a truly liberal society, a spiritual socio-economics, global involvement, and self-sufficiency in energy use. When implemented it is believed that these measures would lead to the realization of New Zealand's future destiny: a peace or real spirituality coupled with creative co-operative endeavour.

The movement launches a protest by the young of the affluent middle class against the society based on the values of the modern secular world-view. It represents a tendency of the spirit for a more human way which rejects materialism and the competitive ethic of modern social institutions and politics. It is a cultural revolt calling for re-assessment of self, of one's relation with others, of man's relationship to his natural environment, and his responsibility to future generations.

The following salient features of new consciousness as discussed by Theodore Roszak[11] can be traced in the philosophy of Ananda Marga:

1. *Potentiality:* a new idea of the essence of man as potentiality, spiritual enhancement of a central need in man to evolve beyond the restrictions of time, matter, and morality;
2. *Upaya:* proven techniques for awakening and controlling visionary energy that features in the Vedic and Tantric traditions of India;
3. *Transpersonal Subjectivity:* the experiencing of mental images not as essentially unreal but constituting another reality which is fundamentally mind-like;
4. *University:* rejection of the possibility of exclusive claims to truth, an acceptance of the value of all spiritual vehicles as variations on a theme, a theme that exists only as immediate, visionary insight and is not directly expressible;
5. *Wholeness:* rejection of the claim of some lesser portion of human nature to be in itself the whole;
6. *Organism:* a new appreciation of the body as an instrument of meditation and transcendence;
7. *Illumination of the Commonplace:* experience of the sacred in, or through the common stuff or substance of life, a seeing through the illusion of ordinariness to the empowered presence of things in the everyday life, a vision that will be a 'new wealth' superseding conventional wealth (merchandise, material plenty, cash hoards, and capital);
8. *Satsang:* a new social form, composed of communities where work, friendship, family, and the transcendent impulse merge in a fellowship of

souls striving for mutual enlightment; voluntary societies of seekers that take the place of the institutions of family, neighbourhood, occupational peer group, trade union, etc.

The role of Ananda Marga is seen by the followers as a unificatory point of religious insight and practice *and* social reform. It attempts to penetrate into a deeper and more meaningful level of life than that offered in the spiritual wasteland of contemporary consumerism. The essential significance of the sect in New Zealand does not lie in its political aspect but in the 'new transcendentalism'. Some of the salient features of this sect which confirm the above spirit of transcendentalism can be clearly seen among these followers. All have in common the rejection of Western/materialism as giving a satisfactory answer to life. For these people, 'the Path of Bliss' (Ananda Marga) provides a spiritual way of life, thereby answering a process of identity destruction and reconstruction. Members are given a new name in Sanskrit, a new life-style, and a new interpretation of reality. The goal is a complete assimilation of one's identity as a timeless, spaceless, qualityless self in a state of oneness with the cosmic self or consciousness and de-identification with the physical body and the individual personality. Members regard their doctrines as a 'uniquely legitimate avenue of salvation'. They view themselves as chosen spiritual messengers for mankind. Self-purification is considered to be very important by Ananda Margis. And finally, in this movement, the level of spiritual attainment (called variously 'higher', 'deeper', or 'inner' realization) subordinates intellect or reason to intuition, which alone can guarantee final salvation. A member's worthiness is continuously assessed in the group. The aid of such a spiritual conviction is sought in order to live in the ideal sphere of existence not by abnegating the world, society, or human relationships, but by harmoniously establishing them in the structure of Reality which is Brahma (Consciousness). The nature of man is one with Brahma. Liberation consists in stripping away from the mind the false idea of oneself as ego, mind, intellect, or separate personality. Margis believe that the *Dharma* of man, i.e. this essential nature is full of bliss. It can be accomplished by *sadhana*: 'Just as all rivers originally come from and eventually return to the sea, the purpose or goal of human life is to return to our source, or in other words, to realise our higher nature. The human being in order to fulfil his or her potential must seek the unity amidst diversity and look inward to realise Brahma as one's own divine self.'

For such a realization, the role of the *Guru* and the *acarya* is essential. Anandamurti or 'Baba' is the only *Guru* of Ananda Marga. Other *acaryas* while teaching are regarded as vessels of Anandamurti. 'The *acarya* becomes a channel for Baba's knowledge to flow through, and while it may be the *acarya* who physically initiates a person, it is actually Baba using the *acarya* to give instruction'. The Margis have their initiation ceremony in which a *mantra* is given to the follower by the *acarya*. Initiation is regarded as the first ladder to the terrace of liberation. The fundamental purpose of *mantra* in Ananda Marga is to generate a feeling of identification with the goal of this movement and total commitment to it. Their *mantra-yoga,* according to Margis, is not black magic but a potent instrument for creating spiritual vibration in the followers, which arouses an intense urge for liberation. Meditation accomplishes this urge. The purpose of meditation is to shift the focus of the mind from the external world of the senses to the inner realm and more specifically to the goal of the realization of Infinite Self (Brahma). It is believed that through repetition of one's *mantra* during meditation, accompanied by de-involvement with external sense objects, the individual gradually realizes the supreme consciousness which is also called *Sachidananda.* Anandamurti has himself instructed:

> The man who performs *sadhana* twice a day regularly, the thought of *Parama Purusha* will certainly arise in his mind and at the time of death, his liberation is a sure guarantee. Therefore every Ananda Margi will have to perform *sadhana* twice a day invariably. Verily is this the command of the Lord. Without *Yama* and *Niyama, Sadhana* is an impossibility. Hence the Lord's command is also to follow *Yama* and *Niyama.* Disobedience to this command is nothing but to throw oneself into the torture of animal life for millions of years. That no one should undergo torments such as these, that he might be enabled to enforce the eternal blessedness under the loving shelter of the Lord, it is the bounden duty of every Ananda Margi to endeavour to bring to the path of bliss. Verily is this a part and parcel of *sadhana* to lead others along the path of righteousness.

Ananda Marga also emphasizes group-culture and co-operation. It represents a social attitude in order to find spiritual and devotional exaltation in the company of others. Margis are encouraged to take part in *kirtan* (chanting) as many times as possible, for during its performance, the mind becomes completely submerged in the supreme consciousness; feelings of separateness and ego are dissolved and replaced simultaneously with feelings of intense happiness and joy. It also creates an atmosphere of sharing a common ideal which generates a sense of sacred group identity. The chant employed during *kirtan* is *Baba Nama Kevalam* (only the name of the supreme father); Baba here refers to the omnipresent supreme consciousness. Occasionally *kirtan* turns into the *tandava*, which is described in the Marga literature as an intense spiritual dance which originated in India thousands of years ago and which is associated with the dance of Shiva. This dance is a symbolic representation of the struggle between the power of life and the power of ignorance, aiming at the eradication of the latter. It is also a sign of conquest over destructive force as mythologically the Lord Shiva exhibited his destructive nature through the *tandava* in order to eliminate the evil forces.

In the preceding sections, we have sought to focus some features of Ananda Marga which appear significant to us in the New Zealand context. Ananda Marga is a religio-social movement. It is evident that this movement has some 'dynamic' implications and earnestly strives to bring vital changes in the present structure of society embracing public institutions as well as individual aspirations. Its eschatalogical theme consists of a movement from darkness into light; a revolt against evil, wickedness, corruption, and depravity. Its attempt to treat the philosophical aspect of Brahma as a significant Indian trend to be applied to the existing social order is quite understandable. Indian thinkers like Tagore, Vivekananda, Gandhi, and Aurobindo have clearly linked Hindu religious teachings to the transformation of man's social life. Whilst stressing the urgent need for a reformation in society, Ananda Margis, it appears to us, become involved in socio-political and economic modernisation in rather a revolutionary and abrupt fashion. These orientations stemming directly from the Marga philosophy have raised suspicion about their motives both in New Zealand and Indian contexts. Beginning with the adverse publicity over the 1975 election period in New Zealand, support for Ananda Marga declined and has never revived here. Its functions, to my mind, might more appropriately be seen not as a device to maintain the poise of the political scene but as an effort to ease the individual passing through a crisis situation and to contribute to the survival of the society by reinforcing the sense of spiritual identity.

The Hare Krishna Movement

The Hare Krishna movement is a monotheistic and devotional type of religious sect. The founder of this movement was A.C. Bhaktivedanta Swami Prabhupada, or Swami Prabhupada as he is affectionately called by his devotees. He was born in Calcutta in 1896 with the original name Abhay Charan De. After completing his graduation from the University of Calcutta with majors in Philosophy, English, and Economics he worked in a chemical firm, from which he retired in 1954. During those years of service he met several spiritual leaders and was greatly influenced by the teaching of his spiritual master, Bhakti

Siddhanta. It is believed that his teacher ordered him to disseminate the teachings of Krishna consciousness not only in India but to the Western world as well. In 1947 the Gaudiya Vaishnav Society assigned him a spiritual name, Bhaktivedanta. Five years after his retirement he took the yellow cloak of the *sannyasi* (mendicant) and dedicated himself to the cause of the spread of Krishna consciousness to the western world.

The movement was founded in the United States in 1966 and has a recent origin in New Zealand. When I came here in 1973 it was à usual occurence in Wellington's Willis Street and Lambton Quay to see several devotees chanting, dancing, and selling pamphlets; the movement was even more widely spread in Auckland and Christchurch. The Journal of Krishna Consciousness, *Back to Godhead,* was available on the streets of many cities to present the authorized, original, and transcendental spiritual science of God-realization. Devotees take pleasure in explaining the bliss of Krishna consciousness and urge people to go back to the original bliss of God-realization: materialism, however glorified it may be, cannot provide happiness: happiness has its root in divine love of which Krishna is the perfect embodiment. The state of Krishna consciousness is described as the normal ecstatic state which lies hidden in human consciousness. The nature of every individual in its original form is in closer affinity with Krishna consciousness, but because of the transmigration of soul to which every individual is subjected, this affinity seems to have been lost. It is within the power and reach of every individual to restore the sense of lost identity. The fundamental discipline prescribed by this movement is the chanting of the great Hare Krishna Mantra which is described as the greatest of all mantras. It consists of sixteen words and runs as follows:

Hare Krishna, Hare Krishna, Krishna, Krishna, Hare, Hare,
Hare Rama, Hare Rama, Rama, Rama, Hare, Hare.

The Krishna conscious devotees claim that this combination of syllables is scientifically formulated to bring about a state of spiritual joy. The *mantra,* according to them, has a purifying significance and if properly chanted with devotional concentration on Krishna, it can purify the mind and senses. They further assert that spiritual happiness can only dawn upon the individual whose mind and senses are completely purified. The work of propagating the great *mantra* is of central significance to these followers. However, the message of this movement is not simply personal happiness but universal peace and solidatrity.

Religion, according to Prabhupada, is not merely a matter of personal convenience. He is a traditionalist and a critic of Western civilization (*not* of Western people), which he sees as suffering a tremendous loss of self-identity accompanied by the desperate need for self-aggrandizement. It is strange to find that despite the conservative and rigorous doctrinal formulations of this movement it has caught on most quickly among young people (members number around four hundred in New Zealand). The reason for the appeal of this movement is the staunch dedication of the founder to meet the needs of the people who are disenchanted with material life.

The life style of the Krishna people is very rigorous in its discipline. Religious activity begins soon after 4 a.m. and continues throughout the whole day and evening. They reject the heterodox religions of India, namely Jainism and Buddhism on the ground that they are antagonistic to the Vedas (*shruti*), which extol Vishnu, of whom Krishna is an incarnation. They also try to identify and relocate the Indian religious tradition in terms of *bhakti* (devotion) to Vishnu in the form of Krishna and Rama in Brahmanical Hinduism. They are very much in favour of Sanskritization of Hindu tradition rather than Westernization of it. The urge for Sanskritizing the movement has directly come from their strict adherence to Hindu scholarship of which Chaitanya, to whom the movement owes its strength and vitality, was the greatest scholar and saint of the fifteenth century. These Sanskritization elements are quite evident in their disciplines and life-styles. The Hare Krishna devotees are required to observe the following disciplines in all details.

1. There are severe restrictions against gambling or any frivolous sports. Any conversation which is not directly or indirectly related to Krishna is considered to be a waste of time. The daily activity of these followers, in addition to chanting and worship, includes the reading of the *Bhagavad Gita*, translated by Prabhupada himself. They narrate and fondly discuss the sacred and mythical stories of Krishna with Gopis in the garden of Vrindavana. The most authoritative literature available on Krishna is prepared by the founder himself.

2. Followers of this movement are strongly against the use of all forms of intoxicants, such as acohol, drugs, tobacco, tea, and coffee. Some of them undoubtedly have previous drug experience but after joining this movement their attitude is completely changed. In their view, our natural state of consciousness is one of ecstasy and bliss. Any attempt on the part of the follower to induce a chemical alteration of consciousness by means of drugs is not only unneccessary but also superficial.

3. The Krishna people, like the Margis of New Zealand, have strict dietary rules forbidding the use of meat, fish, and eggs. They take milk, cheese, honey, and vegetables. Their breakfast consists of fruits and cereals. Lunch is preceded by an offering to Krishna consisting of *puri* (Indian bread fried in clarified butter, *ghi*), *sabji* (prepared mostly with pumpkin and potatoes), and sweets. Because it is offered to Krishna, the cook must be physically and mentally pure before entering the kitchen. According to them the vegetarian meals are light and they calm down the various emotions like anger, sensuality, and hatred, and help the individual in inculcating the virtues of peace, love, contentment, and spiritual alertness. They do not believe in fasting except occasionally such as on the anniversary of the birthdate of Krishna, *Janmashtami.*

4. These devotees have a strong injunction against illicit sex. Even within marriage there is a demand for austerity and minimisation of sexual gratification. The use of contraceptives is strongly prohibited. Swami Prabhupada himself considers sex as an impediment to spiritual growth: 'This does not mean completely forget sex life.. It is not forbidden. If you can forget it good . . . to become a great soul is to completely forget about sex'. One follower in the Krishna temple in Auckland suggested that sexual passion can be spiritually transformed, channelled into love for Krishna. A survey I undertook reveals that 60% of the devotees prefer celibacy, while 20% approve of sex within marriage, and the remaining 20% regard sexual life as unsatisfying in comparison with their intense experience of the love of Krishna. It is important to note here that this type of sexual attitude of the devotees is in conformity with the Vaishnava view of life which strongly condemns lustful life.

5. The Krishna people exhibit a peculiar attitude towards employment. The total number of full-time employed followers in New Zealand is not large. When asked 'to what extent do you think that your job and the work that you do for your employers determine your happiness?' 60% of the devotees deleted the word 'employer' and inserted 'Krishna', the great King and employer. Others found the source of their happiness not in employment but in their dedication to Krishna.

6. All of these followers believe in life after death. The love that exists for Krishna requires more than one life and since their desire is genuine, it is bound to be fulfilled.

7. Their attitude towards themselves, friends, and relatives is of trust and affectionate concern. Most of the devotees have a communal lifestyle inside the temple which they describe as 'spiritual communism'.

8. The devotees see great significance in the structure of common discipline prescribed by the movement. One of them suggested that all acts that are incapable of being performed with detachment and dedication to Krishna are selfish.

9. In accord with their attitudes to possession, their way of life and manner of dress have a great simplicity. Men generally shave their heads but possess a slender tuft of hair (*shikha*) which symbolizes their surrender and dedication to the spiritual teacher. They also decorate their forehead with a wet mixture of clay, called *tilaka,* which they also paint on their faces and other body areas.

10. The position of women in this society may not appeal to 'liberated' women Swami Prabhupada says that all women except one's wife should be treated in the same respectful way as one's mother, and women need protection by men at all times.

11. In the temple it is customary for visitors as well as devotees to sit on the floor and eat the food. Conversation is limited while eating the food (prasadam)

The Krishna temple in Auckland exhibits several features of religious worship performed exactly as in India. Temple priests perform daily worship; they offer worship, water, and flowers to the image of Krishna. Krishna is awakened in the morning with a ceremonial performance such as the blowing of conches and chanting. The actual structure of the temple follows almost all the dominant features of Hindu temples. There are four parts of the temple: the porch, a walkway around the outside of the temple, an inner room called the womb of the temple, and a vertical spire that dominates the whole structure. The porch is the place where religious instruction takes place. The walkway is meant to help the devotees to see the god displayed on the outer walls of the temple. The inner sanctum contains the central image. This is the place where the devotees worship and commune with Krishna. The structure of *Puja* (worship) is not very rigid and can express itself in a variety of ways. Another notable feature in this connection, particularly in New Zealand is that any one can approach the god, whereas this is not the case in more orthodox Indian temples or in the structure of Vedic sacrifice.

Followers of the Hare Krishna movement, in brief, can be regarded as a religious group of people dedicated to a search and propagation of the classical Indian religious goal of life in a Western society. We have no reasons to disbelieve ancient Vedic times looks to be quite fascinating. The Krishna people are scornful of the new values but they are not scornful of conservative views. I do not imply by any means that conservatism is bad; it becomes bad only when it is accepted dogmatically without any appraisal. I have serious doubts in my mind whether this group takes this point seriously. It seems to me that the movement's strength lies more in challenging the structure of Western society rather than providing a solution along Indian lines.

The Divine Light Mission

The Divine Light Mission was founded by Guru Maharaj Ji and first brought to the United States in 1971. His followers strongly believe him to be an *avatar* (an incarnation of God) and an enlightened man. He appears to have manifested some divine glamours and supernatural powers, as a result of which he has achieved immense popularity in America and other parts of the world.

Like most of the movements in New Zealand, this mission also shares the belief that the modern technocratic society is no place for the cultivation of spiritual values. Human life in the modern structure of society has abnormal and unhappy suicidal tendencies. The happy normal condition comes from eternity which in this respect is equivalent to divine mission. Guru Maharaj Ji believes that eternal spiritual reality is not external to man; it is part and parcel of his life. God Himself is our home: the home from which man comes and to which he will return. The first and last state of the human being is divine light and if it is true, man can commune with God here and now. The blissful state that the mission looks back to and longingly looks forward to is a condition in which a man is not separate from the rest of mankind nor from the spiritual reality. A temporary alienation is the price of personality which modern man is paying for most heavily; re-absorption in the supernatural realm of spiritual life is the sequel to the sloughing off of the separate personality that is the feature of life on earth.

The Divine Light Mission believes that the Divine Light is a state in which the incompatability between the physical life and spiritual life can be harmoniously resolved. It does not imply the extinction of life or of consciousness but the further enrichment of blissful life and blissful consciousness. Guru Maharaj Ji himself is regarded by his followers as having reached this point in his enlightenment but then to have retained his incarnate personality voluntarily in order to teach the people the way of release from alienation which he had discovered for himself by his intuitive knowledge.

Guru Maharaj Ji like another Hindu Messiah, Meher Baba, claims to be an ultimate revealer of the main strand of the universal religion, according to which one must have complete love of God by surrendering oneself to him through the perfect Master. All the world religions describe the descent of such a teacher who is a living embodiment of great divine wisdom. Many people seem to be thoroughly impressed by the style of his teaching in which he assures his followers a tremendous reward accruing from his teachings. Thus he asserts: 'It is very simple knowledge. It will give you complete peace of mind, it will give you infinite bliss. Do not complain, later on, that you were never told about this knowledge. Again and again I do nothing but to tell you all to take this knowledge.'[12] On another occasion, he states: 'And I must tell you, that you don't meditate for me, you meditate for yourselves. You should get high. You need to do this meditation because you want to get high. Not me. I am high, I am in the infinite state. You must get high, you must get to this point where you can also go to the infinite state. I have given you this knowledge, therefore your duty is to meditate on it.'[13]

It is clear from this that Guru Maharaj Ji wants to strengthen the belief among his followers that divine knowledge is impossible without a perfect leader. He repeatedly compares his brilliance with the essence of the gospel of Jesus Christ. Unlike other religious movements of Indian origin, the mission stresses that one can remain in a state of knowledge only if one pledges an absolute obedience to Guru Maharaj Ji. His teachings consist of four fundamental meditative techniques as a means to reveal knowledge. These technqiues are (1) a longing for the moment to feel a vibration, (2) perception and realization of a bright light, (3) smelling of nectar, (4) hearing a divine sound. The most important is the first of the four, the vibration (also known as the word of God) which activates and sustains the universe. He repeatedly asserts that this vibration is not outside us but within us, although we are unconscious of it.

The central message of the Divine Light Mission can be briefly summarized as devotional and montheistic. There are approximately two hundred followers of the mission all over New Zealand. Its main teaching was summarized by one of its followers thus:

So anyway, from this you understand that Divine Light Mission is not a religion, though it may look like one. It is not based on beliefs of any kind ultimately, but on the direct experience of God revealed within us . . . When we have experienced that experience ourselves it becomes manifestly clear that this is so, we can really recognize it. However the real meaning of all these words will only sink into an open mind, and in this age of darkness, open minds are less than common. The problem is that we all think we know already.[14]

Transcendental Meditation

Transcendental Meditation was introduced into New Zealand by Maharishi Mahesh Yogi in 1962. At that time many people were initiated into the technique, but not until 1970 did the first New Zealand teacher, Andrew Davey, upon his return from his six months teachers' training course in India, set up the International Meditation society in New Zealand. Since then the society has trained about fifteen thousand people. There are now more than ten branches of the society in this country having fifty teachers. It is claimed that all of them have had personal contact with Mahesh Yogi, the founder of the society.

In order to keep T.M. authentic, it has been thought necessary to retain its link with the Vedic tradition. The fundamental teaching of the Vedas is to live a life of tranquillity and peace which can be directly realized by entering into the deepest level of consciousness. In the East, meditation that elicits the relaxation response is developed much earlier than elsewhere; it has served as a major element in religion as well as in everyday life. Modern man has made tremendous progress in the physical and scientific world, but the limitation of this advancement lies in the fact that he finds himself completely exhausted. The Maharishi attempts to take man back to the classical principle of self-realization and self-knowledge by meditation.

T.M. is defined as 'a natural technique which allows the conscious mind to experience systematically finer states of thought until it arrives at the finest state of thought and transcends it, arriving at the source of thought, the state of pure awareness, the field of pure intelligence'. According to its followers, T.M. is neither a religion nor a philosophy but a scientific method for the expansion of awareness. They seem suspicious of religion, as being mixed up with dogmatism and external requirements. For many followers, religion absorbed with lofty notions is not applied to practical aspects of life. But on a closer analysis, T.M. sides more with Indian religion and philosophical psychology than with Western religion.

It is claimed that meditation relieves stress through deep relaxation which provides the meditator with boundless energy to enable him to realize his full potential. Changes in the physiology during T.M. have been analysed and reported: they consist of a fall in respiratory rate and volume, slowing of the heart beat, muscular relaxation, an increase in the intelligence growth rate, a decrease in blood pressure, a decrease in drug-reliance including cigarettes and alcohol, and more effective use of one's energy. The Maharishi's main attempt was to verify the effect of ancient wisdom in modern scientific terms.

Like Aldous Huxley, William James, and Alan Watts etc., the Maharishi and his followers determine the effect of meditation technique in terms of the specialist knowledge of psychology of consciousness. T.M. suggests that there is a deeper level of consciousness after the realization of which man experiences peace and happiness. He has divided consciousness into various levels along with the trends of the Upanishadic thinking. These levels are waking state, dreaming state, dreamless state, and the highest blissful state. Of these four states, only the first two are well known to us. The purpose of T.M. is to make us aware of the significance of the last two particularly the fourth one. One of the followers remarked on the significance of the realization of the highest level of consciousness thus: 'In this respect the gentle rise to cosmic consciousness is like the gentle change from night to day. As the dawn breaks the intensity of the light increases ten millionfold but the change is so smooth and gradual that we hardly notice it. All we notice is that our vision is becoming gradually clear. Similarly with the dawning of the cosmic consciousness, the gradual brightening of awareness is not itself noticed'.

Conclusion

All these religious movements of Indian origin have one thing in common. Having once plunged into the world of counterculture, they experiment into new paths in search of an alternative style of life with new meaning. Ananda Marga teaches the path of bliss in order to transform the individual and social life. The Hare Krishna movement rejects the culture of the establishment and its forms of religion by providing an authority to give them another alternative. The Divine Light Mission, being a prophetic religion, looks into the ills of life and provides a solution based on Oriental wisdom. And Transcendental Meditation plunges deep into the psychological aspect of human life and establishes the authenticity of ancient meditation technique to elicit the relaxtion response in the individual life. Through some kind of religious truth that each might share with others, they desire to form a basis for a world view that would be compatible with the complexity and needs of our time. Their search for meaning in life has three common factors:

1. They try to give meaning to life when all other authorities seem to have failed.
2. They try to validate and sacralize their perspectives by means of personal experience in order to give an absolute authenticity to their *Weltanschauung.*
3. They try to form their own group, members of which can share something in common and rediscover the sense of identity lost in the secular world. Their devotees all exhibit a different consciousness from that of their parents and

other older adults, with consequent alienation from the culture and so often from their parents too.

Notes:
1. CLECAK, P. The survivors of the counterculture (review of C.Y. Glock and R. N. Bellah, eds. *The new religious consciousness* Washington D.C.) *The Chronicle of higher education,* October 25 1976, p. 16.
2. For details see C.Y. Glock and R. N. Bellah, eds *The new religious consciousness.* Berkeley, University of California Press, 1976. p. 391.
3. JUDAH, J. S. *Hare Krishna and the counterculture.* New York, Wiley, 1974, p. 12.
4. ELLUL, J. *The technological Society.* Translated by J. Wilkinson. London, Jonathan Cape, 1965, p. 404.
5. SPENGLER, O. *The decline of the West.* Translated by C. F. Atkinson. London, Allen & Unwin, 1926, p. 505.
6. LEECH, K. *Youthquake; the growth of a counter-culture through two decades.* London, Sheldon Press, 1973, p. 50.
7. ZIMMER, H. R. *Philosophies of India.* J. Campbell, ed. Princeton, Bollinger Press, 1955, p. 13-14.
8. Quoted from:
TIWARI, K. Major Indian religious movements in New Zealand. Unpublished MS, Wellington, Victoria University, 1976.
9. Ibid.
10. Ibid.
11. Ibid.
Cited from:
ROSZAK, T. *The making of a counter-culture.* N.Y., Doubleday, 1969.
12. Ibid.
13. Ibid.
14. Ibid.

The Pluralist Tendency

PLURALISM AND THE FUTURE OF RELIGION IN NEW ZEALAND
Lloyd Geering

What is the future of religion in New Zealand? There are two ways in which we can set about attempting to answer this question. The first is to confine our attention to New Zealand shores, try to analyse the present religious situation here, look into the immediate past, extrapolate from it the most dominant trends and then project them into the future. Such a procedure is of some real value for the short term even though it becomes increasingly invalid the further we look ahead. The second way is to take a bird's eye view of the long-term religious trends throughout the whole world and see what light it can throw on the New Zealand situation, on the grounds that we live increasingly in a global village, which fact makes it impossible to isolate the religious scene in New Zealand from what is happening elsewhere. Let us briefly attempt both methods in turn.

Fortunately for our purpose, New Zealand, unlike many other countries, has been asking for the religious affiliation of its citizens at every five-yearly Census. Some very clear trends have been showing up over the last fifty years. Since the time of European settlement there have been four major Christian communities in New Zealand; in 1926 they could together claim the allegiance of 86.2% of the population but fifty years later this had decreased by one-fifth. The Anglican proportion of the total population has been declining steadily, from 40.9% in 1926 to 29.2% in 1976. Similarly the Presbyterian component has dropped from 23.5% to 18.1% and the Methodist from 8.9% to 5.5%. The Roman Catholic trend has been somewhat different, increasing from 12.9% of the population in

1926 to 15.9% in 1966, but since that time it also has joined the drift downwards.

The internal evidence from these four major denominations suggests that, by the criterion of regular participation in acts of worship and other church activities, the decline in allegiance has been even greater than the figures show. The Census figures include all who have even the slightest inclination to claim a denominational label. In a period of declining interest in any particular group this understandably leads to a higher proportion of purely nominal adherents among the Census totals. This may be illustrated from the Presbyterian Church of New Zealand, which has collected annually its own statistics of regular church-goers. We have just noted above that between 1926 and 1976 Census Presbyterians dropped from 23.5% to 18.1% of the total population. During the same period the number of regular Presbyterian church-goers declined from 4.76% to 2.26% of the population. This means that in relation to the population the active participation of New Zealanders in Presbyterian worship has declined to less than half of what it was fifty years ago. Further, the decline has been most dramatic since 1961, for in 1956 a peak was reached in which Presbyterian Church attenders (105,047) represented 4.83% of the population.

With the smaller religious bodies the story has been noticeably different. The Baptist component of the total population has remained almost stationary at 1.6% and the Brethren at 0.9%. The Ratana allegiance has grown from 0.8% to 1.1% and the Mormon from 0.3% to 1.2%. In absolute figures, of course, the growth of the latter is quite striking, having expanded from 4,060 adherents in 1926 to 33,290 in 1976. In the case of small but expanding religious bodies the point made in the last paragraph applies in reverse. The nominal component is relatively small and the Census figure therefore is much nearer to the total number of active participants than is the case with the larger denominations. This means that the contrast between the larger and the smaller religious groups with regard to growth trends and effective vitality is even greater than the Census figures indicate.

Among the still smaller religious groups there is a distinct decline shown by those which are closer in character to the mainline churches, such as the Congregational Church and the Church of Christ. But there are others which are growing quite rapidly and this is especially so with those which have a distinctive set of beliefs or practices, such as the Jehovah's Witnesses and the Seventh Day Adventists. More recently, and largely by migration, there have arisen some non-western religious groups such as Eastern Orthodox Christian, Hindu and Muslim communities. In 1971, for example, there were for the first time, more Hindus than Jews in New Zealand. Before 1961 there were no Buddhists. In 1961 there were 350. By 1976 they had increased to 2,618, a growth of 748% in 15 years!

When the Census figures are looked at as a whole the three most significant trends are these. First there is a very distinct decline in the allegiance of New Zealand citizens to the larger and long-established ecclesiastical institutions and during the last twenty years this decline has been accelerating. Secondly there has been a rapid expansion in the actual number of small religious groups and in the particular labels which individuals choose to specify their religious position. Even so, leaving aside the seven largest religious bodies, those who adhere to all of the many others still make up only 9.5% of the population. The third, and perhaps the most significant, trend and one closely related to the first is this: the section of the population which either professes no religion, or objects to state, has grown from 5.4% in 1926 to 18.5% in 1976. In absolute numbers this section has grown in fifty years by a massive 755% and now consitutes the second largest component of New Zealand society from the point of view of religion.

What this brief analysis makes very clear to us so far is that the religious character of New Zealand is becoming less and less homogeneous. Religious allegiance is becoming increasingly diversified and individualized. It must be remembered that the rapidly growing section of the 'non-religious' we have referred to above is itself an amorphous collection of individuals, the only element they all have in common being a reluctance to acknowledge any religious profession on a census paper. All this adds up to a steady increase in what is now referred to as religious pluralism. A non-pluralistic religious situation consists of a completely homogeneous community in which all share the same religious faith without any form of division or sectarianism. An unstable form of religious pluralism occurs in a situation where two or more religious faiths co-exist in the same community and the relationship among them involves persecution or the attempt of one or more to expand by the conversion of the others. A stable form of religious pluralism is one where several different forms of religious faith co-exist and the members of the community freely acquiesce in this state of affairs, feeling neither threatened in their own faith by the diversity nor compelled to convert the others.

To understand the nature of the religious pluralism which exists in New Zealand today we need to compare it with what went before, so far as the European population is concerned. For roughly a thousand years before the Reformation western Europe was in the process of being so pervaded by the Christian faith that it became the more or less homogeneous society known as

Christendom. It was the Reformation which shattered that unity and first introduced, to any real degree, a state of religious pluralism. Admittedly this was a limited form of pluralism, when looked at from the outside, for the several divisions were still contained within an encompassing Christian framework. But when viewed from within, Europe had definitely become religiously pluralistic; they saw one another as belonging to quite different and sharply opposed religions. It was such an unstable form of religious pluralism that it gave rise to bitter hostility and armed conflict.

The post-Reformation pluralism was partly tempered by the fact that particular geographical areas of Europe remained relatively homogeneous, apart from quite small minorities, and this was particularly so with the British Isles, with which New Zealand is chiefly concerned. England was basically Anglican, Scotland and Northern Ireland were chiefly Presbyterian, and Ireland generally was predominantly Roman Catholic.

The migration to New Zealand by settlers from all parts of the British Isles had the effect of throwing together Christian denominations which had, to some extent, been geographically separated in the homeland. Thus New Zealand became somewhat more pluralistic than had been the case in Britain. There were certainly some settlers who expected to be able to transfer to New Zealand the modified form of religious homogeneity they had known at home. There was a move, unsuccessful though it was, to commit New Zealand to the Anglican tradition in the way that this denomination was the state (i.e. established) Church in England. Since Otago was a specific settlement by those who only recently had broken with the established Church of Scotland (Presbyterian), they had no wish for a state-dominated church; but there are indications that, at first, they were expecting that province to remain exclusively Presbyterian. There were other areas in which other denominations were the predominant group. These early religious concentrations are still present today even though, in the course of population movement, there has been a levelling process at work. Presbyterians still have their greater strength, relatively speaking, in Otago and Southland; Anglicans in the East Coast, Marlborough, Nelson, and Canterbury; Roman Catholics in Westland; and Methodists in Taranaki.

It is often claimed that New Zealand is basically a Christian society and the majority of its citizens probably still think of it as such, even if somewhat vaguely. As each year goes by, this judgement becomes more and more open to question. On the other hand, even if this assessment was truer in the 19th Century than it is today, it is not clear that the first waves of European settlers thought of the new colony in quite those terms. To do so would be to project back anachronistically some of the ecumenical spirit of the late 20th Century. The first settlers did not think of themselves as Christians, so much as being Anglicans, Presbyterians, Catholics, and Methodists. It was the lack of religious cohesion among the many Christian bodies and the fact that they viewed one another in a competitive and often hostile spirit, which led to the situation in which governing bodies and other civil spokesman at both provincial and national level were forced to become religiously neutral.

The religious neutrality of New Zealand at its official and governing level (in comparison, say, to Anglican England, Lutheran Sweden, Catholic Spain, and Jewish Israel) is clearly illustrated by the controversy which let to the inclusion of the secular clause in the 1877 Education Act. As Ian Breward rightly points out [1] the secular clause was not *anti*-religious in intent; rather it should be interpreted to mean religious *neutrality*. This had become the only viable way in which the state could provide a national educational system which transcended sectarian narrowness and bitter hostility. We may further appeal to this 19th Century controversy as an example of the way in which religious pluralism is an important factor in promoting the process of the secularization of society. Secularity, among other things, means religious neutrality or non-commitment to any particular religious tradition.

It is in the sense just outlined that New Zealand is properly described today, not as a Christian state, but as a secular state. It means, on the one hand, that there is full religious freedom for all citizens. No citizen is penalized or loses any privilege because of his religious convictions. He is equally free to be a Roman Catholic, Jew, Buddhist, Jehovah's Witness, rationalist, agnostic or atheist. He is free to express his religious beliefs publicly and to practise this religion in whatever way he thinks fit, provided this does not infringe the freedom of his fellow-citizens or endanger the security of the state. (Incidentally, since it has been the policy of Soviet Russia actively to promote atheism and strictly to curtail the activities of some religious minorities, it cannot be said to be a secular state in the way in which New Zealand is. Rather it is to be judged a 'religiously'-committed state, comparable to Catholic Spain or Islamic Pakistan, in that Marxist doctrine is accepted as orthodoxy at the official governing level and the government is in the hands of Party members only).

To refer to New Zealand as a secular state means, on the other hand, that the state itself is not committed to or allied with any religious tradition or ideology, and therefore no religious group enjoys a privileged position. It is true that when state functions seem to call for some kind of 'religious' component, the New Zealand Government of the day tends to look to the Anglican Church for a lead.

But that is not because of any legal affiliation between that Church and the state. It is simply because New Zealand society still retains much of the ethos of the Christian West of its past and the Anglican Church is still the largest religious group in the country. It is theoretically conceivable, even if most unlikely, that should the Ratanas, Mormons or Buddhists ever come to have by far the largest following at some future time, then the government would be free to look for a lead to them if it so wished. As an illustration of this general principle, we may point to the fact that though the national radio and television media are strictly neutral with respect to religion, they nevertheless allot time to cover religious ceremonies roughly in proportion to the national strength of each religious body. This further illustrates that, in being secular, the state is not anti-religious but neutral.

The fact that New Zealand still reflects in its ethos so much of the Christian past of its European ancestors tends to hide the fact that New Zealand has in some respects moved further in the direction of a secular or religously-neutral state than has been the case with most states of western Europe. There Christianity was, and often still is, in a privileged position, and its beliefs and practices are protected by law. There Churches *were* allied to the state. Before the mid-nineteenth century, citizens were not free to express or publish beliefs which were at variance with Christian orthodoxy. Much of this has changed in practice, if not in theory, even in Europe. In New Zealand the change occurred at an early stage after European settlement, and largely because of the greater degree of religious pluralism which the settlers brought to New Zealand.

If at this stage we briefly summarize the present religious trends discernible in New Zealand and project them into the remaining two decades of this century then we arrive at something like this. The chief trend is in the direction of an increasing religious pluralism of what we have called the stable variety. To preserve and guarantee the maximum religious freedom for all of its citizens the state and its departments (e.g. education) will remain strictly neutral. Even Christianity (particularly in its more traditional forms) will lose more of its remaining social privileges. For example, the designation of certain religious festivals as public holidays (such as Christmas and Easter) and the question of trading on Sunday, are more likely to depend in the future upon mutual agreements between trade unions and employers than on the express wishes of religious authorities.

A feature of the growing religious pluralism in New Zealand will be the further decline of the large national religious institutions and the proliferation of small religious groups. Many of the latter will tend to have quite a rapid growth to begin with and, after finding their natural level, will become static, and perhaps start to decline. Other small groups may have even a much shorter life, and be organized on an *ad hoc* basis, providing for their members mutual support and an opportunity for group study and the sharing of experiences. Throughout all this movement individual choice and initiative will become increasingly significant. The individual is becoming freer, than he has ever before been, both to choose and to reject, and this fact tends to militate against the formation of either large or permanent religious organizations.

The only factors which could conceivably alter or reverse the trends just sketched would be (1) the rise of a strong reactionary movement which, because of fear of moral and religious chaos, tries to restore the social supremacy of one of the traditional belief systems and sets of moral values; (2) the rise and rapid spread of an as yet unknown religious movement which would be peculiarly equipped to capture the allegiance of an influential majority; (3) the rise of a militant secularism. (Secularism, as an ideology, is not religiously neutral but acts as a negative form of religious commitment. This actually was stronger in the late 19th Century than it is today.)

Now let us turn to the global scene. If the religious character of the British Isles in particular, and of western Europe in general, had remained close to what it was in the 19th century when the European settlers were first migrating to New Zealand, then we would have to look mainly to local factors in order to explain the trends we have just been pointing to in the New Zealand scene. In actual fact, of course, the trend towards religious pluralism, greater religious freedom for the individual, and the secularization of the state, are all clearly to be seen taking place also in western Europe and North America. This means that there are more important factors than purely local ones in shaping the present and immediate future religious character of New Zealand. Change of a quite radical and far-reaching character is happening on the global religious scene. If we look at New Zealand religious trends in a purely parochial way we may fail to recognize this. Too many New Zealand churchmen, for example, seem to see the present church decline as only a temporary phenomenon, and regard it as similar to earlier ebbings of religious vitality. They hopefully expect the tide soon to turn and run again in their favour. They look for the most effective methods, such as evangelistic campaigns, the modernization of the liturgy, new activity programmes, and so on, which hopefully will enable them to regain lost ground. There has been a certain reluctance to acknowledge the fact that the nature of the present social and religious change is so deep-seated that none of these measures can do any more than bring minor and temporary relief.

What is the nature of this process of radical religious change which is taking place on a global scale? Only the briefest of sketches can be attempted here.[2] In the long and complex story of man's diverse religious experiences over the last five thousand years it is both possible and useful to discern three major phases of religious development which have occurred successively. We may refer to these as primary, secondary, and tertiary phases and see them separated from each other by two transitional periods; the first of the latter has been called the Axial Period, and the second, which is the transition to the modern world, passed over its major threshold during the time of the European Enlightenment of about 1650-1750.

Belonging to the primary phase of religion are the religions of tribal societies (such as the pre-European Maori) and also of the ancient urban societies (such as existed in the Indus Valley, Egypt, Assyria, and ancient Rome). The chief reason for calling them primary is that these religions had no known historical origin. These religions were ethnically based. They had grown up with the people who profess them and had evolved so slowly that their practitioners could think of them as having been more or less unchanged since they were revealed by the gods at the beginning of time. In the primary phase each community, small or large, was religiously homogeneous: all shared the same faith. This faith was carefully transmitted from one generation to another. Each member was born into his religion at birth and had no choice in his basic beliefs and practices, so long as he remained a member of that community. For this reason religion never needed to be named in the primary phase and we still have to speak, therefore, of the religion of the Ancient Sumerians or of the Australian Aborigines etc.

Then came the Axial Period. This was a time of deep reflection, unsettlement, questioning and rejection of many aspects of the ancestral religious traditions, all leading to radical change which brought forth a new phase in man's religious experience. Karl Jaspers and others have pointed out that the Axial Period occurred within a few centuries and more or less simultaneously in several different localities (Greece, Middle East, Persia, India, and China), which do not appear to have been influenced much by one another.[3]

The Axial Period gave rise to religions of the secondary phase and it is a feature of this phase that each religion has an identity of its own and can now be named. Belonging to the secondary phase are Judaism, Christianity, Islam, Zoroastrianism, Hinduism, Buddhism, Confucianism, and Taoism as well as later offshoots from these. These religions all look back to a time of historical origin and not to a mythical beginning. They are sometimes referred to as the historical religions, not only because they look back to historical founders but also because each has a subsequent history as it adapts to changing conditions and spreads geographically.

In the secondary phase religion ceased to be tied of necessity to one ethnic group. Having an identity of its own, it does not depend on the ethnic identity of those who embrace it. In it the individual enjoys an element of choice which was not present in the primary phase. He is free to adopt the faith initially (and this is usually celebrated in an appropriate ritual); he is also free to abandon it in favour of another. This gives religion a mobility it did not previously possess. Religion of the secondary phase therefore may jump over ethnic boundaries and actually has the potential to become global in extent, i.e. universal to all mankind. Of the religions just named, Christianity, Islam, and Buddhism displayed this capacity most fully and became missionary religions, whereas the others remained more closely linked to the ethnic origins.

As religions of the secondary phase spread out from their place of origin they experienced little difficulty in the long run in displacing the primary religions they encountered. Actually they did not *completely* displace them so much as cover them over with a veneer. This veneer provided a vaster and more intellectually satisfying spiritual horizon than had previously obtained, yet much of the folk beliefs and practices of the primary religion lived on beneath the surface in some kind of synthesis with the new faith.

The relationship of the secondary religions with one another, however, has been noticeably different. While they could displace religions of the primary phase in the manner just described, they could not so easily displace one another. From the time of their origin until, say, the fifteenth century, they had spread out until they had divided up the whole of the great land mass of Eurasia, with relatively clear boundary lines separating them from each other. There was the Christian West, the Muslim Middle East, and the Hindu sub-continent, while the Far East was already experiencing the religious pluralism of Buddhism, Confucianism, and Taoism. They spread out until they met each other and then tended to come to a halt. This phenomenon is also well illustrated by the results of the great expansion of Christianity in the 19th century. Greatest success was among the people of primary religion in Africa and Polynesia (as it had earlier been in the Americas) whereas in the Islamic world, Hindu India, and Confucian China, Christian advance was minimal by comparison.

Now we come to the second period of religious transition. Unlike the Axial Period it originated in only one place, western Europe, but it has since been transported round the world and is now affecting the whole globe. This transition to modernity had a gestation period of about five centuries, the 14th to the 19th, the Age of Enlightenment marking the irreversible threshold of no return. This second transition is proving even more radical than the first, so much so that some interpret it as a transition from religion to non-religion. It must be remembered, however, that even at the Axial Period there were some who saw the then new religions as abandonment of the old gods and hence a rejection of religion. In order to do justice to both transitions it has been necessary to find a wider and more all-embracing definition of religion, one which does justice to man's concern for the ultimate but which does not limit the manifestation of that concern to symbols or answers which either of the two great transitions have rendered obsolete.

Like the Axial Period, the transition to modernity has been marked by much questioning, spiritual unsettlement, and, above all, a rapid expansion of the horizon of man's knowledge and experience. Indeed the modern view of the universe is so vast and mind-boggling that it has swallowed up and rendered untenable the world views which accompanied the religions of the primary and secondary phases. The modern world view is the fruit of the empirical sciences, which have not only played a vital role in the transition to modernity but now constitute the chief cultural possession common to all men. Just as religion of the secondary phase jumped over ethnic boundaries, so the empirical sciences have transcended the cultural boundaries formed by the religions of the secondary phase and laid the foundations of a global secular culture.

Important though the sciences have been in formulating the worldview common to all men on a global scale, they cannot in themselves provide the new answers required for man's basic religious questions. These are the questions of ultimate purpose and value which, because he is the only known creature to ask them, make man a religious being. It is outside the scope of science to deal with questions of value, of purpose and of that which concerns man ultimately. Science, among other things, has been instrumental in forcing the religious questions to be raised afresh, by undermining the validity of some of the former answers — answers found in the religions of the secondary phase. But instead of supplying the new answers, science has thrown man back on his own resources.

In the primary phase of religion the individual did not have to concern himself very much with the basic questions of the purpose of life. The tradition of his tribe, city or ethnic group told him all he needed to know. These questions came to the surface for the first time during the Axial Period. In the secondary phase of religion definitive answers were believed to have been authoritatively revealed from the source of ultimate reality itself through prophetic spokesmen such as Moses, Jesus of Nazareth, Muhammad, the Buddha,

Confucius etc. The ordinary individual was freer than he had been in the primary phase; he was free to accept or reject what was being authoritatively proclaimed, free also to choose between the different answers offered. But, generally speaking, even in the secondary phase, he was not required, or expected, to play any major role in formulating the most appropriate religious response to the demands of life. That had already been done definitively for him through the founder and he could safely rely on the experts to interpret the message where this was necessary.

It is a feature of religion in the third or modern phase that each individual is not only freer than he has ever been before but also must shoulder more responsibility for 'working out his own salvation in fear and trembling,' and in a more radical way than even Paul envisaged when he wrote those words. (Incidentally, these words are strangely similar to those which tradition ascribes to the dying Buddha, 'Work out your own salvation with diligence.') One result of this increased freedom in the modern religious situation is that a whole host of new religious spokesmen have come to the fore, each claiming to have the ultimate answers. In the religious vacuum which the transition to modernity has perforce caused to occur, this phenomenon is very understandable but these self-appointed prophets and gurus, in so far as they call followers simply to adopt their convictions and teaching, simply represent a resurgence of the religion of phase two rather than that of phase three.

There are of course many other aspects of religion in the tertiary phase which there is no room to discuss here. This question of both the freedom and responsibility which belong to the individual in the modern phase has alone been taken up because of its bearing on religious pluralism.[4] In discussing religion in the modern era, the sociologist of religion Robert Bellah enunciated as a dominant trend 'the increasing acceptance of the notion that each individual must work out his own ultimate solutions and that the most that the church can do is provide him with a favourable environment for doing so, without imposing on him a prefabricated set of answers.'[5]

If there is any truth in this paradigm of the religious development of mankind through three basic successive phases, then we find it throws some considerable light on what is happening to religion in New Zealand. It not only provides the global and historical context within which to understand the particular trends we earlier noted, but it helps us to appreciate the fact that they point to changes which are more permanent and deep-seated than we may otherwise judge them to be.

If the European settlement of New Zealand had taken place no later, say, than four centuries ago, then the sort of thing which would have taken place is this. The religion of the pre-European Maori would have been displaced by pre-Reformation western Christianity, for that is what happens · when a secondary religion encounters a primary religion. It would have created a situation similar to that of South America of the 17th century. In actual fact the encounter did go some distance in this direction. By the latter half of the 19th century, however, the situation was becoming much more complex than this because of two reasons. The first was that the incoming form of Christianity was already pluralistic, since it came from an area of Christendom strongly marked by the post-Reformation divisions of Christendom. The second is that in the 19th century the western world was already experiencing the birth-pangs of the new religious situation which we have referred to as the tertiary phase of religious development. The settlement of New Zealand happened to coincide in time with the beginning of a new religious era.

The present religious trends in New Zealand, as brought to light by statistical evidence during the last fifty years, are wholly consistent with the paradigm of long-term religious change which we have just been sketching. The fact of this correspondence lends some weight to the validity of the analysis. It suggests that religious pluralism, of a kind much wider in scope and much greater in number, than the relative form of Christian pluralism which obtained from the 16th to the 19th century, is here to stay for the foreseeable future. It will apply not only to New Zealand, but increasingly throughout the world.

The religious pluralism of the modern phase of religion is not in itself wholly new on the scene. It is to be seen as a growth to maturity of seeds sown, not only at the Reformation, but at the Axial Period in the very way it gave rise to the religions of the secondary phase. This is why each of these historical religions has, in the course of history, branched out into an increasing variety of sects, segments, schools, or parties. Judaism, for example, was already doing it on the eve of Christian origins. Primitive Christianity was simply one of several Jewish groups. The phenomenal success of Christianity in the following centuries had the effect of causing Judaism to close its ranks and, in its rabbinical form, become more unified than it otherwise might have been. On the other hand, Christianity and Buddhism could be said to exist today, in each case, as a family of religions. Further, these families are continuing to multiply and even to intermarry, bringing forth offspring of mixed parentage.

Religious pluralism of the modern era does not mean that religions of the second phase die out; it rather means that they will display even further diversification. Just as religion of the primary phase continued to operate underneath the veneer supplied by the secondary-phase religions, so these latter continue into the tertiary phase as viable options for some people, and in ever-increasing variety of forms. From time to time there is likely to be a minor resurgence of one or other of these forms, but it is unlikely that any one of them will ever again embrace a whole society in a homogeneous way. In this respect, Marxism, in so far as it is to be judged a religion, is a very late example of the religion of the secondary phase. Because it is late and more geared to the this-worldliness of the modern era it is likely to wield a collective force for a longer period than the earlier forms of secondary religion. In the long run, however, it too will succumb to the inroads of religious pluralism; the present tensions in the Marxist world are a pointer in this direction.

For similar reasons, Christianity will never become contained in a unified ecclesiastical institution, such as it approximately was for some centuries and as some still hope it will be. The ecumenical movement, even in its post-Vatican II form, has come too late to counter the now accelerated movement to pluralism. Likewise, an ecumenism extended to take in all the historic faiths, such as the World Congress of Faiths founded in 1936 by Sir Francis Younghusband, can achieve but little. Perhaps the only form of ecumenism which will be permanently viable will be that which arises out of the humanity which men of all races and cultures share. It would provide a secular, religiously-neutral base on which each individual is left free to formulate for himself the religious answers most appropriate to him.

The time for large religious institutions is over. That is why the larger and long-established churches are dying. But the historic faiths of which they were for so long a part, belong to the total religious heritage of mankind and will be drawn upon by successive generations of the future in an increasing variety of ways in a process of continuing religious creativity. Thus, for example, Christianity will outlast the structured church, as Buddhism will outlast the Sangha, and the Vedanta will outlast the Hindu caste system.

Religious pluralism really began during the Axial Period with the rise of several historical religions. While these remained in relative isolation from each other it was possible for each to assert its own unique claims to be the absolute truth. The transition to modernity has served to accelerate the phenomenon of religious pluralism and to undermine the former claims of men to be in possession of absolute truth. Religious pluralism brings home to men the relative character of their religious beliefs and practices. While it is necessary for man to adopt *some* kind of religious stance the recognition that it can never be claimed to be absolute means that religious pluralism becomes more readily acceptable and therefore grows in stability.

Anyone who undertakes to prophesy the future of anything is engaging in a very risky exercise for he is almost certain to be proved wrong in some respects. But taking this caveat into account, one may venture to suggest that as we look into the future from 1980 we may expect religion in New Zealand to become increasingly pluralistic, to depend less and less on large organizational structures and more and more on individual choice. Religion will become more tailored to the individual in both belief and life-style. There will be increased fluidity in the social groupings in which the individual seeks to share his religious concerns. The cultural bonding of New Zealand as a nation will not be of a religious character but will consist of a secular or religiously-neutral base, to which each person will be responsible for choosing and adding his own religious component.

NOTES:
1. BREWARD, I. *Godless schools? A study in Protestant reactions to the Education Act of 1877.* Christchurch, Presbyterian Bookroom, 1967, p. 102.
2. For a fuller exposition, the reader is referred to my book *God comes down to earth,* awaiting publication by Collins, London.
3. See:
    JASPERS, K. *The origin and goal of history.* London, Routledge and Kegan Paul, 1953.
4. A fuller discussion is to be found in:
    GEERING, L. *The religion of the individual in the modern world.* Wellington, Price Milburn for the New Zealand Council for Civic Liberties, 1975.
    (J. C. Beaglehole Memorial Lecture, 1974)
5. BELLAH, R. *Beyond belief.* New York, Harper & Row, 1970.

The Academic Contribution

RELIGIOUS STUDIES : NEW ZEALAND AND WORLDWIDE
Albert C. Moore

Viewed from the outside, New Zealand seems "the last place on earth" in which to carry out Religious Studies. Literally as well as metaphorically this is the impression our country makes. As an American once said to me apprehensively as I pointed out my homeland on a map of the Pacific Ocean: "If I had to live down there I'd be frightened of dropping off!" A similar feeling may temper the joy of the New Zealander returning home by ship or by air. The familiar landfall makes one all the more aware of physical isolation from the major continents and civilizations of the world. I should know this, writing as I do at latitude 46 degrees south in Dunedin, the seat of the southernmost university in the world. Even on a fine night when one can admire the lights of the city from the vantage-point of a hill, one realizes with some disquiet that the lights peter out along the coast and that beyond is a vast expanse of water and eventually Antarctica. Most of the time we are able to suppress this realization or at least learn to live with it without disturbance to our everyday concerns. Yet the truth is that human culture and religion have a very tenuous hold on the environment; and while this can be said of all countries it seems much more true of New Zealand than of, say, Bali or Japan or Britain with their many centuries and millennia of human interaction with nature. Perhaps a thousand or more years ago the Maoris began to bring Polynesian language, culture and religion to this land; and the last two centuries have seen the dominance of a Western European culture with mainly British forms of Christianity. Such a late and thin spread of human culture does not provide a very promising basis for a wide and deep study of religion and religions.

Yet the essays in this book (as well as the publication of other books [1] and the expansion of university courses in Religious Studies in New Zealand over the past 15 years) indicate that interest in the wide study of religion has indeed emerged. Why has this come about? It may be that the very factors of isolation and "thin spread" have something to do with this. Aware of their economic and cultural dependence on Europe, New Zealanders have had to look beyond their shores for fulfilment. Traditionally Maoris had dreamed of Hawaiki; then white settlers and their descendants came to think of Britain as "home", with the churches as expressions of Western Christendom. Through literature and travel ("the overseas trip") New Zealanders have been overwhelmingly drawn to their Western heritage. However this pattern began to be modified from the period of World War II when the Pacific theatre involved America and Japan, Australia and New Zealand in the Pacific Islands and South-east Asia. The post-war years brought greater awareness to New Zealanders of their involvment in the Pacific area and Asia and the need to appreciate more positively the life, culture and religions of peoples in these areas. Churches which had previously thought of these people as simply "heathen" to be converted to Christianity began to see them now as people deserving of respect and as fellow workers in the future. Prophetic words in the 1950's pointed out that New Zealanders had a Western heritage but an Asian destiny.[2] Subsequently a number of younger New Zealanders have done volunteer service in the Pacific area and the "overseas trip" has come to mean Indonesia and Asia as well as Europe.

A New Zealand contribution

These experiences supplied the soil in which Religious Studies could grow. New Zealanders have been no more and no less virtuous or intelligent than other nations; but their situation has been of necessity one of conscious dependence on other cultures. The lack of strong local cultural traditions has often resulted in a culture that is colourless or worse. It is possible for New Zealanders to be smug in their isolation and to learn nothing from travel abroad. (I once squirmed to hear a compatriot announce in a European youth hostel : "I've been through all these countries and scenically you can't beat good old New Zealand.") Fortunately the awareness of cultural isolation has led also to a receptiveness to overseas visitors, sometimes even over-eager in its dependence on ideas from abroad. At its best this has led to a genuine interest in and openness to news and experience of life elsewhere but tempered by critical detachment. Being remote from the great historic centres of religion, one can approach them with a certain freshness and independence. There is a two-way interaction between one's local experience and the wider experience of distant cultures and religions.

I am suggesting that this interaction is the living basis for Religious Studies in the latter half of the 20th century. It is a universal possibility and not the monopoly of any one people. Other countries such as America have provided this basis and led the world in the variety of Religious Studies programmes; but America is so large and affluent that it is in danger of absorbing the varied experiences of the world beyond rather than retaining the tension of their otherness. Perhaps it pays here to belong to a smaller country. For instance Holland has produced notable scholars in the field of world religions; but as with other European nations, the colonialist tradition which made possible the exper- ience and careful observation of other cultures and religions (especially of Indonesia) also contributed a sense of the mother-country's superiority with its culture and religion. New Zealand is by no means free of such attitude, but it is probably better placed than most at this point, just because of its comparative isolation. This provides a certain space and objectivity conducive to the study of widely divergent cultures and religions.

Of course New Zealand's geographical isolation should not make us overlook the ready communication of ideas and information from the news media, presses and universities of the rest of the world. Overseas lecturers are sometimes amazed to find their recent works being read and discussed in the Antipodes; but this should not occasion surprise. As far as Western culture goes, New Zealand settlers in the 19th century could keep up with news and literature from the Old Country brought by the slower communications of sea-mail. One could even say that the seeds of interest in Religious Studies were already sown two centuries ago when the voyages of Captain Cook opened up New Zealand and the Pacific to European influence and settlement. For it was the 18th century age of the Enlightenment with its belief in reason and its curiosity to explore and question.It was also the age of Rousseau and romanticism which, with all its idealization of the"noble savage", did contribute the ideals of tolerence, empathy and understanding. And it was also the age of the Industrial Revolution in England which was to make possible further explorations, conquests, and trade communications with other lands. In these great adventures of human ideas and technical activity one can see at work the attitudes which have gone to make up the modern approach to Religious Studies, as a subject world-wide in its scope of inquiry and range of sympathy.

Bridging religious worlds

It is just this world-wide scope of Religious Studies that provides the justification and excitement of the study as it has developed in New Zealand and elsewhere. Through coming to terms with cultures and religions very different from the traditional forms of Christianity familiar in New Zealand one is drawn outwards and stretched in one's understanding; at the same time one learns to see the familiar religion in the context of the religious development of mankind as a whole. To experience this is to switch from one's own world to other very different worlds.

This is a creative experience which is at the heart of the subject called Religious Studies - whether it is given the label of "comparative religion", "history of religions", "scientific study of religion", "phenomenology of religion" or simply "world religions". It can be illustrated time and again in the experience of scholars who became founders and leaders in the subject. For instance, Rudolf Otto, the German philosophical theologian and author of the now classic *Idea of the Holy* received his inspiration on one of his explorations beyond the world of European culture and religion. In Morocco in 1911 he was struck by the awesome power and profound meaning of the "Holy Holy Holy" being chanted in a Jewish synagogue on the Sabbath; and he subsequently pursued this theme through the religions of Asia and of the Near East, including Christianity to which he belonged. [4] A parallel experience of switching worlds is seen in Mircea Eliade, the well-known Romanian scholar now in Chicago.[5] As a young man in 1928 he left the world of Europe (in particular, the Latin culture and Eastern Orthodox Christianity of his native Romania) to spend three years in India, immersing himself in Indian religion, philosophy and yoga. Having switched worlds he returned to Europe, with insights which enabled him to experience many other unfamiliar worlds of religion in the history of mankind. This is an archetypal experience shared by many anthropologists, historians, philosophers, and students of religion; it can also be the experience of many a traveller, teacher, administrator, and missionary who has immersed himself in the life of the people whom he seeks to serve. A further example is seen in the British scholar Ninian Smart. From his Christian tradition as a Scottish Episcopalian he encountered another world in the Buddhist tradition in Sri Lanka. He described his own religious "search" as finding a counterpoise in other religions which may contribute elements lacking in one's own or may stimulate the rediscovery of such elements as meditation. This requires an openness to other influences which feed back into one's own view of religion.[6] It is rooted in the experience of switching religious worlds. And here lies the basic significance of Religious Studies for New Zealand religion and culture.

The purpose and value of the subject

What does this mean in practice? What do we expect the study of religion to provide for the interested layman who may eagerly pursue reading in this area or for students taking courses at school and university? Put differently, we might ask "What sort of person do we aim to produce and with what insights and skills should he emerge from the study of religion?" The answer must surely involve a richer view of religion - on the one hand by way of extended knowledge and on the other by a deeper and more thoughtful personal grasp of religion.

First, the person who studies religion should become knowledgeable about the rich variety of religions in the world; one might call this the "history and geography of religions" and it can be claimed that any educated person should have some awareness of this field. For on the one hand religions haveplayed an enormous role in shaping the life and culture of peoples the world over, as any traveller should know, and on the other hand the variety of religions is a significant fact which we have to come to terms with in the modern pluralistic world. Through the study of religion one should come to a way of seeing and understanding these religions in their variety. One should learn what to look for in approaching religions, to appreciate the religious experience at its core and also the basic forms in which that experience is expressed. (Here the simple framework of Joachim Wach points to the three basic forms of expression - in thought, action and fellowship - which characterize religions.) [7] In using such an approach the student should learn to describe any religion he encounters in a fair and unbiased way and yet also feel himself as far as possible into its basic experience. This combination of objectivity and empathy has been called the "detached-within" approach in the Phenomenology of Religion. [8] It seeks to span the history of religions as a universal human phenomenon and at the same time to get inside the meaning of the specific phenomena as they appear in the religious experience of the people concerned.

Such a combination of knowledge and understanding is of considerable practical value as well as being of interest in its own right. Sound information of religious traditions would help a bewildered traveller. Once I met a group of ladies on a conducted tour of Japan who were confused by the many Buddhist temples and Shinto shrines they had seen; they had apparently not even been told of the distinguishing marks of Shinto, such as the *torii* arch, which would have greatly aided their interest and understanding. Educators and missionaries can all benefit from such knowledge in foreign cultures. Politicians too cannot afford to ignore the importance of religious attitudes, movements and leaders. A current example (1979) is to be seen in Iran where the powerof the Shah had to give way to the massive public following of the exiled Muslim leader, the

Ayatollah Khomeiny. Apparently this came as a surprise to the U.S.A leaders of foreign policy, since there was no advisor sufficiently knowledgeable about the religious affairs of Iran or aware of the deep currents of popular feeling for Islamic religious leaders.

Secondly, in his own thinking, the student should become aware of the significance of the claims made by the different religions about man's relation to the universe, the Sacred, and the ways of life and thought resulting from these claims. He should see the religions not just as museum-pieces but as ways of experience potentially having something to say and from which one might learn. This leads on to a critical grappling with the issues raised by religions. It does not mean a naive acceptance of the views one states, however sympathetically. Rather, one pays true respect to a religious viewpoint by seeking to listen and to give a critical answer. Religion is not all a matter of sweetness and light and the study of religion must raise questions of criticism and the search for truth. Religious Studies courses do not claim to offer "cut and dried" criteria – nor a "consumers' guide to world religions". We seek instead to promote critical awareness by which students can further their own legitimate view of and critical thinking about religion.[9] It will be a large part of our contribution to the changing world to promote the earnest pursuit of truth.

The human experience of adding dimensions to one's life and thought through contact with world religions is at the heart of modern Religious Studies. If it can produce students enriched by this outlook and orientation, the subject will be more than justified in its contribution to New Zealand life and religion. This is its primary and continuing task.

Ongoing tasks.

Many further tasks derive from this and at least the principal ones can be mentioned. Especially for those working in the Pacific area it is important to come to a deeper understanding of the primal (so-called "primitive" or "traditional") religions of Polynesia and Melanesia and Australia.[10] Linked to this is the study of new religious movements in the Pacific area and over the world scene - a rich and interesting field of research.[11] Then in relation to the great world religions such as Buddhism and Islam there is the task of furthering inter-religious dialogue; a Christian missionary teacher in Indonesia incorporates study of the Qur'an along with the Christian Bible and achieves a break-through in opening up meeting with Muslim scholars.[12] Within the areas of Christianity itself there is a continuing ecumenical task of promoting understanding between the churches; and this should not be confined to theological and ecclesiastical discussions but related to shared activities and the wider range of symbolism, art, myth and ritual studied in the phenomenology of religion. [13]

In the academic world Religious Studies is in the process of finding areas of research to pursue at higher levels. Already there is a variety of work in progress, often pursued in related disciplines such as history, theology and the social sciences. Co-operation with scholars and researchers in other fields is important, for Religious Studies is a "subject field" [14] with inter-disciplinary implications. It is like Political Studies in that it focusses on a certain field of human concern while drawing upon a variety of academic approaches, ranging from theoretical analyses in philosophy to concrete ethnological descriptions.

In such co-operative work scholars can be stimulated to see new aspects of the religious dimension in human existence,[15] sometimes in ways hitherto regarded as "secular". They may also investigate new areas which have been overlooked. To take an extreme example adjacent to New Zealand, Antarctica lies dormant as a vast area as yet untapped and not even contemplated in Religious Studies to date. One's immediate response to such a suggestion might well be to see it as merely facetious or as a rather mean comment on New Zealand's isolation. Yet who knows? One day Antarctica may prove to be a new centre for international culture, replacing California as the "wave of the future". [16] The point is that there is a whole world of religion and religions to explore and rediscover.

The studies in this book participate in a worldwide movement of Religious Studies. The subject can bring to people of today an enrichment of life and thought which is not only academic. And New Zealand, dependent and isolated as it is in many respects, is a good place from which to start and to contribute to the wider world.

Notes:

1. HINCHLIFF, J. C. ed. *Perspectives on religion: New Zealand viewpoints 1974.* Auckland, University of Auckland, 1975; and the subsequent collections of essays from the annual Auckland Colloquium of Religious Studies.

   On research interests, see also:

   MOORE, A. C. Religious studies in the Pacific area, Australia and New Zealand. *Religion 5* (special issue): 84-90, 1975.

2. The Rt. Rev. Alan Brash, Presbyterian minister and ecumenical worker and spokesman, who has now returned to New Zealand.

3. Influential Dutch scholars of the past 100 years include C. P. Tiele, Chantepie de la Saussaye, W. Brede Kristensen, G. van der Leeuw and Hendrik Kraemer.

4. TURNER, H. W. *Rudolf Otto, "The idea of the holy"; a guide for students.* Aberdeen, the author, 1974, p. 3-7.

5. ELIADE'S works include *The sacred and the profane: the nature of religion.* N.Y., Harcourt, Brace, 1959, and *The quest: history and meaning in religion.* Chicago, University of Chicago Press, 1969.
   See also:
   KITAGAWA, J. M. and Long, C. H. (eds) *Myths and symbols: studies in honour of Mircea Eliade.* Chicago, University of Chicago Press, 1969. Part III.

6. SMART, N. *Background to the long search.* London, British Broadcasting Corporation, 1977, provides an interesting popular introduction to accompany the TV series on world religions, "The long search," see p. 293-98.

7. WACH, J. *The comparative study of religions.* N.Y. Columbia University Press, 1958. For an application of this approach see:
   ELLWOOD, R. S. *Religious and spiritual groups in modern America.* Englewood Cliffs, N.J., Prentice-Hall, 1973, and the chapter above by P. de Bres on Maori religious movements.

8. KING, W. *Introduction to religion: a phenomenological approach.* N.Y., Harper & Row, 1968, p. 1-8.

9. Helpful paperback introductions on these matters are:
   CREEL, R. E. *Religion and doubt: toward a faith of your own.* Englewood Cliffs, N. J. Prentice-Hall, 1976.
   DONOVAN, P. *Religious language.* London, Sheldon Press, 1976.
   DONOVAN, P. *Interpreting religious experience.* London, Sheldon Press, 1979.

10. HINCHCLIFF, J. et al., eds. *Religious studies in the Pacific.* Auckland, University of Auckland Press, 1978, p. 7 ff.

11. TURNER, H. W. A new field in the history of religions. *Religion 1:* 15-23, 1971.

12. Compare:
    CRAGG, K. *The dome and the rock; Jerusalem studies in Islam.* London, S.P.C.K., 1964 and his other works on the dialogue of Christianity and Islam.

13. MOORE, A. C. *Iconography of religions: an introduction.* London, S.C.M. Press, 1977.

14. CAPPS, W. H. (comp) *Ways of understanding religion.* New York, Macmillan, 1972, p. 7-12.

15. STRENG, F. J. et al. (comps) *Ways of being religious: readings for a new approach to religion.* Englewood Cliffs, N. J., Prentice-Hall, 1973.

16. SMART, N. *Background to the long search.* op. cit. p. 291-2.

Select Bibliography: Religion in New Zealand

Compiled by
Lucy Marsden
Massey University Library

For the most part this bibliography is very selective, being restricted to published monographs of direct New Zealand relevance that should be readily available in all major libraries or through the interlibrary loan scheme, with some unpublished theses where there is a paucity of published material. An exception to this however has been made in the case of the sections on Maori religious movements, to include all items mentioned by Pieter de Bres in his paper, but not listed by him in footnotes. These sections therefore appear disproportionately large and detailed compared with the others.

This bibliography should prove adequate for anyone seeking basic or introductory material on religion in New Zealand: the serious student however would do well to follow up the items listed in the notes after each paper.

GENERAL

DIALOGUE on religion: New Zealand viewpoints 1977. Peter Davis and John Hinchcliff, eds. Auckland, Auckland University, 1977.

The FUTURE of religion in New Zealand: Seminar II. The impact of orthodox Christianity — what is happening now? October 1974. Some papers and comments. Wellington, Dept of University Extension, Victoria University of Wellington, 1974.

PERSPECTIVES on religion: New Zealand viewpoints 1974; a selection of essays given at a colloquium held at the University of Auckland, New Zealand, in August 1974. John Hinchcliff, ed. Auckland, University of Auckland, 1975.

RELIGION in New Zealand. *Landfall 20:* 4-59, 1966.
Contents:
Oliver, W. H. Christianity among the New Zealanders. 4-20.
Davies, W. M. Church and nation. 20-24.
Geering, L. G. Church in the new world. 24-30.
Downey, P. J. Being religious in New Zealand. 31-37.
Harre, J. To be or not to be? An anthropologist's view. 37-41.
Nichol, F. Theology in New Zealand. 42-49.
McEldowney, D. Ultima Thule to Little Bethel: notes on religion in New Zealand writing. 50-59.

The *RELIGIOUS dimension: a selection of essays presented at a colloquium on religious studies held at the University of Auckland, New Zealand in August 1975.* John Hinchcliff, ed. Auckland, Rep Prep, 1976.

RELIGIOUS pluralism in New Zealand: Friday evening, 2 July, Saturday 3 July: study papers. Wellington, Dept. of University Extension, Victoria University of Wellington, 1976.

SECULARISATION of religion in New Zealand: seminar papers; Friday evening 8 October, Saturday 9 October. Wellington, Dept. of University Extension, Victoria University of Wellington, 1976.

BIBLIOGRAPHY

HAMILTON, Alison S. *A bibliography for an outline history of the Christian Church in New Zealand.* Wellington, New Zealand Library School, 1960.

STATISTICS

NEW Zealand census of population and dwellings.
1871 –
Issues in 1871, 1874, 1878, 1881, 1886, 1891, 1896, 1901, 1906, 1911, 1916, 1921, 1926, 1936, 1945, 1951, 1956, 1961, 1966, 1971, 1976. Wellington, N.Z. Dept of Statistics.
From 1951 to date religious professions have appeared as volume 3 of the series; before that the volume or part number varies. For earlier Statistics *see: STATISTICS of the Dominion of New Zealand.* 1853/56 - 1920.

STUDY AND TEACHING

AUSTRALIAN and New Zealand Society for Theological Studies. *The study of religion and theology in Australian and New Zealand tertiary institutions; documentation.* Sydney, 1972. (A survey of the courses available)

BREWARD, Ian *Godless schools? A study of Protestant reactions to the Education Act of 1877.* Christchurch, Presbyterian Bookroom, 1967.

JAMIESON, Ian W. A. *Survey of religious courses at tertiary level.* Wellington, Churches Education Commission, 1975.

CHARISMATIC MOVEMENTS

BAPTIST Union of N.Z. Special Committee. *Report of an investigation of the effects of neo-pentecostalism on New Zealand Baptist Churches.* Wellington, Baptist Union, 1970. Also reprinted in Worsfold, (see below)

CHURCH of England in New Zealand. Commission on the Charismatic Movement. *Report. In* General Synod of the Church of the Province of New Zealand. 42nd, Christchurch, 1976. *Proceedings.*

NEIL, A. G. *Institutional churches and the charismatic renewal. Thesis, S. Th., Joint Board of Theological Studies, 1974.*

PRESBYTERIAN General Assembly, Christchurch, 1967 and 1973. *Proceedings.*

PRESBYTERIAN General Assembly. Doctrine Committee, and, Life and Work Committee. *Reports,* 1974 and 1976-78.

RAYNER, A. *Social Characteristics of Pentecostalism: a sociological study of the Christchurch Apostolic Church,* Thesis, M.A., University of Canterbury, 1980.

REIDY, M.T.V. and Richardson, J. T. Roman Catholic neo-Pentecostalism: the New Zealand experience. *Australian and New Zealand journal of sociology, 14:* 220-230, 1978.

WALDEGRAVE, C. T. *Social and personality correlates of Pentecostalism: a review of the literature and a comparison of Pentecostal Christian students with non-Pentecostal Christian students.* Thesis, B. Phil, University of Waikato, 1972.

The WINDS of the spirit: an introductory study of the charismatic movement. J. Osborne, ed. Auckland, Methodist Board of Publications, 1974.

WORSFOLD, J. E. *A history of the charismatic movements in New Zealand.* Bradford, Julian Literature Trust, 1974.

ECUMENICAL MOVEMENTS

AUTHORITY, conscience and dissent; being the full text of a series of papers presented at three meetings of the Joint Working Committee, set up by the National Council of Churches in New Zealand and the Roman Catholic Church. Christchurch, National Council of Churches, 1971.

BREWARD, Ian *Unity and reunion.* Dunedin, The Author, 1972.

BROOKES, N. E. *New Zealand Methodists and church union: an historical and sociological survey* Thesis, M.A., University of Canterbury, 1976.

BROWN, C. G. The Council, the churches and controversy; the history of the National Council of Churches in New Zealand, 1941-70. *In* Hinchcliff, J. et al (eds) *Religious studies in the Pacific.* Auckland, University of Auckland, 1978. p. 191-199.

JOINT Commission on Church Union in New Zealand. *Background.* Wellington, Office of the Joint Commission, 1971 –

JOINT Commission on Church Union in New Zealand. *Plan for union.* Wellington, Office of the Joint Commission, 1969.

JOINT Commission on Church Union in New Zealand. *The plan for Union, 1971.* Wellington, Office of the Joint Commission, 1971.

JOINT Commission on Church Union in New Zealand. *Reports to the negotiating churches.* Wellington, Office of the Joint Commission, 1965–

PARK, J. A. *The ecumenical movement in New Zealand.* Thesis, M.A., University of New Zealand (Otago), 1950.

MAORI RELIGIOUS MOVEMENTS

See also under the names of individual religions and churches, e.g. Ratana, Ringatu, Hauhauism.

ALPERS, Anthony F. G. *Maori myths and tribal traditions.* Auckland, Longman Paul, 1964.

BEST, Elsdon *Maori religion and mythology.* Wellington, Govt. Print, 1924. (Dominion Museum Bulletin, no. 10)

BINNEY, J. Christianity and the Maoris to 1840. A comment. *New Zealand journal of history 3:* 143-165, 1969.

COTTRELL, Blair C. *Maori religious movements in the 19th and early 20th centuries: a selected and annotated bibliography.* Wellington, New Zealand Library School, 1971.

DE BRES, Pieter H. *Religion in Atene; religious associations and the urban Maori.* Wellington, Polynesian Society, 1971. (Polynesian Society. Memoir no. 37)

The FUTURE of religion in New Zealand: Seminar I. Maori-Polynesian influence, June 1974: some papers and comments. Wellington, Dept. of University Extension, Victoria University of Wellington, 1974.

GIBSON, Ann J. *Religious organisation among the Maoris of New Zealand after 1860.* Thesis, University of California, Berkeley, 1965.

GNANASUNDERAM *Maori theology and 'Black theology' or a theology of liberation.* Auckland, N.C.C., Church and Society Commission, 1974.

IRVINE, J. Maori mysticism in the North. *In Dialogue on religion, New Zealand viewpoints 1977.* Peter Davis and John Hinchcliff, eds. Auckland, University of Auckland, 1977, p. 6-10

JOHANSEN, J. Prytz. *Studies in Maori rites and myths.* Copenhagen, Ejnar Munksgaard, 1958.

KAWHARU, I. Hugh *Conflict and compromise: essays on the Maori since colonization.* Wellington, Reed, 1975.

KING, Michael (ed) *Tihe Maori ora: aspects of Maoritanga.* Auckland, Methuen, 1978.

KING, Michael (ed) *Te Ao Hurihuri – the world moves on: aspects of Maoritanga.* Wellington, Hicks Smith, 1975.

LAUGHTON, John G. *From forest trail to city street. The story of the Presbyterian Church among the Maori people.* Christchurch, Presbyterian Bookroom, 1961.

LAUGHTON, John G. *Ringatuism and the Ratana Church.* Mimeo. Wellington, Alexander Turnbull Library, n.d.

LYONS, Daniel P. An analysis of three Maori prophet movements. *In Conflict and compromise: essays on the Maori since colonization.* I. H. Kawharu, ed. Wellington, Reed, 1975. p. 55-79.

MARSDEN, Maori God, man and universe; a Maori view. *In Te Ao Hurihuri.* M. King. ed. Wellington, Hicks Smith, 1975, p. 199-219.

MOL, Johannis, J. (Hans) *Religion and race in New Zealand: a critical review of the policies and practices of the churches in New Zealand relevant to racial integration.* Christchurch, National Council of Churches, 1966.

NGATA, A. T. *The religious philosophy of the Maori.* Mimeo, n.d.

ORBELL, Margaret The religious significance of Maori migration traditions. *In Perspectives on religion: New Zealand viewpoints 1974.* John Hinchcliff, ed. Auckland, University of Auckland, 1975, p. 5-8.

RAKENA, Ruawai *The Maori response to the Gospel: a study of Maori-Pakeha relations in the Methodist Maori Mission from its beginnings to the present day.* Auckland, Wesley Historical Society, 1971. (Wesley Historical Society. N.Z. Branch. Proceedings v. 25, no. 1-4)

SHORTLAND, E. *Maori religion & mythology.* London, Longmans Green, 1882.

SORRENSEN, M. P. K. *Maori and European since 1870: a study in adaptation and adjustment.* Auckland, Heinemann Educational, 1972.

SUTHERLAND, I. L. G. *The Maori people today.* Ch. X: Religious influences. Wellington, N.Z. Institute of International Affairs and N.Z. Council for Educational Research, 1940.

WEBSTER, P. *Rua and the Maori millennium.* Wellington, Price Milburn, 1979.

INDIVIDUAL RELIGIONS AND CHURCHES

ANGLICAN CHURCH

CHURCH of England in New Zealand *Manual of the constitution, canons and standing orders.* Christchurch, 1972.

CHURCH of England in New Zealand. Liturgy and ritual. *The New Zealand liturgy 1970.* Christchurch, Church of the Province of New Zealand, 1977. 1st. ed. 1970
Parallel texts in English and Maori.
MORRELL, William P. *The Anglican Church in New Zealand; a history.* Dunedin, Anglican Church of the Province of New Zealand, 1973.

CHURCH MISSIONARY SOCIETY – BIOGRAPHY

BINNEY, Judith M. C. *The legacy of guilt: a life of Thomas Kendall.* University of Auckland/Oxford University Press, 1968.
EVANS, John H. *Churchman militant; George Augustus Selwyn, Bishop of New Zealand and Lichfield.* London, Allen & Unwin/Wellington, Reed, 1964.
MACMORRAN, Barbara *Octavius Hadfield.* Wellington, The Author, 1969.
ROGERS, Lawrence M. *Te Wiremu; a biography of Henry Williams.* Christchurch, Pegasus, 1973.
SCHROFF, Gordon W. *George Clarke and the New Zealand mission, 1824-1850.* Thesis, M.A., University of Auckland, 1967.
YARWOOD, Alexander T. *Samuel Marsden: the great survivor.* Wellington, Reed, 1977.

ASSOCIATED CHURCHES OF CHRIST

BLAMPIED, Evan P. *The origin and history of the Churches of Christ in New Zealand.* Thesis, M.A., University of Otago, 1939.

BAPTIST CHURCH

BAPTIST Union and Missionary Society of New Zealand. *Yearbook.* Wellington, 1904 –
Title varies.
BEILBY, G. T. *Road to tomorrow; a popular account of one hundred years of Baptist work in New Zealand.* Christchurch, N.Z. Baptist Historical Society/Literature Committee, Baptist Union of New Zealand, 1957.

HAUHAUISM

BATHURST, K. O. *The Hau Hau movement; a study in social, abnormal and religious pyschology.* Thesis, M.A., University of Canterbury, 1940.
CLARK, Paul *Hau Hau. The Pai Marire search for Maori identity.* Auckland, Auckland University Press, 1975.
GADD, Bernard The teachings of Te Whiti o Rongomai. *Journal of the Polynesian Society 75:* 445-7, 1966.
WINKS, R. The doctrine of Hauhauism. *Journal of the Polynesian Society 62:* 199-236, 1953.
See also relevant chapters in the books listed under Maori religious movements.

INDIAN RELIGIONS

TIWARI, Kapil N. (ed) *Indians in New Zealand.* Wellington, Price Milburn, 1980.

JEWISH COMMUNITY

COLLINS, P. R. *The Jewish community in New Zealand; a contribution to the study of assimilation.* Thesis, M.A., Massey University, 1971.

GOLDMAN, Lazarus M. *The history of the Jews in New Zealand.* Wellington, Reed, 1958.

LUTHERAN CHURCH

BRAUER, A. *Under the Southern Cross: history of Evangelical Lutheran Church of Australia.* Adelaide, Lutheran Publishing House, 1956.

METHODIST CHURCH

CARTER, G. *A family affair: a brief survey of New Zealand Methodism's involvement in mission overseas, 1822-1972.* Auckland, Wesley Historical Society, 1973. (Wesley Historical Society. New Zealand Branch. Proceedings, v. 28 no 3 & 4)

GOING places: a portrait of Methodism in the 70's. Ian Harris, ed. Auckland, Council of Mission of the Methodist Church of New Zealand, 1976.

HAMES, Eric W. *Out of the common way: the European Church in the colonial era, 1840-1913.* Auckland, Wesley Historical Society of New Zealand, 1972. (Wesley Historical Society, New Zealand Branch. Proceedings, v. 27 nos 3 & 4)

LAURENSON, George I. *Layman's handbook: a practical guide for officers of the Methodist Church of New Zealand.* Methodist Board of Publications, 1970.

LAURENSON, George I. *Te Hahi Weteriana: three half centuries of the Methodist Maori Mission, 1822-1972.* Auckland, Wesley Historical Society of New Zealand, 1972. (Wesley Historical Society. New Zealand Branch. Proceedings, v. 27, nos. 1 & 2)

METHODIST Church of New Zealand. Law Revision Committee. *Laws and regulations of the Methodist Church of New Zealand.* Revised by the Law Revision Committee. 4th rev. ed. Christchurch, Printed by Wyatt and Wilson Ltd., 1969.

OWENS, John M. R. *Prophets in the wilderness: the Wesleyan mission to New Zealand, 1819-27.* Auckland, Auckland University Press/Wellington, Oxford, 1974.

OWENS, John M.R. *The unexpected impact: Wesleyan missionaries and Maoris in the early 19th century.* Auckland, Wesley Historical Society of New Zealand, 1973. (Wesley Historical Society. New Zealand Branch. Proceedings, v. 27, no 6)

MORMON CHURCH (CHURCH OF JESUS CHRIST OF LATTERDAY SAINTS)

HUNT, Brian W. *Zion in New Zealand: a history of the Church of Jesus Christ of Latterday Saints in New Zealand, 1854-1977.* Temple View, Church College of New Zealand, 1977.

OPEN BRETHREN

LINEHAM, Peter *There we found Brethren: a history of assemblies of Brethren in New Zealand.* Palmerston North, Gospel Publishing House, 1977.

PRESBYTERIAN CHURCH

ELDER, John R. *The history of the Presbyterian Church of New Zealand, 1840-1940.* Christchurch, Presbyterian Bookroom, 1940.

MURRAY, John S. *A century of growth: Presbyterian overseas mission work, 1869-1969.* Christchurch, Presbyterian Bookroom, 1969.

PRESBYTERIAN Church of New Zealand. *Yearbook . . . and proceedings of the General Assembly . . .* Dunedin, 1962 –

PRESBYTERIAN Church of New Zealand. General Assembly *The book of order; or Rules and forms of procedure of the Presbyterian Church of New Zealand.* Christchurch, Presbyterian Bookroom, 1970.

RELIGIOUS SOCIETY OF FRIENDS (QUAKERS)

WEST, Margaret and Ruth Fawell *The story of New Zealand Quakerism 1842-1972.* Auckland? N.Z. Yearly Meeting of the Religious Society of Friends, 1973.

RATANA CHURCH

HENDERSON, J. McLeod *Ratana: the man, the church, the political movement.* 2d ed. Wellington, Reed, 1972. (Polynesian Society memoir, v. 36)

RAURETI, Moana. The origins of the Ratana Movement. *In Tihe Mauri Ora; aspects of Maoritanga.* Auckland, Methuen, 1978, p. 42-59.

See also relevant chapters in the books listed under Maori religious movements.

RINGATU CHURCH

GREENWOOD, William *The upraised hand: or the spiritual significance of the rise of the Ringatu faith.* Wellington, Polynesian Society, 1942.

MISUR, Gilda Z. From prophet cult to established church, the case of the Ringatu Movement. *In Conflict and compromise; essays on the Maori since colonisation.* I. H. Kawharu, ed. Wellington, Reed, 1975. p. 97-115.

ROSS, W. Hugh *Te Kooti Rikirangi: general and prophet.* Auckland/London, Collins, 1966.

TAREI, Wi A church called Ringatu. *In Tihe Mauri Ora: aspects of Maoritanga.* M. King, ed. Auckland, Methuen, 1978, p. 60-66.

See also relevant chapters in the books listed under Maori religious movements.

ROMAN CATHOLIC CHURCH

The CATHOLIC Church and the development of peoples in the South Pacific: Conference held in Suva, Fiji, August 1972. Wellingtor., Episcopal Conference of the Pacific in conjunction with Corso, 1973. 5 booklets.

GALLAGHER, Patrick O. *The Marist brothers in New Zealand, Fiji and Samoa, 1876-1976.* Tuakau, New Zealand Marist Brothers Trust Board, 1976.

MORAN, P. F. *History of the Catholic Church in Australasia, from authentic sources . . .* Sydney, Oceanic Publishing, 1895.

OFFICIAL yearbook of the Catholic Church in Australia and Papua-New Guinea, New Zealand and the Pacific Islands. Sydney, 1886? — Annual.

SIMMONS, E. R. *A brief history of the Catholic Church in New Zealand.* Auckland, Catholic Publications Centre, 1978.

THOMSON, Jane *The Roman Catholic mission in New Zealand, 1838-1870.* Thesis, M.A. Victoria University of Wellington, 1966.

BIOGRAPHIES

KEYS, Lilian G. *The life and times of Bishop Pompallier.* Christchurch, Pegasus Press, 1967.

LARACY, Hugh M. *The life and context of Bishop Patrick Moran.* Thesis, M.A., Victoria University of Wellington, 1964.

DOCTRINAL WORKS

CATHOLIC Church in New Zealand. *Directory on doctrine.* Wellington, 1970.

GUILD of St. Luke, SS Cosmas and Damian. Wellington Branch. *Modern theology, modern philosophy, natural law, Teilhard de Chardin.* Wellington, 1967 (ie. 1968)

SALVATION ARMY

WAITE, John C. *Dear Mr Booth: some early chapters of the history of the Salvation Army in New Zealand.* Wellington, Salvation Army Territorial Headquarters, 1964.

SEVENTH DAY ADVENTIST CHURCH

MAXWELL, Arthur S. *Under the Southern Cross: the Seventh-Day Adventist story in Australia, New Zealand and the Islands of the South Pacific.* Nashville, Tenn., Southern Publishing Association, 1966.

Index

Abbott, W. M., 64
Aberle, D. A., 53
Abhay Charan De, 160
advice columns, 13
Aglow Fellowship, 75
Alcoholics Anonymous, 13
Alford, M., 147
All Saints' Church, Palmerston North, 90, 105
Allan, A., 80
Alpers, A., 34
Amish, 122
Ananda Marga, 149, 155-60, 168; acarya, role of, 158-9; adarsha (moral means), 156; Brahma, 158; ishta (chosen goal), 156; kirtan (chanting), 159; mantra, 159; progressive utilization theory, 155-6; sachitananda, 159; sadhana, 158-9; yama and niyama, 159
Anandamurti, 155, 158-9
Anglican Church, 15, 20, 26, 73, 76, 79, 81-2, 86-7, 95, 100, 102, 105-6, 109-10, 112-3, 116-7, 121, 126, 128, 171, 174-6; Anglo-catholicism, 26, 87; charismatic renewal amongst Anglicans, 105-6, 114, 120; Church missionary society, 79; communion service, 55; constitution drafted 1857, 74; episcopal bench, 71; evangelicals, 87; fundamentalist groups, 120; laity, voice in church affairs, 68; liturgy, 69; missions overseas, 74; Mothers' union, 75; religious orders, 70; vestments, 69; see also Charismatic movement; Ecumenical movement; census figures
Antarctic, 191
Anthroposophy, 153
anti-catholicism, 18, 19, 21
anti-gambling societies, 24
anti-semitism, 141, 143-4, 148
anti-Nazi feeling, 144
Anzac day, 11
Apostolic Church, 100-1, 103-4, 122, 130; Maori adherents, 123
Assemblies of God, 99-103, 112, 114, 122, 130
Association of Presbyterian women, 75
Astor, Rabbi, 143
Aurobindo, 160
Australasian religious history, 18
Australian hymnal, 70
axial period in religious history, 178, 180, 182-3

Baha'is, 13
Baker, Ian, 125
Balkind, V., 147
Baptist church, 20, 69, 73, 77, 82, 88, 93,

103, 113, 121, 128, 132, 172; presidents of, 71; Womens' fellowship, 75
Barber, L. H., 5, 13, 28-9
Barth, K., 23
Bates, J. M., 72
Bathurst, K. O., 34
Baxter, James K., 70, 77
Beavan, P. 76
Bellah, R. N., 14, 96, 150-1, 169, 181, 184
Bennett, Dennis, 113
Bennett, Keith M., 5
Berger, Peter, 119
Best, E., 34
Bible, 10, 62
Bible Christians, 85, 121
Bible class movement, 75
Biblical Christianity and modern progressivism, 152
Biblical fundamentalism, 109
Binney, Judith, 16-18, 28, 34
Black, A., 96
Black, W. B., 77
Blaikie, R. J., 78
Blaiklock, E. M., 78
Blasoni, E. H., 5, 13, 57
Boer war, 21
Booth, Herbert, 23
Booth, Ken, 93, 111
Booth, William, 23
Borch, R. J., 114
Boys' brigade, 75, 80
Brash, Alan, 191
British and Foreign Bible Society, 91
British Israel, 124
British Weekly, 68
Brem, Mrs A., 146
Brethren, 103, 107, 113, 121, 129, 172; Exclusive, 118, 122
Breward, Ian, 5, 13, 17, 67, 79, 82, 93, 95, 111, 175, 184
Brookes, N. E., 94, 96
Brown, Colin, 5, 13, 17, 99
Brown, Norman, 150
Bruggink, D. J., 76
Brunner, E., 23
Buck, Peter, 16

Buddha, 180-1
Buddhism, 14, 115, 154, 173, 175-6, 178-9, 182-3, 189-90
Builders of the Adytum, 120
Burnett, Bill, 114
Burns, Thomas, 67
Burton, J. W., 74
Burton, Ormond, 21, 26, 28, 78

Capps, W. H., 192
cargo cults, 31
Carr, C., 24
Carter, G., 79
Caton, 34
Cavert, S. M., 89
Cawood, L., 79
censorship, 20
capitalism, 14, 24
Catholicism, see Roman Catholic church
census figures, religious professions, 101-3, 115-6, 134, 171-3; interpretation of census figures, 116, 122-3; tables, 128-32
Chantepie de la Saussaye, 192
chaplains, 15
Chappel, G., 112
Charismatic movement, 13, 14, 17, 26, 82, 96, 99-114 passim, 150; among Anglicans, 90; Baptists, 106-7; Methodists, 106; Presbyterians, 106; Roman Catholics, 89, 96, 105; attitude of Open brethren, 107, 113; attitudes to women, 76; baptism in the Spirit, 99; 'charismatic' defined, 100; Christian advance ministries, 90, 113; clerical participation, 109; effects on union plans, 89, 110; gift of healing, 99, 100, 110; glossolalia (speaking in tongues), 99, 100, 105, 110; liturgy, 110; New life centre, 101; social concern, 104, 110; see also Pentecostal churches; Apostolic church; Assemblies of God; Ecumenical movement; census figures
Chatham Islands, 35

China inland mission, 79
chiropractic, 13
Christian endeavour, 75
Christian Science, 125-6
Christianity, expansion in 19th century, 179
Christianity, nominal, 12
Christadelphians, 116, 119, 123-4, 130
Christian (National) revival crusade, 100-1, 103
church buildings, 68-9
church financing, 73
church historians, 15-17
Church of Christ, New Zealand, 101
Church of Jesus Christ of Latterday Saints (Mormons), 13, 16, 26, 52, 102-3, 112, 124, 129, 132, 172, 176; Maori membership, 124
Churches of Christ, 82, 86-7, 95, 103, 106, 122, 129, 172
civil religion, 11, 12, 13, 91-3
civil rights, 21, 25
Clark, P., 34, 55
Clark, S., 96
Clecak, P., 150, 169
Clements, K., 94
clergy, shortage of, 67
Close, Leo, 71
Colless, B. E., 55
Collins, P. R., 146
Colloquium, 72
Commonwealth covenant churches, 100-1, 131
commune movements, 124-5
Community of the Sacred Name, 70
communism, 14
Confucianism, 178, 181
Congregational churches, 23, 73, 82, 86-7, 95, 106, 129, 132, 172
conservation, 53
Cook, captain, 187
Cook Islands Christian church, 83
counterculture, 168
Cragg, K., 192
Creel, R. E., 192
Curnow, E. J., 65

customs, Maori and Pakeha, 12

Daniel, book of, 23
Dansey, H., 34, 36, 54
Darby, John, 122
Darwinism, 19
Davey, A., 167
Davies, W. M., 78, 92, 94
Davis, P., 55, 111
Davis, R. P., 16, 27
Deane, J. H., 77
de Bres, P. H., 5, 13, 34, 192
dechristianisation, 60
democracy, 12
Depression, 15, 16, 22, 24
devotional books, 69
dianetics, 126
Dickey, John, 25, 29, 78
Divine light mission, 149, 165-6, 168; avatar, 165; central message, 166; Guru Maharaj Ji, 165-6
Dixon, C. I. L., 69
dogmatism and variety, conflict between, 25
Don, Alexander, 68, 76-7
Donovan, P., 192
Douglas credit, 22
Downey, P. J., 52, 55
Droppers, G. H., 76
drug culture, 154
Duncan, James, 19

Easter, 11
Eastern Orthodox, 172
Eastern religions and the west, 150-5
Ecumenical movement, 13, 81-97, 183; Act of commitment to union 1967, 86; Anglican charismatics and union negotiations, 90-1; Campaign for Christian order 1943, 83; conference on Christian order 1945, 83; intercommunion, 91; Joint commission on union, 85, 88, 95; oikoumene, 91; Plan of union 1969, 86, 90; voting on, 86-7, 95; Selwyn society, 87, 95; union discussions, 85; union negotiations,

slowing-up, 88; union parishes, 88; union schemes at local level, 87; see also National council of churches
Education, see Religion in education
Eisenstadt, S. N., 145
Elder, J. R., 15, 27, 79, 94
Eliade, M., 188, 192
Elim church, 100-1, 103
Ellul, J., 152, 169
Ellwood, R. S., 192
emigrants, 13
Enlightenment, 178, 180, 197
Epstein, B., 148
Epstein, I., 145
ethical issues, discussion of, 72
European Christianity, concept of superiority of, 59
Evangelical alliance, 18-19
evangelical ecumenism, 91
Evangelical magazine, 68
Evangelical Presbyterian, 72

fascism, 14
Faulkner, J. E., 114
Field, A., 148
Fischman, A., 147
flag, 11
folk religion, 11-13
Forster, A., 148
Fowler, 34
Fox, C., 74
Fraser, Peter, 24
Free church of Scotland, 20
Free Methodists, 85
Friedmann, G., 144, 148
Fulham, Terry, 113
fundamentalism, 23
future of religion in N.Z., 171-184

Gadd, B., 34, 54
Gallagher, P., 16, 28
gambling, 20
Gandhi, 160
Gee, M., 25, 29
Geering, L. G., 14, 26, 71, 78, 94, 171, 184; heresy trial, 18, 26, 72

Gerlach, F. P., 113
Ghana, 67
Gibb, James, 21, 25, 28
Gibson, A., 34, 37, 54-5
Gibson, Colin, 70
Gibson Smith, J., 77
Ginsberg, Allen, 150
Girls' Brigade, 75
Glasner, P., 14
Glazer, N., 145
Glenny, D., 71
global religious consciousness, 150
Glock, C. Y., 169
Gnanasunderam, A., 51, 55
God, Maori concept of, 54
God's own country, 12, 13
Golden Kiwi, cult of, 78
golden rule, 27
Goldman, L. M., 16, 28, 135, 147-8
Good Friday, 11
Goodall, N., 94
Goodman, Paul, 150
government departments, 9
Greek Orthodox church, 82
Green, P., 78
Greenwood, W., 34
Gregory, K. S., 79
Gurau, A. M., 146
Gurdjieff, 153
gurus, 117, 149

Hamilton jet boat, 73
Hare Krishna movement, 127, 149, 160-5, 168-9; Back to Godhead magazine, 161; Bhagavad Gita, 162; bhakti, 162; Chaitanya, 162; discipline of devotees, 162-4; Gaudiya Vaishnav Society, 161; God-realisation, 161; Hare Krishna Mantra, 161; Janmashtami (birthdate of Krishna), 163; Krishna and Rama, 162; Krishna consciousness, state of, 161; Krishna temple in Auckland, 163-4; puja, 164; shikha, 164; tilaka, 164; Vaishnava view of life, 163; Vishnu, 162
Harper, Michael, 113

Harré, John, 73
Hay, James, 75
Heard, Gerald, 153
Hegel, 152
Henderson, J. M., 29, 54
Hepburn, George, 68, 76
Herberg, W., 97
Hercus, D. M., 69, 76
heresy-hunting, 25-6
Hertz, J. H., 147-8
Hickey, Pat, 24
higher criticism, 19
Hill, Michael, 5, 14, 94, 112, 115
Hillel, 142, 147-8
Hinchcliff, John, 5, 55, 111, 113, 191-2
Hinduism, 14, 115, 154, 172, 178, 183
Hine, V. H., 113
Hislop, J., 76
Hoare, M., 80
Hokianga, 81
Holland, H. E., 24
Hort, Abraham, 137
Hunt, B. W., 16, 28
Hunter, John, 69
Huxley, A., 153, 167
Hymns ancient and modern, 70

Indian religious movements, 14, 149-169;
    common factors, 168; gurus, 149, 154;
    Krishnamurti, 149; Meher Baba, 149,
    165; Radha Soami Satsanga, 149;
    Ramana Maharshi, 149; Sai Baba,
    149; upaya, 157; Vendanta, 153, 183;
    yoga, 149; see also Ananda Marga;
    Divine Light Mission; Hare Krishna
    movement; Transcendental medita-
    tion.
inter-religious dialogue, 190
Iran, 189
Irvine, J., 34, 55
Isherwood, C., 153
Islam, 178-9, 190

Jaffe, R., 146-7
James, William, 167
Jaspers, Karl, 178, 184

Jehovah's Witnesses, 21, 102-3, 112, 116,
    119, 123, 130, 132, 172, 175
Jesus marches of 1972, 107
Jesus of Nazareth, 180
Johansen, J., 34
Johnston, archbishop, 88-9, 92
Jones, D. G., 14, 97
Jones, Tim, 125
Judah, J. S., 150, 169
Judaism, 13, 14, 16, 17, 26, 124, 133-148,
    175, 178, 182; aliyah (return to Israel),
    135, 141; Ashkenazim, 141, 147; as-
    similation, 138, 144, 146; 'Auckland
    crisis', 137-8, 147; B'nai Brith, 142;
    B'nei Akiva, 135-6; customs, cere-
    monies and observances, 136-7, 139;
    Cheder (Sunday school), 143; com-
    munity leadership, 143; conflicts,
    140-1; emigration and immigration,
    134-5; family and kinship, 139-40;
    Habonim, 135-6; Hillel group, 140; Is-
    rael, State of, 124, 135, 141, 144; inter-
    marriage, 135-6; involvement in
    Christian world, 137-8; kashrut (food
    laws), 136, 139; Liberal temples, 134;
    Maccabis, 142; Sephardi, 147; social
    problems, 146-7; status conflicts, 141;
    status spread, 142; synagogues in
    N.Z., 134, 137, 146; Yom Kippur, 137;
    youth groups and activities, 136, 143,
    146-7; Zionism, 124, 138, 144; Zionism,
    political differences over, 141

Kawharu, I. H., 54
Kelley, D. M., 114
Kemp, J. W., 77
Kemp, W., 77
Keys, L. G., 93
Khomeiny, ayatollah, 190
King, Michael, 34, 54-5
King, W., 192
Kirk, Norman, 81-2, 91-3
Kitigawa, J. M., 54, 192
Knight, C. R., 76
Knight, G. A. F., 73, 78, 148
Kohere, R. T., 77

Kraemer, H., 192
Kristensen, W. Brede, 192

Labour movement, 23-5
Laidlaw, R. A., 77
Lamb, W., 23
land wars, 19, 33, 59
Lange, E., 96
Laracy, H. M., 17, 28, 64-5
Laughton, J. G., 34, 39, 54-5
Laurenson, G. I., 34
law and order, 24-5
Lawson, R. A., 68
League of mothers, 75
League of nations' union, 24
Leary, Timothy, 150
Leech, K., 153, 169
Lessa, W. A., 54
Liberal Catholic church, 126
liberalising theology, 107
Lipset, S. M., 146
Liquor interests, 16
Liston, archbishop, 21, 29
Little Gidding, 125
Lloyd, captain, 48
Loane, M., 79
lodges, 12
Long, C. H., 192
Lowe, Bob, 27, 71
Lutheran church, 83, 129, 132
Lyons, D. P., 34, 54

MacDiarmid, D. N., 79
McDonnell, K., 113
MacGregor, J., 72, 77
McKessar, M., 94
Mackey, J., 79
makutu, 40
mana, 37, 50
Maori contributions to Christianity, 49-53, 62; angelology, 48, 50; clergy of Maori churches, 47; exorcism, 51; marae, religious concepts expressed, 62; Maori and Biblical concepts compared, 50; Maori and Christian sacraments, 50; Maori Bible, 42, 52;

Maori chants and hymns, 41; Maori culture as sacred heritage, 52; Maori preaching, 71; Maori sections in Anglican liturgy, 70; Maori theologians, 62; Maori theology, 35, 49-51; National council of churches Maori section, 51; Presbyterian service book in Maori, 70; tangihanga (funeral wake), 52; Wairua (Holy Spirit), 49; worship services for Maori occasions, 51; see also Maori religious movements; Ratana church; Ringatu church
Maori religious movements, 13, 31-55 passim; angels in Hauhau belief, 37; Bible in Maori movements, 33; Bible, Te Kooti's interpretation, 35, 48; hau (spirit) and niu pole, 33, 37; Hauhaus, 32-4, 42, 124; Hauhau symbols, 37; Hawaiki, 186; Holy Ghost mission, 49; holy wars, 33; Hurai (Jews), 32; Ihowa (Jehovah), 32; Io in Maori religion, 39-40, 50; land, significance for Maori, 35, 53; 'Lost tribes of Israel', 32; mana, 37, 50; marae, 52; Maungapohatu, 35, 47; miracles of religious leaders, 49; Pai marire religion, 32, 34-5; prayer, 44; prophecy, 32, 48; Rua's temple, 37, 47; Ruru and Riki, gods, 37; tapu, 46, 50; Tariao, 32; tohunga, 50; traditional gods, functions, 42; see also Maori contributions to Christianity; Ratana, Rapana and Ringatu churches
Marcuse, H., 150
Maria Pungare, 32
Marsden, Maori, 34, 50
Marshall, John, 75, 104
Martin, D., 94
Marx, 152
Marxism, 183
Marxism and Judaism, 146
Matheson, J. G., 73
Mbiti, J. S., 48, 55
Medding, P. Y., 145
Mehl, R., 96
Melanesian mission, 73, 79

Mere Rikiriki, 33, 35, 49
Merrington, E. N., 70
Methodist church, 13, 16, 20, 24, 26, 68-9, 70, 76, 81-2, 91, 95, 100, 102, 113, 116, 121, 127-8, 132, 171, 174-5; missions, 74, 79; presidents, 71; union negotiations, 85-7, 94
Methodist New Connexion, 121
Methodists, Primitive, 85, 121
millennialist movements, 17, 22, 31
Miller, G., 77
Miller, John, 19
Mirams, 34
mission churches, 73
missionaries, 15, 17, 18, 31, 33-4
Missionary movement, 85
Misur, G. Z., 34
Mitchell, Austin, 21
Mol, Hans, 34, 78
Moon, Sun-myung, 124
Moore, A. C., 14, 185, 191-2
Moran, P., 28, 65
Morley, W., 16, 27
Mormons, see Church of Jesus Christ of Latterday Saints
Morrell, W. P., 15, 27, 79, 93, 95
Morton, J., 78, 90
Moses, 33, 42, 180
Muhammad, 180
Muller, R. J., 90, 105
Murray, J. S., 79
music and hymnology, 70
Muslims, 13, 14, 172
Myers, M., 112-3
myths of origin, 11

Naseby, 68
Nash, W., 24
National council of churches, 70, 82-5, 90-1; campaign for Christian order, 94; chaplaincies, 83-5; Inter-church aid (Christian world service), 83; inter-church committee on immigration, 83; joint secretariat with Roman Catholics on development, 83; joint working committee with Roman

Catholics, 82-3, 93; Maori section, 51; programme to combat racism, 83-4; refugees settled, 84-5; Pentecostal churches, contacts with, 104; Vietnam war, 94; youth council, 84; see also Charismatic movement; individual churches; Ecumenical movement
naturalization, oath of allegiance, 11
nature - protection societies, 13
Navigators, 75
Neil, A. G., 111-4
new consciousness (Roszak), features of, 157
new religious movements in Pacific, 190
New Zealand, accent, 69, 71; Christianness, 10, 174; cultural isolation, 186; flag and coat of arms, 11; national hymn, 11; present religious trends, 177, 182; religious freedom, 175; religious history, 15-29; writers, 70
New Zealand Hymnal, 70
New Zealand Legion, 22
NZ Journal of Theology, 72
NZ Theological Review, 72
Ngata, A. T., 34, 49, 50
Nicholas, H. G., 78
Nixon, R., 12
Nordmeyer, A., 24
North, J. J., 23
Novak, M., 145

occult, 13
O'Connor, P. S., 17, 28, 93
O'Grady, R. M., 97
Oliver, W. H., 17, 27-9, 55
O'Neill, J. S., 78
Openshaw, R., 29
Oppenheim, R. S., 147
Orbell, M., 34
ordination of women, 76, 90
Otto, R., 188
Ouspensky, 153
overseas missions, 74-5
Owens, J., 17, 18, 28

Pacifiç Islanders Church Hymnary, 70

Pacific Islanders' sermons, 71
pacifists, 21
Page, F., 21
Pai Marire, 32-5
parliament, 11
Parr, S., 72
patriotism, 11, 21
Pentecostalism, 90-1, 99-115 passim, 122, 131; Associated Pentecostal churches of NZ, 101, 103; Maori membership, 101-2, 122-3; pastoral care and mutual support, 109; possible causes for growth, 107-9; theology, 111; see also Charismatic movement; Apostolic church; Assemblies of God; Elim church; Ecumenical movement; census figures
permissive morality, 107
phenomenology of religion, 189, 191
Pitkowski, Rabbi, 143
Pitt, D. C., 5, 14, 133, 146-7
Pitt, M. S., 146
pluralism, religious, 14, 111, 171-84
politicians and public figures, 10
Polynesian language, culture and religion, 185
Polynesians, 26, 144
Pompallier, bishop, 59, 81, 93
popery, 19
post-Reformation divisions in Christianity, 182
Poynton, Thomas, 81
Prabhupada, swami, 160, 162
prayers to open parliament, 11
Presbyterian church, 13, 15, 20, 23, 25-6, 68, 70, 73, 76, 79, 82, 86-7, 90, 94-5, 102, 109, 116, 128, 171-2, 174-5; Bible class movement, 75; Book of common order, 69; church architecture committee, 68; church hymnary, 70; church stewardship movement, 73; local church service society, 69; missions, 74, 79; moderators, 71; union negotiations, 85; Westminster directory, 69; Young women's bible class union, 80; see also Charismatic

movement; Ecumenical movement; census figures
President Johnson cult, 124
primary (primal or 'primitive') religions, 179, 190
prohibition, 21, 24
Protestants, 13, 67-81, 107, 151
provincialism of the spirit, 67
Pulkingham, G., 113
Purchas, H. T., 15, 27
Puseyism, 19

Quakers, see Society of Friends
R.S.A. (Returned Servicemen's Association), 12
race relations, 73, 78
racial prejudice, 17, 31
radio and television, religious coverage, 27, 176
Rakena, Rua, 34-5, 48, 51, 54-5
Ranaghan, Kevin, 113
Rangihau, John, 77
Ranston, H., 78
Rapana church, 34, 36, 44-6; Absolute established Maori church of Aoteoroa, 36; church rules, 44; customary dress, 45; dreams of revelation, 41; Easter observance, 46; see also Maori religious movements; Ratana church
Ras Tafari, 124
Ratana church, 17, 31-55 passim, 91, 103, 115, 172, 176; baptismal rites, 43, 45; belief in angels, 40-1; church finance, 47; contacts with NCC, 83; creed, 40; festival days, 42; flag, 52; healing, 35, 43; Holy Trinity, 40; hymns, 42-3, 48, 77; influenza epidemic 1918, 22; Mangai (mouthpiece), 22, 38, 40-1, 43; Māramatanga, 38; organisation, 45; Ratana pa, 34, 42, 46-7; service book, 42-3; symbols, 37-8, 45, 52; Te whetu mārama, 42; temple, 37, 46-7; tohunga, 22, 38; use of Bible, 42; see also Maori contributions to Christianity; Maori religious movements
Ratana, T. W., 22, 26, 32, 35, 38, 49, 52

Raureti, M., 40, 52, 54-5
Reach out, 72
Reaper, 72
Reeves, W. P., 16
Reformation, 118, 173-4, 182
Reformed church of Scotland, 19
Reich, C., 150
Reidy, M. T. V., 113-4
Religion in education; Baptist college, 72; charismatic Christians and education, 111; Churches' education commission, 91; churches' role in education, 74; College house, 71; Congregational college, 72; Education Act 1877, 20, 74, 79, 93, 175; Holy Cross college, 72; Joint board of Christian education, 77; Knox college, 71, 104; Nelson system, 74; St John's college, 71, 104; Trinity college, 72, 104; university religious studies, 14, 185-93
religious allegiance in NZ diversifying, 173
religious expressions, endeictic and discursive modes, 36, 48
remarriage, 26
revivalism, 18, 22-3
Rex, H. H., 78
Richards, Alun, 21
Richardson, J. T., 113-4
Richey, R. E., 14, 97
Ringatu church, 31-55 passim; basic values, 43; Bible, use of, 39; Bible tapu, 43; cleansing ritual, 43; contacts with NCC, 83; eight covenants, 39; fellowship meal, 47; God concept, 39; healing services, 42; infant baptism, 45; karakia, 41; leadership and organization, 45; makutu rejected, 40; no church buildings, 46; noa (profane), 43; prophecies, 77; ritual, 41; sacred times, 46; seal, 37; services, 42; taro in Maori Bible, 42; tohungas, 40-1; traditional exorcism not practised, 40; 'upraised hand', 37, 41; see also Maori contributions to Christianity; Maori religious movements

Ringer, B. B., 145
rites of passage, 116, 136
Riverside community, 70
Roman Catholic church, 13, 16, 26, 57-65, 81, 88-9, 93-4, 102, 105, 107, 110, 113, 116-7, 128, 171, 174-5; decentralisation in administration, 57; development of doctrine, 58; ecumenical activity, 64; incorporation of Polynesian ritual, 62; indigenization, 58; International theological commission, 61, 65; Irish clergy, 59; form of life in NZ, 58-60; local forms, 61; magisterium, 58; mission, development and liberation, 63-4; missionaries, 59, 81; new forms and structures, 60; orthopraxis, theology of, 62; pentecostals, 114, 120; Pope, 57, 61; ritual and discipline, 58; spirit of inquiry, 62; Vatican council II, 57, 60-5, 183; Pastoral constitution on church in modern world, 61, 65; Decree on church's missionary activity, 61, 65; Decree on ecumenism, 63-4; Declaration on non-christian religions, 60, 65; Dogmatic constitution on church, 64-5; Dogmatic constitution on divine revelation, 64-5; see also Charismatic movement; Ecumenical movement; census figures
Roszak, T., 150-1, 157, 169
Rousseau, 187
Rua Kenana, 32, 34-5, 39, 49
Ruether, R., 65
Ryburn, W. M., 74

sabbath, 20, 137
Sage, C., 79
Salmond, J. D., 78
Salmond, W., 25
Salvation Army, 16, 23, 82, 103, 107, 122, 129, 132
Sanders, J. O., 74
sangha, 183
Sarkar, P. R., 155

Savage, M. J., 24
Schwimmer, E., 37, 54
scientology, 125-6
scouts and guides, 12, 75
Scrimgeour, C., 67-8
Scripture union, 75
Sects, 14, 115-132; appeal of in modern society, 127, 153; 'church' and 'sect', 118; dynamics of development, 120; typology of (Bryan Wilson), 121; working definition, 118-20; see also individual sects by name
secularism, 14, 22, 26-7, 177
secularization, 114, 120, 122, 151-2, 175-7
Seddon, R. J., 16
self-Christianisation, 33
Selwyn, G. A., 67-8, 73-4
Selwyn society, 87, 95
Selwyn, bishop — wife's letters, 68
sermons, 70-1
settlers' denominations, 174
Seventh Day Adventist church, 91, 103, 123, 129, 132, 172; Maori adherents, 123
Shammai, 142, 147-8
Sharot, S., 145-6
Shaw, G. B. — visit to NZ, 14
Shenken, L., 148
Shieff, B., 146
Shinto, 14, 189
Shortland, E., 34
Shove, H. W., 77
Siddhanta, 161
Simpson, G. E., 145
Sinclair, K., 54, 146
Sing a new song, 70
Slater, P., 150
Smail, Tom, 113
Smart, Ninian, 188, 192-3
Smith, J. M., 68
Smith, P. F., 76
Snook, I. A., 28
Snowden, Rita, 77
social Darwinism, 22
Socialist action, 122
Society of Friends (Quakers), 82, 116, 122, 124, 131-2

sociologists on religion, 117-9, 151
Songs of praise, 70
Sorrensen, M., 34
Spengler, O., 152, 169
Spiritualism, 125-6, 131-2
Sprott, T. W., 77
Stacpoole, J., 76
Stamford hill, 137
Steiner, R., 153
Steele, J. T. V., 72
Stewart, W. D., 76
Streng, F. J., 193
Stringer, Mr Justice, 21
Strizower, S., 145
Strong, Josiah, 22
Stuart, P. A., 95
Student Christian movement, 75
Sullivan, Martin, 72
Sunday trading, 176
Sunitananda Avadhuta, 155
supernatural, 13
Sutherland, I. L. G., 34
sweating, 20, 24

Tagore, R., 160
talkback sessions, 13
Taoism, 178
Tariao, 37
Tawhiao, King, 32
Taylor, Jim jnr., 121
Te Aka Rapana, 36
Te Atua Wera, 32
Te Kahupukaro, 32
Te Kooti Rikirangi, 32, 35, 39, 41-2, 46, 49
Te Mahaki, 32
Te Ua, 32-3, 37, 48
Te whakapā (consecratory rite), 50
Te Whiti O Rongomai, 32-3, 54
Telethon, 13
Tertiary students' Christian fellowship, 75
theological scholarship, 72
'theology of crisis', 23
Theosophy, 125-6, 131-2, 149, 153
third world, churches' interest in, 25
Thompson, R., 78

Tibetan Buddhism, 149
Tiele, C. P., 192
Till, B., 89, 96
Tiwari, Kapil, 14, 149, 169
Towler, R., 96
Trade union movement, 24
Transcendental meditation, 149, 167-9; claims to be scientific, 167; consciousness levels, 168; International meditation society, 167; Maharishi Mahesh Yogi, 125, 167; vedic tradition, 167
Troeltsch, E., 127
Troup, George, 75
Turner, H. W., 39, 54, 192
'two swords', doctrine of, 21

Unification Church, 124
United kingdom, migration from, 67
uniting symbols for NZrs, 92
Urquhart, Colin, 113

van der Leeuw, G., 192
van Gennep, A., 138, 147
van Staveren, rabbi, 143
Veitch, James, 17
Viard, bishop, 59
Vidler, A., 20, 28
Visser't Hooft, W. A., 94
Vivekananda, 160
Vogel, prime minister, 141
Vogt, E. Z., 54

Wach, J., 38, 54, 189, 192
Waddell, R., 20
Waitangi day, 11
Waite, J. C., 16, 28
Wakefield, E. G., 134
Waldegrave, C. T., 113
Walsh, J., 77
War cry, 122

waterside strikes, 24-5
Watts, Allan, 150, 167
war dead, 11
Weber Max, 117, 151-2
weight-watchers, 13
welfare state, 12, 24
Wesley historical society, 16
Wesley, J., 121
Wesleyans, 85
West-Watson, bishop, 82
western Christendom, 186
western materialism, 158
Westminster confession, 25
Williams, J., 112
Wilson, Bryan, 88, 96, 114, 121, 124-5
Wilson, J. J., 16, 27
Winiata, M., 46, 55
Winks, R., 34
Wolter, F. F., 21
women in colonial society, 75
Wood, G. A., 93
working-classes, 23, 25
World congress of faiths, 183
world war I, 17, 18, 21, 23-4
world war II, 21, 25, 186
Worsfold, J. E., 29, 100, 104, 111-2

Yahwist, 22
Yinger, J. M., 145
YMCA, 75
Young Maori party, 16, 22
Younghusband, F., 183
Youth for Christ, 75
Yule, R. M., 78
YWAM, 75
YWCA, 75
xenophobia, 21
Xmas cards, 12
Zimmer, H., 154, 169
Zoroastrianism, 178